Somewhere Else

BY JAN GUENTHER BRAUN

SOMEWHERE ELSE A NOVEL

ARBEITER RING PUBLISHING · WINNIPEG

Copyright © 2008 Jan Guenther Braun

Arbeiter Ring Publishing
201E-121 Osborne Street
Winnipeg, Manitoba
Canada R3L 1Y4
www.arbeiterring.com

Printed in Canada by Transcontinental Printing

Cover and typesetting by Relish Design Studio, Ltd.

With assistance of the Manitoba Arts Council/Conseil des Arts du Manitoba.

We acknowledge the support of the Canada Council for our publishing program.

ARP acknowledges the financial support to our publishing activities of the Manitoba
Arts Council / Conseil des Arts du Manitoba, Manitoba Culture, Heritage and
Tourism, and the Government of Canada through the Book Publishing Industry
Development Program (BPIDP).

Printed on 100% post-consumer-waste recycled paper.

Library and Archives Canada Cataloguing in Publication

Braun, Jan Guenther, 1979-
        Somewhere else / Jan Guenther Braun.

ISBN 978-1-894037-32-7

        I. Title.

PS8603.R383S64 2008   C813'.6   C2008-906336-8

For you, in spite of myself

If I speak, my pain is not assuaged,
and if I forbear, how much of it leaves me?
—Job 16:6

THE BRIDE OF CHRIST

What if I were dead? What if flight was a single bullet in the chamber of a gun, a pulled trigger instead of packing bags and disappearing into the night? Maybe that's where the dreams came from—a premonition of sorts—kill something, or be killed. Before I hit puberty, I started waking up in the middle of the night in a cold sweat, breathing heavily. It gradually got worse. I would wake up screaming and shaking and then, after awhile, I could remember bits of my dreams. It's easy to wake up, put your clothes on, and walk around pretending that you remember nothing of the night before—that's the truly scary part. It wasn't that I was afraid to look my parents—my profoundly dedicated, pacifist, Mennonite parents—in the eye and tell them that that I had slaughtered hundreds in my dreams the previous night (please pass the milk). That was a hurdle I felt we could jump as a family. What I could not tell them was why my subconscious was a killing machine.

In my dreams it was never a choice; my hand was forced as I defended myself. The scenario was always the same, an invading army would launch an unprovoked attack on my people—although I had a strong sense of who my people were, it was never defined by borders or blood relations; it was never as clear as nationality. Either I would fight back immediately or somehow escape the initial round-up of captives and come back to launch a surprise attack. Whether my dream was set in medieval times or World War II or in the present, I was always an incredibly efficient killing machine with whatever weapon was at hand. I felt an impossible remorse for actions that went completely against my conscious self.

In my dreams I was never killed. That just wasn't an option.

.....

For better or for worse, a church is a family. I didn't choose my parents—two members of the Mennonite church—I didn't choose the other members of the church, I didn't choose my Sunday school teachers or their lessons, I didn't choose what Martha Wiebe brought for the after-service potluck every month, and I didn't choose the God. I've always known, even now after the arduous labour of putting light years between me and what I didn't choose, that it doesn't matter what I would have chosen for myself, only that what I have exists. If I were dead now instead of alive, it would just be another point of acceptance.

I always wanted to go to church, every Sunday; there was no question in my mind. Church—the building, the concept, the people, the beliefs—was where I understood myself.

Our service started at five to eleven—not eleven, not ten-thirty, but five to eleven. The benches were upright wooden and the walls bare. There were five things at the front of the church, four of which were furniture—the pulpit, and three chairs for the worship leader, song leader, and whoever is giving the sermon—and one of which was an instrument—the piano. There was nothing ornate about our church; the walls were generally barren to prevent you from focusing on anything other than God. There were no stained glass windows; that's just a waste of money. There were no statues of Mary for us to pray at the foot of—false idols! We congregants are creatures of habit. Sheldon Wiens always sat at the back of the church to the left of the pulpit and Mr. Peters always took his spot high above everyone in the balcony. Mr. and Mrs. Petkau were always about ten minutes late for the service, and you could count on Vic and Shelley Neufeld to be the first ones to arrive in the morning (or perhaps tied for first with my dad). It's like the spot you have at the family dinner table, and when visitors or new members take someone's spot on a particular pew, there's always an adjustment period.

Sitting in church one beautiful Sunday morning, I received the answer to a question that I had been avoiding asking myself. It was the last time I attended my home church and certainly my most vivid memory of being there. I was sixteen.

When I entered the sanctuary earlier that morning, I was greeted with the usual enthusiasm of the usher handing out bulletins. Mr. Klassen's (no relation) handshake was a comfort for me despite his hands being the texture of sandpaper from the daily milking of his cows. Dipping his hands into a wash bucket repeatedly for thirty years to clean the udder before putting the milker on had converted the skin on his hands into one big callous. Moisturizing was out of the question and probably would have proved futile. He had lost one of his index fingers in a bailer accident. Apparently, when he had made it up into the cab of the tractor to radio to his wife for help he had merely said, "Daut's mi waut o'raicht" (there's something wrong with me). His wife had managed to find it before driving him to the hospital. They re-attached the finger, but his ability to manipulate it was never the same and when you shook his hand you had to cradle the dead weight of his index finger. I found the transformation from milk-splashed, shit-covered overalls to neatly combed back hair, suit, and tie poetic.

That morning, the usher handed out an additional piece of paper to our bulletins. It was information regarding the upcoming national church conference: the agenda for the conference and a list of corresponding Bible passages to study and think about.

I was sitting three pews from the back of the church to the minister's left with my usual church service partners, Amy Kraus and Kevin Doerkson—my two closest church friends, whom I had known since before I started attending school. We were all born the same year and had been "dedicated" at the same time. Anabaptists don't baptise their children at birth, there's no place in the scriptures that instruct that. Instead, parents promise to do their best to convince their children, when they grow into adults, to choose baptism on their own. The three of us had "wild" ideas, according to some of the members of the church. One time, after some careful scripture study, we found that dancing in church was perfectly acceptable in God's eyes so we started planning a Friday night dance. We were promptly told in no uncertain terms that there would be no Friday night dance, even if we called it "The Friday Night Dance for Jesus" (and maybe especially because we wanted to call it that) and to not bother arguing, because no one was listening.

My parents practised the same parenting techniques of their parents, which was to discourage every natural inclination I ever had. Most of these can be eliminated before the age of ten and, judging from my own experience, require a good many years of sweat to reclaim.

I noticed that the issue of homosexuality and church membership was to be on the agenda. This was a polite way of confirming that there were "no gays allowed" in our fold.

I nudged Amy's elbow. "What is this?" I whispered, pointing down at the sentenced that mentioned homosexuality. She, Kevin, and I were all pretty much on the same page as advocates for gays and lesbians in the church—advocates being the operative word. Words like "they" and "them" were always being used between the three of us.

She rolled her eyes dramatically and reached for the hymnbook as we were about to sing our first hymn. Amy jerked her thumb behind her without looking, "These olds are going to be gone soon enough."

I looked behind me and saw faces that I thought would live forever, had been there forever. I turned my attention back to the conference information. Suddenly I felt my face go hot and red and I looked around again to see if anyone was watching me read. I knew that my hands were shaking, because I saw them shaking, but I felt nothing. I couldn't feel my legs either, and I thought for a moment that I wasn't breathing. One of the scripture passages being used as biblical evidence against the admittance of homosexuals as members of the church was Judges 19:22-26. Again, I looked up and around to see if anyone was watching as I pulled the Bible out of the slot in front of me and flipped to the instructed passage.

Judges 19:22-26, NRSV: *"While they were enjoying themselves, the men of the city, a perverse lot, surrounded the house, and started pounding on the door. They said to the old man, the master of the house, 'Bring out the man who came into your house, so that we may have intercourse with him.' And the man, the master of the house, went out to them and said to them, 'No, my brothers, do not act so wickedly. Since this man is my guest, do not do this vile thing. Here are my virgin daughter and his concubine; let me bring them out now. Ravish them and do whatever you want to them; but against this man do not do such a vile thing.' But the men would not listen to him. So the man seized the concubine, and put her out to them. They wantonly raped her, and abused her all through the night until the morning. And as the dawn began to break, they let her go. As morning appeared, the woman came and fell down at the door of the man's house where her master was, until it was light."*

I looked up from the passage, my heart racing, and I felt my breathing stop. My body threw flames. A violent, involuntary twitch escaped, making my torso pivot to the right as the congregation stood up in unison to sing the second hymn.

I looked around and, for the first time, cast from this family, a stranger to everyone. Dead.

They were talking about me at a national church conference. My heart fell out of my chest. I watched it beating on the pew in front of me. My legs knew it wasn't safe as they started walking me to the end of the pew and up the aisle to the foyer. I turned around— tasting salt on my lips—and looked back into the sanctuary, seeing maybe four people that I thought would stand by my side if right at that moment I marched to the front of the church and stood behind the podium. I saw myself for a second, adjusting the microphone to my height and clearing my throat, "Brothers and sisters in Christ...." My vision stopped short as fear overwhelmed me. I clutched my chest; it felt tight, like someone was grabbing my shirt. A silent violence was being enacted on my body.

As I took my coat off the rack I heard the congregation, united in song, in beautiful four-part harmony. "Praise God from whom all blessings flow, praise Him all creatures here below...." They are the opening lines of our congregation's favourite hymn, and I felt both comforted and betrayed by those words. I stumbled out of the church, my stomach heaving its fear and betrayal onto the front steps. I stepped around the mess and walked home.

When I got home, I carefully took off my shoes and jacket, and went downstairs to my bedroom. I closed the door behind me quietly and crawled under the blanket. Burrowing my nose in the blanket, I let the words that I had just read sink in. The biblical passage scrolled in front of my eyes again, but this time it was like a movie. I saw the action, positioned the characters in the house, and saw the women cowering in fear wondering if they would be sent out to the crowd of men. I saw the dead woman lying on the steps, gasping for her last breath. What was the sound inside the house after the crowd had taken the concubine away to gang rape her?

I reached for my copy of *Questions I Asked My Mother* by Di Brandt and thumbed to a favourite poem, "missionary position (1)," when my parents walked into my room.

let me tell you about what it's like
having God for a father & jesus
for a lover on this old mother...

"Did you throw up on the steps of the church this morning?" My mother asked, taking the book out of my hands.

"Yes," I replied. "And have you heard of knocking before?" I said, pointing to the door, my hands shaking.

"Why would you throw up on the front steps of the church?" My father snapped.

"I wasn't feeling well," I responded weakly, leaning over to take the book back from my mother. "Why are you so mad?" I put the book down next to me on the bed. I felt suspicious; they knew something.

"You need to go back there right now and clean it up," mom said, hands on hip.

"But I don't feel good," I said, shifting my eyes from my dad to my mom and back again.

"No," my dad said suddenly, as though he had just walked into the conversation. "You will not go back there right now, the last thing we need is for people to think that members of our family are cleaning the church on a Sunday." He looked at mom for agreement and then crossed his arms, as though it was time to really get down to brass tacks. "Did you sneak out last night and go drinking with your friends after we went to bed?"

"What?" I said, almost laughing, relieved that maybe we could all settle on an alternate reality.

"Don't you laugh about this," mom said, crossing her arms.

"I was here, reading this book, in fact," I said pointing to the book of poetry I had taken back from my mom.

"Yeah, that's another conversation we need to have," dad said pointing to the book.

"Wow, accusing me of going out drinking and now are you trying to restrict my reading? What's going on with you guys?" I said, trying to keep a smile of defiance on my face. I felt my spirits lifted with the accusation that I had been drinking—something much safer than the truth.

"You are sixteen," my dad said, waving his arms around, as though it would lead him to the insight he seemed so desperate to find.

I cut him off before he could find it.

"Wow, I'm pleasantly surprised that you remember that, dad. Or was that just a shot in the dark?" I sat smug, proud that I had beaten him to some kind of punch.

"Excuse me?" he said holding his mouth open, not blinking. "This is my house!" He crouched down, pointing his index finger in my face. "And you are my child and you will not drink alcohol and you will not speak to me like that and you will not throw up on the front steps of the church. And if I," he said, turning his finger toward himself, violently tapping his chest, "me—your father—thinks that what you're reading or what kind of music you're listening to or what television you are watching is not appropriate for your age I will restrict it because that's what a good father does."

I raised an eyebrow in response to him and was about to open my mouth when mom spoke. "What's really going on here, Jess?" she asked, sounding slightly conciliatory, sitting down on the edge of my bed, touching my elbow.

Something inside me melted. This is it, I thought. But what was "it" exactly? I put my face into my palms for a few seconds. I thought of my brothers—John, I would find out later that week, had gone to the church late that night and shovelled the half-frozen vomit off the sidewalk—and how I had overhead my dad once say that, "You think parenting is easy until you get to the youngest one."

I tried to gauge the shadow behind my mom's eyes. My dad took a deep breath and I saw something familiar—his head was slightly bowed, ready to nod with understanding. The body language of the man I had witnessed in conflict with one of his students at the college who had gone astray, one he desperately wanted to show compassion toward.

My silence seemed to put them at ease. Dad removed his glasses and rubbed his eyes. Mom crossed her legs and smoothed her skirt. I had a perception of morality that was shaped while I slept—there was no other explanation for where it came from—that in most cases nothing was right or wrong, it was all a matter of being honest. I wanted an honest relationship with my parents, however difficult. I was ready to pay the emotional price. It seemed so simple—be honest and everything will work out in the end.

"I was reading the conference material," I said, haltingly, "and there are those 'reference Bible passages' for each of the issues that they're going to discuss. So I read the one from Judges with the concubine who's raped to death, which I've read before but never like this and I just can't believe," I shook my head as tears ran down my cheeks, "I mean, I think I need to talk to you guys, I think," I trailed off, looking for support from my mom, but in her eyes was something I didn't expect.

My mother's face went white and her breathing shortened. She brought a hand to her heart for a moment and looked like she was about to fall backward. I saw fear in her eyes, and it made my jaw freeze in place. I had never seen my mother that afraid. That tiny bit of held-over belief that my parents feared nothing vanished into my stomach. Then there was anger in her eyes; the same look that she would shoot to us kids when she needed to silently say "Don't you dare" in the strictest possible terms.

"This discussion is over!" she shrieked, startling dad.

Terror rushed through me. My stomach dropped into my bowels. A cold sensation spiked down into my body like lightening making contact with earth.

Dad's shoulders lifted. He took a deep breath in but didn't dare look at his wife.

"You have been acting so selfishly lately! You will go to the church tonight and clean up that mess; I don't care why you were upset, there was no call for that," she seethed between clenched teeth as she turned and left the room.

My father stood stunned and, yet, still angry. He watched his wife leave and then followed her quickly up the stairs.

My hands started shaking and the side of my lip curled up. My stomach knotted and a force went through my body—it pushed me out of my bed, fist first hurled toward the wall, punching a hole in the drywall. The knuckles on my right hand were bleeding from having caught a hidden stud. I put my left palm over the bloodied knuckles and stared at the hole in the wall. When I looked down again, the blood was threatening to spill onto the carpet. My breathing was still short and choppy. I touched my jaw—it felt like I had been punched in the face but I think it was temporarily locked. I stood up a little taller, and my shoulders squared straight across like an ox as I made my way upstairs with a body full of rage.

Mom looked aghast when she saw my hands. "What happened? Did you just punch something?"

I said nothing as I stood in front of them.

"This is what I'm talking about!" my mom's voice was high pitched.

I opened my mouth to shout back, but she cut me off. "You have lost your privilege of speaking Jess! It's abundantly clear that you need to do a lot more listening!"

"I never had that privilege in the first place!" I shrieked back. I paused at the top of the stairs, hoping for some semblance of tenderness from her before exiting.

My mom's lips were tight together, and I knew that she was angry with me for making her angry enough to yell. Neither my mom nor my dad was big on yelling at their kids; they preferred to remain silent if they were angry, assuming that the guilt would eat me alive. Most of the time that assumption was a good one.

Downstairs in my bathroom I cried silently as I held my hand under cold water and watched it run red. My hand started to swell where part of my fist had caught the stud. I opened the drawer in the bathroom vanity and reached for the bottle of painkillers. I stared at the full bottle of pills and finally set it on the counter. I took my clothes off and stood in front of the floor-length mirror, staring at myself. I cried harder and watched the tears made their way down to my breasts.

"Why is this happening to me?" I said, whispering again.

I contemplated walking out of the house naked; I wanted someone to see me. I felt my throat tighten, my breathing shorten. I picked up the bottle of pills and looked inside to make sure that I hadn't taken any; the bottle was still full. I sat down on the cold linoleum floor and tried to calm myself. I felt that if I didn't remain conscious, I would stop breathing. I crawled on my hands and knees toward the toilet and threw up.

There was no one to rub my back or hand me a glass of water. As I sat still on the cold floor, there was a stillness above me. I thought my parents had left the house or had gone to bed earlier than usual. There was no more sunlight streaming into the basement.

.....

Silence follows silence, our house was built with bricks of silence. Naturally, I moved away to build my own brick house: sturdy and strong, haunted by my own ghosts, occupied by its own unspoken words. I remember grandma Loewen, silent all those years, nodding approvals and wiping her hands on her apron to say hello. Grandma Klassen was one of those women of few words; she waited for invitations and, when none came, she would sing hymns or remain gently silent. And when you didn't know how to send the invitation it was you who would sing hymns. What her head was filled with, I'll never know; she died when I was just ten years old. She never looked at me and said "Why do you dress like a boy?" She never commanded me to do anything or chided me for my actions. She only ever asked me questions. "Do you think that you could help me?" "How are you doing?" "Do you know how happy I am that you've come to visit me?"

After the funeral the grandchildren were all allowed to choose something of hers to remember her by. On her scratched Formica kitchen table was laid out several aprons, her Bible, a fountain pen, and her Gesangt Buch (hymnbook)—all the most important things to a woman who never asked for anything. I refused to take anything. I was holding out for one last conversation with her.

Monday morning I woke up to a searing pain in my hand. When I sat down to eat my breakfast my hand shook as I tried to hold a spoon and raise it to my mouth. My hand not only hurt, it was immobilized. I winced, setting the spoon down. When I opened my eyes again my mom was staring at me, lips pursed, eyes flaming rage, waiting for me to admit defeat. I grabbed the spoon again and brought the cereal to my lips while my swollen hand shook violently. When I was finished I put the bowl into the sink, dutifully rinsed it, and neatly wrapped pieces of ice in a tea towel as I went back downstairs to my room. I didn't go to school that day, nor the rest of the week. When the school secretary phoned to inquire about my lack of attendance, I overheard my mom simply say, "She's very sick and I think I need to keep her home for the rest of the week." And then, "Oh, thank you, that's so thoughtful of you," before hanging up the phone.

I spent the week pacing the length of my room and reading. By the end of the week it was as though I really was sick with some common illness that I would recover from without incident but wasn't worth mentioning. I took meals with my family, bowed my head before we ate, did all my chores, watched TV, answered the phone, read the newspaper, cleaned my room until it was spotless, and did several loads of laundry. I started making piles in my room. Sifting through my belongings, I put every item through a simple test: If I knew that an invading army was coming to kill me in twenty minutes, what would I pack? It was a surprisingly difficult test, but eventually I had a pile.

By the end of the week, I was ready.

GENESIS 19:1-29; JUDGES 19:1-30; LEVITICUS 18:22,
LEVITICUS 20:13; I CORINTHIANS 6:9; ROMANS 1:18-29

"I'm not going back."

My mom and dad's individual jaws dropped collectively. I had said some shocking things to them but I had never before refused to go to church.

"Get—your—shoes—on—now," my dad said with a long pause between each word of the sentence before locking eyes with me.

It was a tactical mistake to allow me into his pale blue eyes because I saw weakness.

"No," I said simply.

My mom's eyes went to the clock near the door.

"Ruth Marie Klassen," mom said, invoking my given name and taking a deep breath. "Your father and I weren't going to tell anyone before church today, but there's a very important announcement. Your father," she said, allowing a smile for just a second, "has been picked to be the president of the college."

I stumbled backward slightly, feeling as though a tremor had just shifted the house.

"Shocking," I said sarcastically in an effort to hide my dismay.

Dad had been teaching at the college since I was born. I had never known a life without him working there—it was who he was in my eyes. That building was the site of so many childhood adventures and revelations. His former students made up so many chapters of my early narration. I could find my way down the narrow halls of the college buildings with my eyes closed. His evenings and weekends were dominated by one thing—the college. My mom's Tupperware had made the trek from house to car to college reception room far too many times to count. The trek always starting in our kitchen with mom saying, "Now don't eat these squares, kids, they're for the reception after the lecture at the college tonight."

He was single minded in his devotion to his work, genuinely loved his students, and never hesitated to take on committee work or host visiting lecturers. Dad's job was more than full-time, which meant that it was more than full-time for mom as well.

I looked him in the eye and saw something I didn't recognize. Nothing.

"Don't do it," I said, surprising myself. "You don't have to take the job, you don't have to go," I said pointing in the general direction of the church. "They'll make you choose every day, dad. Every day.". The words stumbled out of my mouth not knowing exactly what they meant or where they came from.

"We're going to be late," he said, turning to mom while motioning her toward the door. "You," he said, "will be dealt with later." He shook his head, "You can't even be happy for me." He looked like he might cry. He looked genuinely hurt. He slammed the door, which sent the clock hanging on the wall next to it flying to the floor.

My eyes felt like two little potholes with flames licking the edges as I started to cry. I hadn't slept well the night before, which made the burning sensation more painful.

I watched mom and dad walk in the direction of church. Dad, his hands jammed into his pockets, his shoulders stooped, kept his head swivelled away from my mom, yet managed to walk in a straight line.

I hesitated before walking to my dad's office and letting myself in. It was never locked but it didn't need to be because of the explicit understanding among all family members that no one was allowed to enter the sacred space without dad's consent.

I felt pulled in, like it was a duty. I thought about how, once a year, when the Jewish priest would enter the "holiest of the holies" in the temple, they would tie a band of cloth around his waist. If he was struck down by God for doing something wrong within that sacred place the other priests would be able to drag his dead body out without putting themselves at risk by entering.

I sat behind his desk, touching the wood with the tips of my fingers. I knew that my dad had spent a significant amount of his summer earnings on the wood, hand crafting it in anticipation of his first year of university. John told me that dad started working on the desk

20

the day he got his university acceptance letter. When grandpa entered the wood shop to see dad working away on the desk, he asked what was going on. Dad told him the news of his acceptance, grandpa shouted at him, telling dad that he wasn't going to allow him to go. There was a moment of silence, after the dust had settled and grandpa had yelled himself out. Dad said calmly, "I'm eighteen now, dad. I'm going." Grandpa punched him in the face and tried to walk away, but dad turned him around and pinned him down by the shirt collar on the surface of the desk, cracking the wood. With a forearm across Grandpa's neck he said simply, "It's not your decision."

It amazes me now that dad would still speak to his father. Grandpa, as I remember him now, was not a good man. Grandpa seemed to think that it was his son's fault that he didn't have any more children. Apparently, the birth of my father was so difficult that grandma was unable to have any more children, a fact that grandpa never hesitated to blame on dad. It was as though grandpa felt doubly cheated—not only did he get the bookish child uninterested in making money or *really* working for a living, that child prevented him from having a whole corporation of children.

Grandpa managed to screw over pretty much the whole community of farmers with one business transaction or another and eventually bought all the tractor dealerships in the area. He went on to buy up all the seed and chemical dealerships, rendering escape from his clutches almost impossible. It was as though he was determined to make up for his lack of children by buying as many children to his parent company. He tried to buy us, too, always making comments about how he needed to buy his grandchildren things because my dad's job couldn't possibly pay the bills. We would come home from spending time with grandpa and grandma with a new pair of shoes or a winter jacket or a haircut. I remember bursting into dad's office one day after a shopping trip with grandpa saying, "Look what grandpa bought me." Before I could get another word in, dad violently slammed his fist down on the desk. I stood, breathless and astonished, as dad grabbed the new shoes out of my hands and marched past me. I never saw the shoes again and I wasn't allowed to accept gifts from grandpa and grandma anymore unless it was my birthday or Christmas.

Grandma and grandma as a couple don't make sense to me now. Grandpa was the hipster child he and grandma never had—she in her apron and homemade dresses and he in his smart golf shirts and hand-made, leather cowboy boots. My child-self thought that they were a magical combination, though, of gift buying (grandpa) and gentle, unconditional love (grandma).

Dad's desk was in need of being oiled and although there were chips missing and cracks along the surface, it was still solid. I couldn't imagine my dad pinning grandpa down by the throat on the surface of this desk. I also couldn't imagine the circumstances under which dad would have shared the story of an act he undoubtedly saw as shameful with his oldest son. A teachable moment maybe.

I opened the top right-hand drawer and started pulling things out. There was an old Swiss Army knife, a stapler, a pad of sticky notes, a Dictaphone, an assortment of fine point Uni-Ball pens (all black, a package of which I stuffed into my pocket), a roll of breath mints, an ancient pair of scissors, and a family photo from a time when I was still small enough to sit on his lap.

I stared at the photo, my tiny body fitted into a matching pink skirt and jacket. I remembered when I was maybe four or five and we were preparing to go to grandma and grandpa's for an extended family gathering. My mom was trying to get me dressed and out the door but I refused to put clothes on. I pointed to a pair of overalls while she, almost to a point of hysterical tears, held out a Raggedy-Anne printed matching skirt and blouse. I threw the offending blouse and skirt at her as she stormed out of my room in frustration. That was a point of absolute impasse—I could not understand why it was necessary for me to wear certain clothes only because they were deemed to be for girls. I wanted to know who made the rules and how those rules were established. I wanted to know how it was possible to run fast in a skirt like that. My mom couldn't understand how her beautiful little girl had ended up being a boy.

I wore the overalls that night as I ran outside on the lush summer grass. My second and third cousins swarming like mosquitoes during a game of freeze-tag. I found myself surrounded, and the questions started. Are you a boy? Why are you wearing boy's pants? Are you really a girl? If you're wearing boy's pants how can you be a girl? I understood in that moment why my mom wanted me to wear certain clothes but I could never accept that clothes could somehow make me less of a girl. I couldn't forgive my mom for bowing to the pressure; I wanted her to be on my side.

My father, typically Mennonite—most people put pictures of their family on their desk, not in their desk. I wondered what else was inside the drawers, hidden away. It occurred to me that my father could have a whole life hidden away in his desk drawers and I would never know. I wondered if mom had her own hidden spaces that we didn't know about—unknown secrets (as opposed to known secrets) lurking at the bottom of her closet or dresser drawers.

I got up from the desk and paced around the room, eye-balling all of the shelves, searching for what I didn't know. I took a photo album off the shelf and, flipping to the first page, found my parent's wedding picture. It was the first time I had seen that picture—perhaps the first time I had seen any of their wedding photos. It made sense; their wedding seemed private with nothing to do with John, Francis, or me.

Dad's hair was neatly parted to one side and slicked down, as though he had seen himself in the mirror that morning and thought, "I will make my hair look good for her." Mom's smile looked positively joyous—like a stolen moment. The picture wasn't posed. It was as though someone had shouted their names and a slight turn was all they needed to square into the frame. I couldn't help but smile back at them and their perfect moment of happiness. I wonder what my mom's family thought of their marriage.

Her family was fourteen strong, including her parents. Dad was an only child. They were a bit of an odd couple. Dad was very involved with the more liberal General Conference church and mom came from a staunchly Old Colony Mennonite church that seated men on the left and women on the right for services. The church my mom grew up attending shunned any musical instrument other than the human voice, and the minister delivered his sermons dressed in a an all black suit and never smiled—at least that's what she told me for the bedtime stories that I would beg for. Mom was the youngest and the last one left in the house after her siblings moved away to start their own families. Her mother died when she was just seven of a cause that has never been entirely clear to me. I imagine that mom must have been lost in that sea of children. It occurred to me that the only reason anyone would have noticed her absence was if there was no supper waiting on the table.

The shelves of dad's office were lined with books about Mennonite history, theology, and dictionaries of English, German, Latin, Greek, and Hebrew. There were no books of literature on the shelves, no self-help guides, no books about philosophy or even the history of the other religions or cultures. The place for any kind of bookish diversity was a small shelf beside mom's side of the bed.

I knew that shelf well. It was the one I stared at in the dark of night when I would stumble into mom and dad's room, unable to sleep and in need of comfort. I would stare at her and feel waves of guilt wash over me, asking myself if my nighttime fear was worth waking her up. I would sit beside her bed staring at her collection of books as an internal debate ensued. Sometimes that was enough to soothe my fears and send me back to bed alone. Eventually, I was able to read the titles to myself. *Peace Shall Destroy Many* by Rudy Wiebe, *The Chronicles of Narnia* C. S. Lewis, *Sophie's Choice* by William Styron, *Jane Eyre* by Charlotte Brontë, *Fifth Business* by Robertson Davies, *Paradise Lost* by John Milton, *To Kill a Mockingbird* by Harper Lee, and on and on. In the evenings, after the housework was finished and while dad was working in his office mom would sit down on the one chair in her room and read. She would leave her room and shoo us to bed or make sure that we were doing our homework or check on what kind of television program we were watching or make a cup of tea. I was always amazed by her ability to completely ignore us children while reading. John, Francis and I would often have to stand around her in a semi-circle and chant "mom, mom, mom" before she would look up from her book, startled, and say, "You guys snuck up on me again." She never sounded angry, just genuinely surprised by our presence.

Between two bookcases in dad's office was a quiet looking wooden box—it had the appearance of a treasure chest that was first hauled by an ancestor across the old motherland of Russia and then across the sea. It was a blond wood with an imbedded lock that automatically locked when the lid was down. A quick search of the other desk drawers resulted in an obvious candidate for the key. I put the key in the lock and lifted the lid effortlessly.

I felt awe and terror. Although I knew the Sunday habits of my family like the path from the dinner table to my room, I was still scared that my dad would walk in and catch me digging through his personal belongings.

Nothing looked very interesting on the surface, but I assumed it was locked because the contents were private and, therefore, interesting. I lifted a big stack of papers on the left-hand side of the chest and thumbed through. I soon realized that dad had kept every paper he had ever written. I felt the effort of dad's labour pour onto my lap as I read through the titles and checked for the grades. Neatly typewritten, they all had a grade of A or higher. On the other side of the chest was a pile of family documents, correspondences with people whose names I didn't recognize, and clippings from newspapers—there was an article about the murder of Martin Luther King Jr., one about the work of Thich Nhat Hanh in Vietnam, and what looked to be excerpts from a longer piece entitled "Why War?" by Albert Einstein and Sigmund Freud.

I wouldn't have put anything in that chest under lock and key. But maybe the secret about secrets is that they live in a big wooden chest with a built-in lock in someone's private office. When you sneak into the office, find the key, and open the lid, it turns out to be just a pile of papers. Light a match and they're gone. Send them into the wind and you'll never see them again. Sit down and read them and you'll be bored to tears by the musings of someone's undergraduate essays. Maybe what's more interesting is how we hide our secrets; the wrapping paper around the magic trick of deception. I saw nothing in that wooden box of supposed treasures but, for some reason, I kept looking.

Near the bottom of the pile of family documents, newspaper clippings, and random photos was a brown manila envelope that had an unusual thickness to it. Inside was a small booklet made of plain brown stock paper, stapled in the middle, with a title typed crookedly. *In the Wilderness* by Martha Wiens looked to have been printed shortly after the invention of the printing press and threatened to blow away into bits at the slightest hint of air movement in the room. Who was Martha Wiens and why would dad keep a book of poetry in his possession? I turned to the first page.

"73 Verses"

73 verses
that's all it takes
Jesus got off with 39 lashes
One short of death

"Nun danke all Gott
mit Herzen, Mund und Handen"
Tell me,
How can I thank you God, with all my heart
When loving You leaves nothing for me?
How can I thank you God, with the fullness of my voice
When my tongue was cut out like a female circumcision
generations ago?

How can I thank you God
When it is my hands, absolutely thankful
that finally reach out to touch her skin
which releases my voice, sweating out of my body
in a purging ecstasy enveloping my body in love?

You make me choose between my lover
And You, my distant threat
    (so much more distant when I see the righteous anger glowing
    in their eyes)
I anticipate the lash attacking your skin and I will not allow that
Because I'm the bastard child
I understand how it is to have your father drive past in his pick-
up without a care that you exist

And now 73 verses—just some more of the same nails driven
through my palms
    Crucifying me
    A death I will die forever

I assure You
    My love for Her will not relent

I read the capitalized pronoun over and over again. Her. Her. Her. I checked the front cover of the small chapbook again and knew by the last name that the poet was Mennonite.

It was like finding a joint or pornography or a photo of my dad having an affair. I couldn't quite grasp what I was holding in my hand; I knew that I needed to take it.

I touched the page reverently and then felt terror, convinced that at any moment mom and dad would burst through the door and catch me red-handed. That they would see the tiny book in my hand and invoke the wrath of God. I slid the chapbook back into the manila envelope, replaced the stacks of paper in the chest, and closed the lid. I exited the office, chapbook in-hand—a tomb raider.

FEAR AND TREMBLING

I put the book on my bed and paced around my room with my back to it. Occasionally I would turn and look at it. I felt like I was hosting a fugitive. I didn't know what to do with that little criminal of a book and I was way too scared to read any more of the poems. I thought God would strike me with a lightening bolt just for having it in my room.

I wanted to find this woman. I had an idea of who she might be; there was a woman who lived on the banks of the river who I would sometimes see in the hardware store and thought I had heard her name. I remembered a time when I was child in the hardware store with dad when, for some reason, I mistook her for my mother— maybe she was wearing the same coloured pants as my mom that day. I followed her up the aisle and grabbed a hold of her legs, yelling, "Mommy." Dad charged over, ripping me away from the woman without saying a word. I remember the woman saying, "Dave, it's fine," with a familiarity that didn't make sense considering I had never seen her before. My father said nothing, carrying me to the cash register and quickly out the store. I felt awful and never again mistook my mom's pants for anyone else's.

I looked at the book thinking it was a direct sign of what I couldn't say out loud but desperately wanted to. Finally, turning to the book, I addressed it directly.

"Look, little book, I'm not afraid of you. OK, I'm terrified of you. Here's the truth, though, I'm going to read the rest of your pages anyway."

.....

Martha Wiens was saying what I couldn't, articulating my fear, making hidden thoughts known to me. In the darkness of my parent's house, reading that little book changed me. In the world of Anabaptist Mennonites, private reformations are discouraged, that much I knew, even then.

Looking at that book of poetry I knew I wasn't going to survive in my community. It felt like me and that little book were going to have to get the hell out of Dodge before a mob of silent, slowly moving Mennonites, wielding nothing more than their averted eyes like pitch forks, pushed us out.

Is that all community is? A collection of people who fear the same thing? I remember that it was strangely comforting when the fully illustrated version of *The Martyr's Mirror* was released. To think, a collection of stories chronicling the many harrowing tales of our Anabaptist and Mennonite forbearers being tortured to death for their faith was somehow comforting? I guess it was comforting to know there was a time when my people weren't afraid.

I tucked the small book under my shirt and, putting my ear to the door, listened to make sure that there was no one in the house. As silently as possible, I shut the door behind me, found the keys to the family car, and left the house.

TRUST ME, I'M A PROFESSIONAL

Hours after church had finished, my family returned home. Both John and Francis had moved out of the house by this time, but it was their custom to always come home for lunch after church on Sundays. Our family was always the first to arrive and the last to leave, but their return that Sunday was exceptionally late.

Part of the reason that I loved Sundays was that John and Francis would be home. There would be some friendly sibling pushing and shoving at the door when we took our shoes off. The lunch table conversation was always more animated with me and my brothers trading barbs, directing as many as we could get away with toward our parents.

When I reached the top of the stairs, mom and dad were seated at the table, while Francis and John were milling around the fridge, emptying its contents onto the table.

"Ruth Marie," my mom said, sounding tired, "we need to talk to you." She pointed to a chair across the table from her.

I didn't like this situation at all. My parents seemed far too calm. They seemed crazy, in fact, like while they were away at church they had snapped into insanity. Most importantly, mom called me by my given name, making it clear she was angry.

"What's going on?" I asked, suspicious, afraid that they had figured out I had been in dad's office and taken the car without permission. I moved toward my brothers at the fridge, helping them put things on the table. I couldn't allow my parents to look me in the eye.

"Well," dad started uneasily, "it's your behaviour of late. We think that…" dad trailed off looking at mom for help.

"You have not been keeping up your end of the bargain." She bit her top lip and nodded to herself.

"What exactly is my 'end of the bargain,' I didn't realize that there was a bargain."

"We've spoiled you so much," my mom said, shaking her head. I thought she might cry. "Always let you have your own way."

"What are you talking about?"

John and Francis stopped their emptying and turned to face me. I looked to them for help but they both looked at the floor.

"We think that you'd be happier at private school in Ontario," my dad said in his professor voice. "A friend of mine is the principal there and you can stay with them."

"What? No, I'm not going to be happier at a private school in Ontario." I rolled my eyes to heaven. "All my friends are here," I said in a tone that indicated that what I was saying was nothing short of obvious.

"You don't have a choice, Ruth," dad said, fingering his wedding band, barely looking at me. It looked like he might pull his finger right out of the socket. He said my name like I was being referred to, not addressed. Like he was rehearsing his lines.

I looked around for signs warning me that I had stepped into the middle of a minefield. My dad looked volatile and I had no map. Mom's expression was changing by the millisecond between tears and nothing.

I stood, holding the tub of yogurt I had pulled out of the fridge. "Francis and John didn't have to go to any far off school. You're just going to ship me? What have I done that's so bad?" I threw the yogurt at the kitchen sink. Its contents exploded onto the floor and neighbouring cupboards.

The family stood frozen as a collective until mom walked to the kitchen window and closed the blinds.

"Stuff like this," my dad said, pointing to the sink. "Believe me, Jess, this is a hard decision for us but we would feel even guiltier if we didn't do something to deal with your problems. We're your parents and we need to make hard decisions sometimes." He looked at me with disappointment in his eyes. "You didn't even come to church this morning," he said in a startlingly high-pitched tone at a volume just below a scream.

Mom's head jolted to the side as though dad had reached over and punched her.

I looked at John shaking my head in disbelief.

"Mom, dad," John said after what seemed like an eternity, "I know that you're frustrated right now, but what about if Jess and I go for a ride and talk?"

Dad shrugged. John put his hand on my shoulder and directed me to the door. Mom stood expressionless.

"Come on, let's go buddy," John said before I could respond.

"I haven't eaten," I protested.

"I'll buy you food in town," John said, pushing me toward the door.

I said nothing as I sat down on the bench seat and pulled the door closed sharply.

"Hey," John said, annoyed, "take it easy, you're going to pull the door right off the hinges." His brow was furrowed for a moment before it relaxed again. The only thing that really got under John's skin was mistreatment of his truck. He was Zen-like in most other respects, but abuse directed toward his truck in any way always provoked a response.

John started the truck and tapped the pedal to make the engine rev more slowly. He then reached down to a pile of tapes in a box on the floor, selected one, and pushed it into the cassette deck. He had showed me how to install that cassette deck the previous summer. I wasn't particularly interested, but he had insisted that it was the least he could do as an older brother, so I eventually acquiesced.

Loon calls came to life from the stereo speakers and soon the slightly maniacal voice of Gord Downie sang, "Sun down in the Paris of the prairies/ Wheat kings have all their treasures buried." *Fully Completely* was one of the four tapes my brother and I could agree upon while in the car together. Another one was Blue Rodeo's *Five Days in July*. I can't remember the other two. As we accelerated out of Blaurock toward Saskatoon, I rolled down the window and stuck my head out like a dog.

This was not the first time he had brought me out of Blaurock to convince me to stay. I had been running away from home since birth. I had never been asked to leave before, though; that part was new.

"John, I think that I want to smoke some weed."

"What? No, absolutely not....and I don't even have any or do that," he said, eyes focused on the flat highway in front of us.

I reached down and opened the glove compartment, pulling out an unmarked cassette tape cover that I had spotted before pulling out the *Tragically Hip* tape. John gave me a sideways glance but said nothing as I pulled out a joint.

"OK, fine, I guess if you're going to smoke it should be with your older brother," he said, still not looking directly at me.

"Busted," I said.

He smiled. "We have to wait until I'm not driving though; I'm not driving while stoned because that's dangerous. And you have to promise not to tell any of your friends, I don't want this getting back to mom and dad. Not even one friend," he said, wagging his finger at me.

"What, are you afraid that mom and dad are going to ship you off too?"

"Ah, buddy," he said. "They're just upset. This will blow over, trust me."

The night had started to set in, but it was still easy to see the mounds of snow that remained despite the warm and sunny days.

My fists curled up and tightened; my right hand was still scabbed and sore from going through the wall the week before. I mentally patted myself on the back for the pre-emptive action I was going to take. I wasn't going to be sent away.

John pulled the truck into a parking spot near the Bessborough Hotel. The old CN hotel sitting on the banks of the South Saskatchewan River is easily the most beautiful building in Saskatoon, bringing some sort of stability to a struggling prairie city even while it sinks into the riverbank. We walked toward the river in silence and found a dry bench. The day had been very warm for early spring, but as the sun went down the temperature dropped.

We lit the joint, passing it back and forth several times before declaring it cashed. Every muscle in my body relaxed and released as the stone quickly set in.

"Why didn't you go to church today?" John asked, yawning.

"I went to see that lady who lives down by the river just east of where we used to pick Saskatoon berries."

"Who?" John said, trying to stifle another yawn. And then, becoming more alert, shook his head slightly. "Are you guys friends or something? Why would you go and see that lady?"

"I don't know her. I actually didn't get a chance to talk to her." It was one of the first times I had lied to John; it wasn't much of a lie, but a lie none-the-less. I had only had about five minutes before I realized that if I didn't head back home my absence would be discovered. "Don't tell mom and dad, OK? I just wanted to ask her about poetry."

"OK."

"I had a dream last night, John."

"Did it have to do with not going to church?" John said, grinning slightly.

"John, I am a homosexual," I said with as much enunciation I could muster.

John's smile appeared and I felt at ease. "Dude," was all he said before starting to giggle.

I giggled, too, because the only options were to join him or freak out.

"Maybe it's for the best if I do just go away, John. There's no way that with dad's new job I can be his daughter. Fuck, John, it's better if I just go away."

"Jessie, stop, what are you thinking?" His eyes were wide, "This will pass, there's no need to contemplate things like suicide."

I rolled my eyes. "John, I'm not thinking about suicide. Let's not get too dramatic here," I said. "I think that we should get some food; it feels like I haven't eaten in six hundred years."

"Yeah, yeah," he said nodding his head slowly. "Let's talk about this. We should really talk about this."

When he said "this" I knew that he couldn't name it. I stood up, found a rock, and threw it into the river.

"*This?* 'This' is me John," I said, turning to face him again.

John was the only one in my family that I felt had a set of ears. He was the only one that I could truly be myself around. More importantly, he was the only one I felt comfortable around while in a state of disagreement.

"I miss you already." I said, looking toward the river again.

"Come on, stop it. Let's get some food and video games," John said as I followed him back to his truck. "Don't talk like that, we'll get this figured out, I promise. You know, maybe it would be better if I started spending more time at home during the week." He sounded as though he genuinely thought that would make the situation better.

We drove over the Broadway Bridge toward Fifteenth Street. We got to his house and John served up ice cream as I loaded the game.

We always played the same skateboarding game, which was an exercise in futility. John's hand-eye co-ordination was much better than mine to begin with, not to mention that he had spent hour after hour procrastinating from writing both an undergraduate and masters' thesis playing this particular game. I never had a chance except that night, he started nodding off. The controller slipped from his hands as his head rested on the top of the old couch. I watched him fall asleep.

I took the keys to his truck from the table—he was always losing them, so I reasoned he wouldn't be horribly upset when they weren't around, failing to consider that I also wouldn't be around. As I put my shoes on, I avoided looking at my snoring brother. I made my way out the door as quickly as possible.

I took Broadway to Fourth, cut across to Second, then drove along until it became Warman Road and then Waneskewan Road and, finally, Highway 11. As I reached highway speed, I rolled down the window and closed my eyes for a second. I was so tired that I had to will my eyes to open again. "Fuck," I said to myself, "fuck, fuck, fuck. Don't cry. You are not going to cry."

The lights were all out in the house. I checked my watch; I had no time to spare. I prayed to the stealth gods that mom and dad wouldn't wake up as I crept downstairs, opening my closet door as silently as possible. After retrieving my pre-packed belongings, I found my mom's grocery/to do list on the fridge and left it on the middle of the table where I knew it would be found.

Dear mom and dad,

Sorry this didn't work out. Just tell people I went to private school in Ontario.

Jess

MY GODDESS: ABUNDANCE, DESIRE, LOVE, FERTILITY, AND SPRING

When I got to the meatpacking plant on the west side of the city, I turned the truck north again and followed a dark little street to the train station. It was hidden amongst the freight cars and seemed to be a little light shining just for me.

John had taken me there a few times to look at the trains coming through town and to explain the virtues of train travel. He always told me that the train was the most interesting and beautiful way to travel.

Parking John's truck, I checked my watch again—12:45 am. Locking the keys inside the truck, I touched the hood—a warm feeling against the cold night that had set in.

"I'm sorry, John, I hope you find her."

My eyes had to adjust to the bright lights of the station as I opened the door. I caught my breath as I spotted the baggage cart being loaded. The rag-tag assortment of luggage was being loaded onto a wooden cart with big wheels that looked as though it might be hitched behind the train and pulled down the rails. Despite the relative modernity of the building, everything seemed so old-fashioned and otherworldly. There were no armed guards or X-ray machines or sniffer dogs; the only thing holding back passengers was a polite velvet rope and a sign saying "Line Forms Here." The lack of security struck me as a harkening back to days of implicit trust—a time before my birth.

I felt giddy, like I was walking through a lucid dream controlling the events at will, able to do things that I could not do in my waking life, such as buying a train ticket. I had never spent that much of my own money before that night. The cash felt unreal—it had to be unreal, because my parents would have never allowed me to take that much out of my account, let alone spend it. The money didn't feel like mine despite having spent many summers toiling away for a few of the many farmers who attended our church. I wondered if I would step foot in a field again. Dedicated lobbying on my part had finally convinced a farmer from our church to teach me how to drive a tractor and let me out onto his field alone to pick rocks. For hours and hours I wandered around the field looking for rocks that might give the cultivator, seeder, swather or combine trouble. The dust would come over the field, finding its way into every nook and cranny of my body, painting itself as another layer of my sunburned skin.

My parents had always been clear about the fact that they knew how to manage my money much better than me. "Nothing I owned was truly mine" had been instilled in me from an early age. The body of Christ, after all, is corporate, and the fifth commandment—don't forget—is to honour your mother and father.

"A student one-way to Winnipeg," I said, producing my high school student card, which the attendant barely glanced at. I had rehearsed saying those simple words all the way from Blaurock to Saskatoon to make sure I sounded as calm as possible when saying it in the heat of the moment.

"One-thirteen forty-two," he said, focusing on his computer screen.

The computer spit out my ticket and I walked away from the counter staring at it with a sense of pride. I sat down amongst my fellow travellers and smiled as I heard the train pull in, howling its arrival. In response to the sound, people started hugging each other with the usual words of travel: "Have a good trip" and "Call me when you get there." I looked around half-expecting my parents to walk in the door. I put my hood on and zipped my jacket all the way up. My heart was racing.

I sprinted toward the first available car when the gate was opened onto the platform. I kept thinking that someone would ask me what I was doing there alone or where my parents were. I tried not to meet anyone's eyes, afraid that they would see "I'm running away" hanging in my eyes like a sign.

When I boarded, I walked as far as I could into the bowels of the car and finally found a spot out of the general vicinity of anyone else. I heard the train moving away from the station before I felt it. As the train lurched forward, I looked out the dark window and saw my reflection against the backdrop of Saskatoon. It smiled and stared back at me. I took a deep breath as the conductor came to check my ticket and bring me a blanket.

"You should go up to the observation car," the man said as he clipped my 'seat claimed' ticket above me. "It's a few cars back," he said, gesturing with his thumb behind him. "We turn the lights out up there so you can have a better view. It's pretty fantastic."

"Thanks," I said.

The train chugged away from Saskatoon, no questions asked.

I grabbed my wallet and the blanket and headed in the direction he had pointed. Finally I made my way to the dome car but, to my surprise, at the bottom of the stairs leading up to the observation deck was the smoking lounge. The car was a smoky blue. A few men sat at a table with packs of cigarettes cracked open. They all had worn and dirty hands and were sporting clothes that had the name and logo of the train company they worked for.

I sat down at the table across the aisle from them and started checking my pockets as if I had lost my cigarettes. "Shit!" I swore, in a staged whisper. I stood up and continued to check my pockets.

"You need a smoke?" one of the men said from the table across the aisle.

"Yeah, you know, I think I forgot them at home," I said, hoping to sound as though I had smoked before. I decided that if Hagar Shipley could start smoking in her senior years, I would start preemptively, in my junior years.

"Thanks," I said, grabbing the cigarette and lighter from the man. I lit my cigarette. Behind the glow of the flame a woman sat in the corner by the stairs going up to the observation deck. She caught my eye just as the smoke hit my lungs and I realized that smoking a cigarette was much different from smoking weed. I looked over at the men at the table and tried to smile in spite of myself.

"You OK?" The man said, chuckling.

"Yeah, yeah," I stuttered, "I think that maybe I smoke lighter cigarettes than you do." Nervous laughter escaped from my mouth like a puff of smoke.

"The blacker the better," the man said, laughing in that good old boys kind of way. The rest of the men joined him. "Here, have the pack, I've got to quit before I see the wife tomorrow. I'm getting too old for this." He tossed the pack to me and smiled as though he was handing down some sort of family heirloom.

The men went back to their conversation about a garage that one of them wanted to build in the back yard but 'the wife' wouldn't let him. I sat, amazed, looking at the pack of cigarettes, unable to comprehend my good fortune. I went back to staring out the window while out of the corner of my eye I concentrated very hard on the woman sitting in the corner.

As we rode through the gut of the prairies, the gentle sway of the train and the quiet dark made me feel like I was in a dream. The full moon lit up the fields surrounding us. All I heard was the warning cry of the whistle and the wheels below grinding out space and time.

I pulled out the battered copy of *In the Wilderness* as I tried not to stare at the woman. She was deep in thought and several times took the pencil she was chewing on out of her mouth to underline sentences and passages. A large blue stone hung at the base of her throat, and her blond hair was messed up in just the right places. A matching blue stone ring ran the length of her left middle finger from the base to the knuckle. With Thai fishing pants, a pair of sandals (no socks) and a halter-top, she looked impossibly underdressed for the cold soon-to-be-spring weather. It was like she had her own bubble around her that kept the weather temperate and the sun shining, giving her in a perpetual tan.

I turned to the second poem and started reading.

Quilts and wooden furniture
Neatly stitched decorative wall hangings
Earnest four part harmonies praising God in heaven
Rows planted straight
Hair in place
Neatly coiled cinnamon buns rising in the oven

A crescendo of Kraft! ...

I looked up to see if she was still there and put my hood on in an effort to make myself small. Leaning against the window, I brought my knees up to my chest and held myself in a little ball wedged between the table and the bench seat. I read on, not sure what the author meant by "Kraft!"

Horse tackle unmatched
Mother's komst borscht bubbling on the stove
Cords of wood stacked perfectly against the night
33 bushels of potatoes from just one acre
Carefully cleaned-out pig intestines ready to be stuffed full again

A crescendo of Kraft!...

"Do you want an apple?"

38

I jumped and turned my head to see her heavenly face hovering above me and her hand holding the fruit out to me.

"Yes, I would. I kind of forgot to bring food," I said in a stutter, reaching for the apple. Bringing food along hadn't even crossed my mind.

"A virgin smoker," she said smiling and squinting her eyes as I took a bite of the apple. "The train's a good place to start."

"I've smoked before," I said, scoffing at her.

She leaned across the table, getting closer to my left ear and whispered, "It's OK, your secret's safe with me as long as you share one of those with me." She leaned back, pointed at the pack, and laughed quietly, a slightly devilish smirk on her face.

"Jess," I said, reaching my hand across the table, "and yes, you're welcome to have a cigarette."

"So, Jess, my name is Freya and I want to give you a little piece of advice, the next time you want to meet someone, just get up and introduce yourself." She smiled again, her tone friendly and inviting.

I could feel myself turning crimson and averted my eyes out the window. "That obvious, hey?"

"Yes, but that's OK because you're very cute," she smiled again, squinting slightly. "You also appear to be in a worse mental state that I am." This time she was serious. I felt like she could see right through me.

"That obvious, hey?" I said, averting my eyes again.

"Yup. But you know, it takes one to know one, so spill, Jess, because we've got nothing but time, a pack of cigarettes, and open prairie right now."

"Well," I said, looking around to see if anyone was listening in, "I've got a little bit of shit to work through with my parents so I'm kind of taking a break away from them."

"Yeah, distance helps sometimes." She lit her cigarette and exhaled slowly through her nose. "I'm just coming back from a trip to visit my dad and I'm really glad that I don't have to spend too much time with him. We're just so different. It's soul sucking." She tapped her cigarette on the tin ashtray.

"He can't even whisper the word 'dyke,' and he's so interested in making money. He's this lawyer who's got a serious case of little-man syndrome—he's always totally overcompensating. He pretends to be so cool and worldly about everything but really he's just so small town." She shook her head.

At least, I think that's what she said. I didn't hear much after she said the word "dyke." I had never heard anyone say it so casually. Never had I heard anyone own it and be angry that someone wouldn't call them that.

"So what's the plan, Jess?"

I shook my head, trying to come back to the conversation, and smiled. "I have no plan. I didn't really think past the part where I get on this train."

"Spontaneous," she said, ashing her cigarette. "I like that." This time her voice was thick and low, her tongue barely moving as she said the words.

I laughed, shocked that anyone would peg me for that kind of person. I looked out the window and watched the passing glow of white snow outside the car.

"What are you reading?" she asked, pointing to the book of poetry I had instinctively tried to conceal under my elbow. It felt like I had been caught with porn.

"Ah, it's a book of poetry."

Freya laughed, "Yes, clearly, but who's the author?"

"Martha Wiens," I said suddenly, with more confidence, hoping that someone like Freya might be able to shed some light. Maybe Martha Wiens was famous and I was simply unaware of her existence; maybe she was one of those authors famous everywhere but her hometown.

She smiled and shook her head, "I've never heard of her. Is she from Canada?"

"Actually, I think she might be from my hometown, but I'm not sure, I just discovered her."

"How did you discover her?"

"Rummaging through my dad's personal effects," I said casually.

She threw her head back and burst out laughing. "You're so funny," she said, still laughing. "It's just the way you say things. You have great timing."

"Yeah, I think I do," I said, trying to sound as sexy as possible.

"We should go upstairs," Freya said, motioning to the observation deck. "You'll love the view and, if we're lucky, there might be some northern lights."

I followed her up the stairs where she led me to the back of the dimly lit car. The rounded roof was clear plastic, giving passengers a full view of the sky. Two people sat near the front across a table from each other, engaged in an intensely silent game of chess.

"There," Freya said, gently cupping my chin to face my eyes in the right direction.

My stomach melted into my bowels when she touched me. I thought I might throw-up onto my lap, but instead I stared out the window and tried to calm my racing heart.

I didn't see anything, maybe it was temporary blindness or she was looking for a reason to touch me. I didn't care.

"When I was a kid," I said, trying desperately to maintain the illusion of calm, "we used to stand out in the fields that surrounded our town and scream at the top of our lungs because we were convinced that you could make the northern lights dance if you screamed loud enough."

"Did it work?"

"I'd like to think so."

"You're not going back, are you?" Freya asked, hushed and reverent.

I inhaled quickly and tried to stop the stinging in my eyes. Freya took my hand in hers. "What's going on? In three sentences or less, tell me how you're feeling right now," she said brushing my hair back from my eyes.

I was used to John pushing me quietly to speak my feelings but there was a quality to her caring that was new to me.

"Um, well, I guess that I am not straight and we're Mennonites and my parents will never accept me so I left." I wanted to cry, but I didn't feel that safe. I saw myself as an injured animal that had to wait until I got into the thicket to recover.

"It's so ridiculous how people can let their religion get in the way of loving their kids, especially when I could tell within two seconds of meeting you that you're amazing," she said.

It was different from John's reaction—she seemed genuinely outraged on my behalf. She seemed ready for a fight. I felt that after knowing me for only thirty minutes she understood me in a way that I'd never been understood. I felt like a new land being discovered by a seasoned explorer and I was happy to be mapped.

"I grew up in Winnipeg, and all the Mennonites I know are either total hicks from hell or have completely walked away. Good for you for walking away." She furrowed her thin eyebrows and shook her head.

41

I said nothing. Was it that simple? *Good for you for walking away?* I didn't know what to do with that comment; it didn't seem remotely that simple.

Although I was on a train chugging away from my family, friends, and church it hadn't occurred to me that I was walking away from anything. I was covered, like a skin—I couldn't just walk away from being Mennonite.

"It doesn't seem that simple," I mumbled to myself.

"Then why are you on this train?" She moved her head and looked me directly in the eyes.

I laced my fingers together as though I was about to pray. "Leaving before I'm forced to leave."

"Now that sounds like an over-simplification," she said, not letting go of my eyes.

My lips were frozen. I took it as an insult.

She smiled. "What do your parents do? What's their story?"

"My mom is a housewife and my dad's a prof at the U of S—well, I guess now he's the president of the Mennonite College there."

"So, if your dad's an academic why isn't he a little more liberal or open minded—he should be." It wasn't a question so much an expression of disgust.

"My dad wasn't supposed to go to university," I said, feeling defensive. "You know what happened when my dad got his university acceptance letter, my grandpa punched him in the face."

"Why?"

"I don't know, I guess grandpa wanted my dad to do what he was told—join the family business—and I guess he felt like maybe dad was trying to insult him by becoming educated. I guess some Mennonites are kind of suspicious of education or something."

"Suspicious that it might change their minds about things? That they may start thinking differently about the world?" she said, laughing.

"Well, it has more to do with the split between the wave of immigrants who left Russia in the late nineteenth-century and those who left in the wake of the Russian Revolution—more class differences than anything," I said. "A division emerged between the highly educated Mennonites who owned land and those who were landless," I continued, slowing down, realizing that I sounded like a dork. "And my relatives were landless...sorry, I'm not making sense, I know."

"It's OK, it's just not the answer that I was expecting," she smiled again. "My dad is constantly trying to exceed expectations," Freya offered. "Icelanders have always been great champions of higher education, so both sets of grandparents really pushed their kids to succeed and now my parents are total over-achiever, workaholics, especially my dad." She paused for a moment to massage her neck. "My dad just told me this weekend that he's accepted a position with some fucking evil law firm in Toronto and he's moving there in a month."

"My parents wanted to ship me off to a private school in Ontario— I think my dad's afraid of me, that he might get fired or something."

"Why would he get fired because of you?"

I felt breath sharp in my throat and a familiar tightening around my neck. "I guess that they think I'm a trouble or something; that I'll shame him."

"Because you're queer?" she said.

"I don't know," I said quickly. "Um, OK. Yes," I said, finally.

Silence fell between us. I rested my head on the back of the seat and closed my eyes, trying to figure out how to respond to her in the way that she wanted me to. I wasn't sure, so I said nothing.

"What happened to your fist, Jess?" She was quiet as she picked up my hand to examine it more closely. "Did someone hit you or something?"

"Umm," I said, hesitating, "I punched a wall. But please don't think that I'm a violent person," I added quickly.

She laughed, "You don't strike me as the violent type, and besides, you're a Mennonite. Aren't you supposed to be all peace-loving, pacifist-types?"

"Yeah, exactly, but I was just really pissed-off and then there was a fist through the wall and that fist was mine."

"You have really beautiful hands," she said in a low voice. "Here," she said, reaching into her bag, "you need some calendula for this bruise. It will heal better."

She took my hand again and gently rubbed the ointment on it. Leaning in, she hesitated while biting her bottom lip. She kissed my ear and neck very softly.

"How about we get off the train in Winnipeg and spend some time in my bed?" She almost giggled.

"Yeah," I grunted, unable to say anything coherent, "I think that's a good idea."

Just as the train bent itself around a corner and the whistle howled again, an elderly couple came into the observation car and sat down across the aisle from us. I pulled away from Freya in response.

"Hmm," she said, "maybe it's time for another cigarette." Standing up, she led the way back down the stairs to the smoking car below.

"So," she said, taking a cigarette from the pack I had thrown back onto the table, "any siblings to distract your parents from your absence?"

"Yeah, I've got two brothers, John and Francis. They're both kind of perfect though. John's studying to be the next Carl Jung or something and Francis is happily selling tractors with our grandpa. They don't really do anything wrong except for spending too much time playing video games and perhaps loving their trucks just a little more than they should." I smiled, taking another drag of the cigarette; it was becoming easier with every inhalation.

"I'm an only child," she said, gently ashing her cigarette. "It's just me and my divorced parents." She stopped and stared at me for a moment. "You know what the secret is, Jess? You will never make your parents happy. They're parents and by their very nature they will always be disappointed in you because that's what they do, they just want you to be the greatest person that ever walked the planet."

"I think my parents would just be happy if I was the most normal person who ever walked the planet." I looked out the window but could only see my own reflection.

She smiled and, touching my arm, said, "Well, I'm glad that you're not."

One of the conductors walked into the smoking car and in a loud I've-said-this-a-million-times voice said, "We're now entering into the Province of Manitoba."

"Daut freit mi sea," I said, raising an imaginary glass.

"What the hell was that?" Freya said, snorting. "That sounded like gibberish. I almost mistook it for Icelandic."

"It's Low German; it just means 'that makes me happy.' We don't really have a word for 'cheers,' because we're not really supposed to drink. Anyway, I'm happy that we're out of Saskatchewan, but I miss her already."

"Saskatchewan is the asshole of Canada; enjoy your new-found freedom from the depths of that asshole." She raised her own imaginary glass to that statement and threw it back with a dramatic flare. "Skald!"

"I think that you just hate it because your dad lives there," I said more seriously than I had intended.

She flinched slightly and then regained her composure. The expression of weakness in her eyes lasted the duration of the car going over one cross-tie on the track.

"Gotta go to the bathroom," I said, motioning to the tiny door three feet away, "I'll be right back."

I locked the door securely, checking it twice before lifting the lid of the toilet, crouching down half way, and throwing up violently. After it was all out I fell backward, hitting my head against the sink, and crumpled to the floor. I held my hand out and watched it shake. Finally, I got up, washed my face and hands, checked myself in the mirror, and walked out.

To my great surprise, Freya was still sitting in there, waiting for me.

"Let's go back upstairs," was all she said.

.....

She fell asleep curled up beside me in the observation car. I watched the passing bits of light that I could find out the window. The laughter from the smoking car spilled upstairs as the rail men continued to talk long into the night, sipping coffee, lighting cigarette after cigarette, and playing rounds of cards. The train chugged along, slowing down at times but never fully stopping. The motion was relaxing and the sound of the whistle comforting. It occurred to me that train travel served the very important purpose of suspending the traveller between departed and arrived. I knew that I had to leave, but arriving was a mystery to me. I felt thankful for the time it was taking me to travel, affording me the opportunity to fully leave while gaining a sense of where I might arrive.

The reason I considered relocating to Winnipeg was my visit the previous summer for a national Mennonite youth conference. I thought I could call a few people I had met through the conference and see if they would put me up for a few nights. My plan was to tell them that I was spending a few days in Winnipeg to decide whether I wanted to go to university there.

I opened *Into the Wilderness* and turned to the third poem.

I shovelled shit long enough
To recognize the motion miles away from the farm
I made my hasty exit and shut the barn door behind me

I brushed my boots off

Watched the caked mud and manure, straw and grain
Join the grass beside the house
Bathed the smell of cows from my hair

I clicked my clean shoes down the mopped halls of academia
Right into your office
I thought you might understand –
Your thick Low German lilt
Your squared face
Your last name declaring shared heritage on your office door
The smell of smoke still caught up in the hairs of my nose
They burned your books
Your mythology began rising from the ashes
I was like the bison herds chasing fresh sprouts of grass

What were Martha's instructions to me in this poem? I couldn't decide if she was suggesting that university education was a good idea. A comment on people like my dad, to be sure, but was it an invitation to walk away or fight? I hadn't had a chance to ask her about whether she had graduated from university or what sage advice she might have for me regarding that matter. I hadn't really had a chance to ask her any questions at all. When I started asking her about whether she was a poet or not she started asking me questions like "Exactly what poems are you speaking about?" and "Is your father David Klassen?"

I went over the story in my mind, developing my parents as characters, imagining what one would be doing if pretending to look at university options, figuring out how to respond to the question of why I hadn't called ahead of time.

I watched Freya sleep and thought about how lucky I was to not have to call anyone and make up stories. The gentle rhythm of the train lulled me to sleep as the last vestiges of adrenaline seeped out of my body. I succumbed.

I dreamt that I was in Africa wandering through the Kalahari with my brother John. Suddenly we were surrounded by every kind of African danger in animal form—lions, tigers, cheetahs, panthers, rhinos, and jackals. Luckily, John and I had brought a gun along, but when I took aim and fired at an animal I missed. I was scared to death and turned around, looking to John for support. But he had vanished. I was angry, but it quickly passed as I realized that the animals were getting closer. I needed a plan. I moved closer to one side of the circle of animals and took a couple of shots at close range, hoping to escape their circling. As I got closer and raised my rifle to take a shot, I saw that what I thought were predators were really goats and sheep. They were lying peacefully in the grass as I walked past them safely.

I woke up just outside of Winnipeg.

.....

I followed Freya and the gaggle of friends who greeted her at the train station. My feet shuffled along the marble floor as we opened the large doors and I took in the intersection of Broadway and Main. The sun shone brightly on that Monday afternoon. Somebody named Eyes helped me with my belongings, eagerly and enthusiastically welcoming me to Winnipeg. No one seemed to find it odd that I was following them home.

THIS IS MY STORY (AND I'M STICKING TO IT)

Oh, my stomach. The pain. Bathroom. Where the hell was I? Please, darkness. Top of stairs. Cold porcelain. Expulsion.

"Jesus, how long have I been in here?"

"I'd say at least ten minutes."

"What the hell…oh, Freya."

"Were you really expecting Jesus?"

"It controls me. I get upset and it sends me packing." She wasn't buying it. Blank stare. Realization. "I don't have a fucking eating disorder, if that's what you're thinking."

Finally laughter.

"Um, I'm not sure if drinking a mickey of gin is called an eating disorder, an introduction to alcoholism perhaps, but let's not insult those with eating disorders." She handed me a glass of water. I gargled until it was gone. "I guess you have officially welcomed yourself to the house," she said, laughing. "Do you always drink to the point of puking when you're nervous?"

"When I was a kid," I said, leaning against the cold toilet, "my grandpa came over one night." I reached for a couple of squares of toilet paper to blow my nose. "My dad opened the door and there he was—his father. Before my dad could even say hello my grandpa started screaming at him. I have no idea what grandpa was screaming about but I know that the screaming started just as I rounded the corner to launch myself into his arms for a hug. Rage spilled out of his every pore, and it hit me like a wave. I assumed that it was something that I had done so I turned around, ran to the bathroom, and threw up." I puffed up my cheeks and let out a big breath.

"Jess," Freya said, her hand extended to me.

I followed her to her bed. In bed I kissed her like it was my idea.

.....

"So that's sex, huh?" There was something between us. How can it be—strangers 24 hours previous and now that? What was I? The *Oxford English Dictionary* isn't helpful in these situations. Even the complete twenty-four-volume edition couldn't help me.

"Oh my God, you've never had sex before? I've deflowered you?"

"Um, no and yes respectively. Although I've never really understood what deflowered means."

There are looks of shock that one can witness. Like when you tell your cousin, who's just barely younger than you, that grandpa drove over her puppy. Or the look of horror on your parent's faces when you walk in on their afternoon "nap." But there is nothing like the look of horror and shock when you tell someone that they were your first, after the fact. I guess that's the kind of thing you're supposed to discuss before hand. Well, she never asked.

"I've never even kissed anyone before, but you seem like you're pretty good. Thanks." I also failed to reveal my age, but again, she never asked.

"Oh good, well, I should have known, I guess," Freya said stuttering. "Promise me that you'll never just jump into bed with the first girl who comes along again, OK?" A smile was cracking across Freya's face. It was the first time that I would have the upper hand with Freya. Like the second, and last, time, it was gained unwittingly.

"I can't promise anything," I said earnestly. At least I got her laughing again with that. I fell asleep with her smiling face pressed into my back.

In the morning, there was no one lying beside me.

You find out things later, after the fact, in hindsight, but it doesn't help in the moment, because you will never have that moment again. I was a child, being carried in the womb of my new lover, and I was alone that morning to contemplate how in love with her I was. I imagined Freya and I as old women sitting on rocking chairs on the front porch smoking cigarettes and reflecting on our fifty-five years of marriage.

She walked into the room and I looked up at her. "I'm in love with you," matter-of-factly, just like that.

"Oh yes, I know," she said in the curt manner that I would both come to love and hate. "Isn't that the only reason people have sex," she said sarcastically.

"Yes." I said earnestly. "Hey," I said just as she was about to turn around, "is your real name Freya?"

"Yes," she said, grabbing a book from her dresser, "is your real name Jessica?"

"No, it definitely isn't." I was about to tell her a story, but she cut me off.

"I have to go to class now. I'll be back later. Don't leave the house, you'll get lost." She turned to leave, then turned back toward me and crawled into bed for a second, kissing and touching me, making me wet and warm. That's the way love is, I reasoned. It's confusing, warm, panty-soaking, life-stopping sweetness.

My thoughts went to the night on the train and the party the night after. I realized I wanted to get on with the business of really being a real smoker. A conversation with Eyes made up my mind outside the house during the party. He told me, while lighting my cigarette, that if I wanted a way out of any uncomfortable situation it was best to start smoking. It was always an excuse to leave a conversation. If you arrive early and you don't know anyone, you can linger outside with a cigarette and not look creepy. Also, he said, finishing his argument, it kills your hunger when you've got nothing.

She took her hands off of me, as if she was a doctor finishing surgery and rolled out of bed. "Do you feel better now?" she said, grabbing her bag.

"Yeah," I said breathlessly. "We smoked all my cigarettes on the train, do you have any?"

"Yes," she said, tossing her pack onto the bed beside me. "Just don't blame me when you're hopelessly addicted."

"I will never blame you for anything, Freya." The moment it came out of my mouth I knew it was a lie.

"We're going to a book launch tonight. You'll love it."

And that's the way it was with her after that night. She would tell me things and we would have sex. I read the books she brought home. I went to the rallies, protests, and speeches she instructed me to attend. I became a chain-smoking vegan without a job. She directed me through the process of applying for welfare—making sure that a sixteen-year-old run-away was able to receive benefits with no questions asked.

Every day I would wake up, still amazed by the wonders of the night before. I thought I knew what it meant to be truly loved with Freya, but really I was tasting food I couldn't identify. And for all her

vegan leanings, she was a cheeseburger with fries; a comfort food at
its finest, neatly decorated in recycled, post-consumer cardboard and
with fifty per cent less fat. I thought that I was in love with her, and
she let me believe that. I thought that she was in love with me, and
she let me believe that too.

Freya rented a house with friends on Walnut Street, just north
of Westminster in Wolseley. The house was three stories, with every inch of space occupied by people or belongings. The basement
was a jam space for the various bands that the various housemates
played in, which ranged from hard-core punk music to traditional
bluegrass. There was always a damp smell in the house, and despite
their best efforts to keep the elements at bay with plastic covering
the windows, the wind found its way in nonetheless. The garage was
a bike storage and repair space and housed a "free" store, which was
the cause of some serious debate. The problem being that people
wanted to leave the free store open at all hours for people to peruse
at their leisure, while others were concerned about the safety of their
bikes. That debate was never resolved while I lived there.

They were neo-hippy anarchists who dumpster dived for food
and paid rent occasionally. How they survived was almost primi-
tive—they were hunter/gatherers at their urban best and I admired
them for it. When I think about it now, Freya was probably financed
by her mom and dad while the rest of them lived in varying degrees
of poverty.

They were all kind and generous. What they had, they shared. I
was shocked to find that the radical Mennonite/Christian ideals of
community, simple living, and civil resistance that my parents had
talked about, and exhibited in their own way, was being played out
within my adopted community without the use of God to justify or
propel their actions. I was so small town but I tried my hardest to
keep people from seeing it, which is why I mostly kept my mouth
shut and watched life from my favourite couch in the living room.

Freya had about six housemates, including me, and a wide range
of hangers-on and couch hoppers. There were extensive bookshelves
circling the living room—a collection of everyone's textbooks, and
books purchased, borrowed, and stolen. There was also a TV but
there were strict house rules regarding its usage for MOVIES ONLY.
The kitchen was also wall-to-wall shelving units with every type of
spice, canned good, dried good, cookbook, and condiment imagin-
able. The whole house was crammed to the rafters with books, food,

flyers, blankets, art projects, tools, potted plants, CDs, random furniture, and people.

Every night was scheduled and busy for Freya. She was, first of all, the co-ordinator for the university GLBT Centre, sat on the board of directors of the student's union Womyn's Centre, and volunteered for Food Not Bombs. She, along with her roomies, attended every rally and protest and critical mass bicycle ride. They made posters and handed out handbills informing their fellow Winnipeggers of the latest global disaster. They had huge parties that lasted well into breakfast time of the next morning. They cooked for each other, had sex with each other, played in bands with each other, and shared most everything else. All the while I sat on the couch making my way through the house library and listening in on heated debates.

Whatever was happening, Freya was either co-ordinating or somehow involved in.

One of Freya's housemates, Sam, questioned me one day about my coming out. I made some sort of joke about cumming a lot and lit a cigarette.

"I'm serious," she said. "From what you've told me since moving in here, which isn't much, you come from a pretty religious background. Are you struggling with that at all?" She was chopping up carrots for a soup that she was making and was able to continue with the rhythm of her cooking while talking to me. I found her very relaxed rhythm of cooking comforting, reminding me of the intuitive way that my mom put meals together.

Her expression turned to horror when I absent-mindedly ashed into her bowl of guacamole. I wasn't prepared for her question, not because I hadn't thought about it—it was always on my mind—just that no one had, up to that point, engaged me in that kind of discussion. Certainly not Freya. She was busy counselling young undergraduates through their sexual identity crises. Her idea of listening to me was increasingly becoming a combination of telling me to fuck my parents and to just "not feel that way anymore."

I was so caught up in my own mental/spiritual/emotional struggle, it was so all encompassing, so pervasive through my every thought, it hadn't occurred to me that I needed to talk to someone about it. I was the observer on the couch, fully immersed in the lives of others and in the books I read that my own life turned into a foreign concept that somehow inhabited every fibre of my being. Maybe my detachment was for my own preservation, maybe there was too much for my little brain to handle. I think that Freya felt she was doing everything she could for me by having me live with her.

As I stood staring at Sam, I realized that I was crying. I walked to the recycling box, fished a piece of paper out, and found a pen. On the kitchen counter I wrote as Sam quietly scooped the cigarette ash out of the guacamole. It was a pseudo-mathematical equation.

I am a homosexual

(My parents cannot have a homosexual child because
they think it's a sin) X (My father can't be the president of the
Mennonite University College if he does not reject his daughter
as a sinner) + (My father is an academic, accustomed to using
his rational mind in developing well constructed arguments
but when it comes to homosexuality the buck simply stops at
"It is a sin" (and mom agrees)) =

(My father (and mother) must reject me as a sinner because
apparently God thinks that I'm a sinner)

+ (One of the greatest sins is being a practising homosexual)

/ (My parents cannot be outside of community standards on
what God deems sin)

= Jess, as a practicing homosexual, must leave her family.

I handed the paper to Sam as she handed me her hankie. I blew my nose and wiped my tears. She held the soggy piece of paper in her hands and shook her head.

"I love you. I think you're wonderful," she said as she pulled me into her arms to hug me.

"I just don't know if I did the right thing. I feel guilty every day for hurting my parents, my family. I feel guilty for who I am."

Sam pulled me closer and with a fierceness that I had never experienced from her, said, "Never—don't you ever feel guilty about who you are. It's not your fault that your parents can't accept and love you for who you are."

"Maybe it is."

"Oh God, Jess," Sam whispered. Tears started to tickle down her face, dropping off her cheeks and hitting my forehead. "That's a lie you can't believe."

I pulled away from her and said, "Don't tell Freya I was crying today, OK?"

"Why?" she asked, surprised.

"Just don't, please. This is good enough," I said as I walked out of the kitchen.

Still, I missed my parents, my family. I wanted Freya to offer her family to me as a sort of makeshift replacement, but that was not to be. Freya would go to visit her mom without me, and I would hear snippets about the woman, but I was never allowed to go with Freya to her mother's house. Freya was never one for apologies; she simply said that I wasn't invited to visit her mom, end of conversation. I assumed that there was a very good reason for my not being allowed into that part of her life and never pressed her on the issue.

I wanted to be taken home and I hated myself for that.

When Freya talked about her mom, it made my heart hurt a little bit. I think that it was partially because she was a minister and I hadn't been to church for months. I mentioned several times that I might like to visit the Unitarian congregation that Freya's mom presided over, but that suggestion was always met by Freya with silence and then I would forget about it for a while.

One day, as I sat listening to an old Hank Williams record on one of those rare moments when I had the house completely to myself, the doorbell rang—also a rare occurrence, to be sure. No one ever rang the doorbell. Opening the door I saw a woman with hair the colour of snow, smiling brightly, a large turquoise stone hanging around her neck. She was wearing robes. After consideration, I realized that they were not robes of a religious order, simply the style of dress the woman obviously preferred.

"You must be new," she said, smiling, "at least, I'm pretty sure that we haven't met before."

"Jess," I said, extending my hand, knowing in that moment that it was Freya's mom. "Come in, I'll make coffee," I said, motioning toward the kitchen with my head.

She followed me inside as I went to the kitchen.

"I don't recall Freya mentioning anyone by the name of Jess. Did you just move in?"

I turned, holding the coffee canister in one hand and a cigarette that had somehow found its way out of the pack in the other. "I've been here for quite some time," I said, trying to hold back the feeling of knives in my throat.

She sat down at the kitchen table and crossed one leg over the other. "And how is it that you've found yourself in this kitchen at this very moment?" she said, her hands folded in front of her. Her eyes were too bright to stare into for long. Her small smile looked slightly mischievous.

I put my hood on and jammed my hands into the pockets of my sweater. "By your unexpected arrival," I laughed nervously. "I suppose that I was an unexpected arrival, too. But you know, everything seems to be unexpected, so it seems to make sense."

She smiled quietly.

"I met Freya on the train back from Saskatoon. I guess we were both on the way from visiting family."

"So you have family in Saskatchewan too?"

"Ah, yeah," I laughed despite myself, "all of my family." I was nodding my head as I turned around to attend to the coffee grinder.

"Did you runaway from them?" she said, slightly higher pitched, after the noise of the grinder stopped. She was chuckling to herself.

"Ah," I said, swatting my hand in the air, "I'm too old for stuff like that."

She nodded her head slowly. Her expression changed as she realized that while she had been joking, I wasn't. "Why did you have to leave your family?"

I chewed on the end of the string circling the hood of my sweater, hesitating to answer. "I'm glad that most people don't ask."

"Feel free to not answer that," she said.

"I don't think that you're most people."

"How come I'm so special?" she said, furrowing her eyebrows.

I shrugged, wanting to explain how she had a place in my heart without having met her, but couldn't.

"Is it complicated—your running away? Or do you mean you ran away by going to school in a different province, away from your family?"

"It's simple really," I said, letting go of the end of the string between my teeth, "but it's still hard. And it has nothing to do with school." I gripped the edge of the kitchen counter and looked down for a moment. "I like girls and not boys, like I'm supposed to. I kind of tried to talk to my parents about it but that went really badly, well, not badly in the fact that they hit me or anything, it's just that they..." I trailed off for a second, ashamed that I held so much fear in the face of no violence life-threatening actions from my parents. "I just felt so afraid, like something really really bad would happen if I tried to talk about it with them."

"Sometimes," she said, throwing me a line, her words paddling out to rescue me, "parents can provide everything for their child—food, shelter, an education, clothes, and opportunities. They can be the type of parents that I'm sure your parents are in that they love you and would never hurt you in any physical way, but they get scared. Without wanting to, I think, sometimes parents scare their children with the threat of taking away their unconditional love. To me, that is one of the most dangerous and scary things for kids; for anyone really." She stopped, as if lost in thought or a memory. "I don't blame you for running for your life," she said finally.

"I do," I said, gently pounding my fist on the counter in front of me. "There's nothing wrong with my life—I'm not like some kid in Sudan being forced into the army and my parents are selling me into prostitution or anything, and now I've ruined their life by leaving."

"How have you ruined their lives?" she said, catching my eyes for the brief moment that I would allow.

I started crying and felt like I might never stop. It occurred to me that my time without tears was a reprieve and not the norm. The time I slipped away into the bathroom to have a quick cry was adding up.

"People will ask my parents questions."

"Jess," she said, her voice cracking, "you did what you honestly and truly felt like you needed to do and that's all anyone can ask of you."

I bit my tongue and stood silent as the kettle whistled insistently.

It was Sunday afternoon. The sun was starting to wane. The curious feeling of nothingness began its once-weekly attack on me.

I poured the hot water into the French press and stirred the black liquid before forcing the grinds to the bottom with the plunger.

"Do you want to go outside and smoke that?" she said, pointing to the cigarette I had transferred to my mouth.

We sat down on the front steps of the house and just as I lit the cigarette Freya rode up on her bike.

"Jess," she said, not looking at me, "will you please excuse my mother and I."

I exhaled, "What? Why?"

Freya took the cigarette from me. "Thanks, I'll finish it up for you."

I went in the house, desperately wanting to overhear their conversation. Instead, I sat down on the couch and put the needle back down on the record. There was something about Freya's mom; I felt transparent in her presence. I wanted her to reach into me and wave her hands around like a faith healer.

Freya came into the house as I watched her mom walk down the street back to her car.

"Freya," I said as she walked past the living room on her way up the stairs, "what was that all about? Why are you mad at your mom?"

"I'm not."

I took the needle off the record again, "Really? Because it seemed like there was something wrong. I added, "I really like her."

"Of course you do. Of course you would."

"What's that suppose to mean?" I said, standing up, indignant and confused, as though I had done something wrong in speaking to Freya's mom.

"Well, I definitely need space from her overbearing nature, so it's a good thing that we're leaving for the lake soon." She continued up the stairs as I called up to her.

"Freya, what lake?"

She stopped at the top of the stairs and turned around. "Babe, we're going to Lake Winnipeg, I've mentioned this before," she said smiling.

"No, you've only said that you spent a lot of summers there but you didn't mention that we were going there."

"Well, why would that change?" She laughed, making me think that she was pulling my leg. "There are certain things I'm not willing to compromise on Jess, and this is one of them," she said, her tone changing. Turning sharply, she continued on her way closing, the door behind her as she went into the bedroom. I wandered the house, touching appliances around the kitchen and wondering if I wanted to go away from Winnipeg for an entire summer.

My Sunday afternoon malaise was kicked in fully as I opened the fridge door, looking for something to comfort me.

When you grow up going to church every Sunday, you might expect it to be difficult to sleep in on Sunday morning, but it wasn't. I would wake up late and make my way downstairs to join a throng of people making waffles or pancakes or breakfast burritos. I would enjoy my mornings thoroughly, perfecting my pancake flipping while listening to discussions of the local political landscape or comparisons of dumpster findings from the previous night or gossip about people's latest crushes.

All the while I didn't think about the fact that it was Sunday morning. I didn't think about sitting in a pew and listening to a sermon. I didn't think about the hour or so after church spent visiting with our fellow church members whom I had known my whole life. I didn't think about the safety that it offered me or the unqualified love I received whenever I played any small part in the service. I didn't think about the way my heart would lift into my throat while singing certain hymns. It wasn't a matter of thinking about anything.

In the morning I was fine, but everything I hadn't thought about in the morning would show itself in the shadows of the afternoon. I would become despondent, walking around the house aimlessly, vacillating wildly between wanting to be around people and wanting to be alone. My regular regime of smoking and reading did nothing to dissolve these feelings. I had always been taught that Sunday afternoons were for naps—*matta schlops*—but sleeping in the afternoon was not an option after sleeping until noon. Four o'clock would roll around and a quiet hell would break loose.

The pacing would start and then, as if playing a game of freeze-tag, I would stop to stare out the window for long periods of time. At the sight of the dirty dishes a wave of guilt would come over me, but halfway through washing them I found couldn't go on because I felt guiltier doing work on a Sunday. One time I rented four movies, determined to spend the day on the couch under a blanket, watching TV, but that just made me feel lazy, which then made me feel guilty.

I described it as Sunday PMS—a subconscious ache whose source, while so obvious to the casual observer, remains hidden to you.

Finally, and to my great surprise because I thought I was hiding it well, Freya noticed. The next Sunday afternoon, after I had stared out the front window of the living room for nearly half an hour, Freya walked into the room.

"Oh for fuck sake, Jess," she exhaled loudly, disgusted, "that's it. This is bullshit and it's gone on too long." I didn't turn around but I could hear her leave the room and race up the stairs.

Five minutes later she came down with a piece of paper in her hand.

"Here, here," she said, getting my attention, "here's a list of all the fucking Mennonite churches in Winnipeg; the names, the addresses, and the times. I never thought that I would ever utter these words, but GO TO CHURCH," she shrieked before exiting swiftly.

I smiled at the paper, wondering if everything would be solved if I just tried a different Mennonite church.

The next Sunday morning, I woke up at an appropriate hour, showered, and watched myself in the mirror as I put on my Sunday best, which certainly wouldn't have been considered my best by my parents. I took the neatly folded paper off my shelf in the bedroom and stared at the names. I kissed Freya on the forehead.

"Where are you going?" she said in a half sleeping state.

"To church," I said, smoothing her hair.

"Which church?" she said, almost frantically, becoming more conscious.

"This one," I said, pointing at the name on the list.

"Oh, OK, that's OK," she said, turning over and pulling the blankets back over her face. "Are you sure you don't want to stay home and have sex instead?" her voice muffled by the blanket.

"I think that I should do this."

I got on my bike and rode over to the closest one on the list. After locking my bike, I stood in front of the homely church, staring at the entrance. It was just after the official start time of the service.

The sign read "Sherbrook Street Mennonite Church, Sunday Service at 9:30 am. All Welcomed." On the sign was the insignia of the national church body—the same insignia my church in Saskatchewan had on its sign. I read the sign over and over again as my guts ran up and down the sides of my stomach, threatening to spill over. I paced in front of the door and then started crying.

I picked up a stone in front of me and threw it. It bounced off the large wooden door, making a soft sound. I picked up another rock, one that was a little bigger, and threw again. I scrambled around finding rocks and throwing.

I started banging on the door with my fist, still crying, and with another stone started carving into the wood.

"Dear God," I carved, the wood giving way easily to my makeshift pen.

My tears blurred my vision—I think I was screaming—and then I threw up onto the door. The vomit bounced off and caught part of my shoe.

With all the noise, I could no longer be ignored; someone opened a side door. "What are you doing? What's wrong with you? Do you want me to call the cops?"

I ran all the way back to Walnut Street, checking back to see if I was being followed. I got into the front entrance of the house, panting, tears still streaming down my cheeks.

Freya poked her head of the kitchen and said, "So how was church? Do you wish you would have stayed home in bed with me instead?"

I couldn't respond because I was trying to recover from my running and my fear and my tears.

"Hey," she said cheerfully as I ran up the stairs, "start packing your things. Jess, we're leaving bright and early tomorrow morning."

"Leaving for where?" I said, not turning around, wiping my cheeks with the back of my hand.

"For the lake. Come on, we've talked about this. Why are you flaking out on something that's important to me?" She sounded annoyed, and I felt that if I turned around I would see her standing with her hands on her hips.

"I just don't know if I want to leave Winnipeg for a whole summer. All my friends are here."

"You'll love it," she said.

When I did turn around she had already disappeared into the kitchen, end of discussion.

Snot ran down my chin as I walked toward one of the shelves in the kitchen. I took a liquor bottle with clear liquid in it outside with me to the front porch, along with the cordless telephone.

After hours of taking gulps from the bottle, it was almost empty. I realized that I had been clutching the phone in my other hand the whole time I had been sitting out there. I started sobbing uncontrollably as I dialled the familiar 306 area code.

"Hello?" My mother's sounded half-asleep.

I checked my watch to find that it wasn't late at all—only the afternoon.

"Mom," I said between sharp intakes of breath that sounded like a frog's night-time cry. "Mom," I said again.

"What?" She was silent for a moment while I sobbed. "David, is that you?"

"No mom, it's me, Jess." I waited, hoping that she would wake up from her haze and lead me through the conversation that we needed to have.

I heard the breathing on the other end of the phone increase rapidly. "I don't have time for this," she said between quick inhalations. "You're not the only one with problems on this earth," she said with a slight slur before hanging up the phone.

I laughed as I lit a cigarette. I took a deep breath and threw the empty bottle onto the lawn in front of the porch. My whole body shook, but I wouldn't allow myself to exhale. I slapped myself in the face hard before standing up, tossing my cigarette into the street and walking back into the house.

That night I slept on the couch. Or rather, I fell asleep on the couch and when I woke up I chose not to go upstairs to Freya. Instead I opened the creaky front door and lit a cigarette. A cat stood in the middle of the street, cleaning its front paws. I wondered who would let their cat roam free at that hour.

.....

The stories that we tell—misnamed or correctly named (I still can't decide) as history—are instructive. At least, that's what stories meant to me growing up.

John, Francis, and I used to say, "Dad, tell us the story," and dad would recount some random story from his vast knowledge of Mennonite history. My dad used to tell us "the story," usually over supper or during long rides in the car. Dad would take up the narrative at any point in history he felt like, sometimes starting with the early history of the Anabaptist movement. Other times he would explain how Mennonites left Canada for parts of South America and Mexico in the early 1950s when they felt the government was infringing on their fringe lifestyle choices.

The stories always involved Mennonites fleeing persecution from either the Roman Catholic Church or bands of roving marauders. For some reason, the history of the defeated was very appealing. Maybe that's why my parents never came looking for me. Because they respected running away as my ancestral right.

A BRIEF HISTORY OF WILLOW ISLAND

Late in the day, Freya woke me up with a cup of coffee and a plate of pancakes.

"I packed for you, your stuff is in the car."

I ate, dressed, and followed her to the car. It always seemed to take us forever to leave the house for whatever occasion and for no particular reason. We would always end up sitting around saying things like "Well, I guess it's time to leave," but no one would take the initiative. I think we found it both maddening and endearing.

"Where did you get this car from?" I asked, securing my seatbelt.

"Aren't you excited about going to the lake for the whole summer?" she said, turning the key to start the car.

"What do you mean for the whole summer?" Either Freya hadn't been very explicit in discussing her/our plans for the summer or I hadn't been paying attention. "We're going back into the city on the weekends, right?"

"Lake Winnipeg," she said, as though I was still confused as to where we were going. "I spend every summer at the lake, you know that. My family cottage." She started nodding her head in time with the song playing on the radio. "Amma and Afi's cottage, I talk about them all the time."

"You didn't spend last summer at the cottage. How am I supposed to know that?"

"Oh my God, do you not pay attention? I've mentioned this, like, sixty times."

I had no idea if she had mentioned it 'sixty times' but I didn't recall hearing anything about a cottage and how she spent every summer there.

"Whose car is this?"

"What?" Freya said, apparently not having heard me.

"Where did you get this car from?"

"From my dad." She shoulder checked and changed lanes, without thinking it might be odd that she had a car from her dad who lived in Toronto.

"Did your dad buy you a car, Freya?" I said, smiling, wondering if she had been hit by lightning, which would explain why she was suddenly in possession of a death machine, as she had many times referred to them.

"Yeah, I don't know. I didn't want it, but then he just showed up with one and sometimes it's important to just accept gifts."

"What do you mean, he just showed up with a car? I never saw him."

She turned the radio up, making it impossible to have a conversation.

Freya drove us over the Arlington Street Bridge, then made some turns. Eventually, we made our way outside the city and onto the highway. It was a beautiful spring day which apparently had the effect on Freya of making her speed; for someone who abhorred the car culture, we were often "being forced" to drive somewhere. She had a smile on her face and sang along with every song on the radio. After about an hour I read a sign that said "Gimli."

Freya turned toward the lake, into what appeared to be a vast marshland.

"This is the causeway," Freya said to me. The sun was setting rapidly; we were almost out of daylight. "It was built awhile ago. Willow Island is really not an island at all. It's too bad, really, because now people totally overrun the place every year. It's become so commercial."

"They've stolen your Icelandic paradise, have they?" I said looking out the window.

"What the fuck is that supposed to mean, Klassen?" Freya snapped at me, turning the radio a little louder.

I smiled to myself. I had scored a small victory, considering I was being brought out to this Icelandic paradise against my will. Or rather, if I had had a will, it would have been against my will.

"Now listen up, because I'm going to tell you a short history of our fine little used-to-be island," Freya looked serious now.

"You have my full attention," I said, poking my hand into the pack of cigarettes on the dashboard.

I was smiling at her and she grinned back before starting.

"This is where the Icelanders first settled. There's a big white rock to mark the event. So my great-grandfather, or my great-great-grandfather, I can't remember which one, built a cabin on the island because he got the land for free or something and started fishing. Then my grandmother—my Amma—almost gave it all up. But just as her father was dying she told him that she wanted to keep it and that's how we have it now." She nodded to herself with an air of satisfaction.

I laughed, "What? That's your history? That makes no sense. Where's the passion? The exact dates? The actual account of what happened?"

"We're here!" Freya said as she threw the car into park and the lights that illuminated the large cabin died.

"Amma! Afi!" Freya screamed as she launched herself out of the car toward the blanket clad, matronly woman poking her head out of the door. Her shrieking reminded me of a six year old; it was jarring.

"Oh, it is you," the woman replied, waiting for Freya to land in her arms. "Your mother said that you were coming, but I didn't realize that it was going to be so soon."

Afi made his way to the car to unpack the contents. I was smoking and standing beside the open car door, transfixed with the lake that stretched out before me.

"Lake Winnipeg is the tenth largest fresh body of water in the entire world," he said by way of introduction.

I jumped and turned to see the old man standing beside me. I was either going deaf or the man moved like a ghost.

"It's amazing," I said quietly, matching his tone.

"Isn't it?" he said, lifting Freya's bags out of the back seat.

Although Freya had packed for me, at the last minute I had decided to bring all of my belongings, which at that point was just enough to fill two milk crates, a Rubbermaid tub and a backpack.

I wandered around the side of the cabin and up the stairs that went up to the large deck facing the water. The lake was quiet, and night had set in. It was almost spooky—the type of place where you always thought you heard someone calling your name. Everything was at rest—in a calm, relaxed state. The jagged rocks that reached out to touch the lake appeared soft and meditative, like in an Emily Carr painting. As the waves came to shore they seemed to be muted whispered "Shhh" as if asking for a little peace and quiet.

The contrast between the Afi and Amma's cabin and our Walnut Street house was immediate. This place was about minimalism and restraint. How, I wondered, could Freya survive out here for an entire summer? The tiny island didn't seem big enough to hold Freya's attention.

I walked closer to the water. My eyes focused but couldn't see anything save a dark glassy mass stretching out in front of me. It was so beautiful, straining to be nothing but itself—a dark, vast body of water—and nothing more. "Hey, I'm Jess," I said. I don't know why, but I started walking into the water. When the water was waist deep I crouched down and submerged myself fully. A fraction of a second later I felt a sharp pain in my head, like I had smacked it on a rock. I pulled my head out of the water and gasped for air; it felt like my lungs were collapsing. Turning around, I walked out of the water, soggy clothes dragging me down until I had to crawl the last few feet to the shore. In a blind panic I scrambled up the steps of the deck and pushed all my weight against the door as I turned the knob. I was shaking uncontrollably as I picked myself up and said, calmly, to Freya and her grandparents who were sitting around the fire, "Freya, do you think you could get me a towel?"

She swung her head around and laughed, "Um, it's a little too early in the year to be taking a swim there, genius." She got up from the couch and disappeared, returning a moment later with a towel.

Freya's grandparents stared at me in shock.

"Are you all right?" Freya's Amma said, obviously horrified as she too got up to fetch towels.

"I just...slipped in," I said between the chatter of my teeth. I removed my shoes and socks and followed Freya to the bathroom on the main floor.

"I'll get you some dry clothes. Take a shower," Freya said. "What are you, six years old? Do I have to supervise you around water?" She smiled for a moment before a look of worry came back into her eyes.

She left the bathroom and I crawled into the warm shower, my hands and legs screaming in pain as the blood started to flow.

After my shower I stood in the threshold of the doorway, quietly looking at Freya and her grandparents.

Inside the cabin the fireplace was situated between two sets of large doors that went out onto the back deck facing the lake. A set of recliners and two small couches formed a semi-circle around the fireplace. A large cozy rug filled the centre of the half circle. To the right of the fireplace was a corner area with two more recliners, a couch, and a large TV. A stairway led to the second floor where there were four good-sized bedrooms. The downstairs living area was huge and hall-like. It was hard to imagine that anyone could own a cottage like that. The dining room table looked to seat twelve easily and there were two small bedrooms and a bathroom down-stairs to the right of the TV area. The cabin was spectacular not only for its sheer size but for the love and care clearly put into crafting it. It was obvious that when someone had built an addition to the cabin they had done so with a desire to make it blend perfectly with the original.

Amma was wrapped in a thick wool blanket, her reading glasses sitting on the tip of her white nose. Her round cheeks and salt and pepper hair fooled me for a second—she seemed an amiable matri-arch—but behind those reading glasses was a fierceness that imme-diately scared the shit out of me.

"Jess," Freya said from her spot on the couch, "Afi and Amma, Jess. You can just call them Afi and Amma. As you can tell from her trip into the lake, she's very excited to meet her death."

"Hi, nice to meet you," I said weakly. And then, gaining a better sense of my surroundings I went to shake their hands. "You have an amazing house."

"Thanks," Afi said, as he settled back into his chair.

"Don't they feed you in Winnipeg?" Amma said, looking me up and down.

I felt my face redden as I looked down at myself. It was true, I was skinnier than ever. My diet of soy products, random dumpstered canned goods, cigarettes, and copious amounts of alcohol was not helping me pack on any pounds.

"She's just joking, geez," Freya said, tugging at my pant leg.

"I don't like this vegan business," Amma said, almost spitting out the V, "it just doesn't seem healthy. How can anyone go through life without eating fish? At least a little fish now and again," Amma said, trailing off.

Freya got up from the couch, "Come on, Skinny," she said, "I'll introduce you to the beverages."

I uncorked the wine bottle and poured. "Freya," I whispered, "I don't think that your grandparents like me very much. I guess my dip into the water didn't impress them."

"What?" Freya said, laughing. "Don't be ridiculous, they don't even know you yet." She put her hand on my waist.

I flinched and wondered if her grandparents were watching us. "And the not eating comment and the way that she stared at me. She hates me, I can see it. She took one look at me and gave me nothing but venom," I said, taking a sip.

"OK well, falling into the lake is certainly not helpful. But, Jess, you're being ridiculous. She was having a discussion with you. That's what Icelanders do, we discuss things. Just calm down. You're acting like a child. And don't fall into the lake again." She laughed, turned, and walked out of the kitchen, but not before grabbing my ass.

"Well," said Afi as he propelled himself out of the armchair, "I think we're going to bed. We'll acquaint ourselves in the morning," he said, looking at me.

"I know I'm ready for bed," Freya said.

"You know," I said to the backs of the trio, "I haven't been out of the city for a while and I think that I'm still in a state of shock from the water, so I'm just going to sit by the fire for a little while."

"Suit yourself, here's a blanket," Afi said, holding up a blanket toward me that he had grabbed from the couch. It looked like a kite caught in the limb of a tree. Well over six feet tall, and weighing at least two hundred pounds, he had an imposing structure. He moved like a ghost, though, and I reasoned that all those years on the boat had conditioned his body to move breathlessly, keeping the boat centred and true to the waves.

"I'm not going to have to worry about you this summer, am I?" Amma said pointing at me, as I turned toward the fire.

"I don't..." I stuttered. Her fierce eyes were burning a hole in me.

I suddenly felt very guilty for being there. Guilty for drinking their wine, guilty for sleeping with their granddaughter, guilty for taking up space, guilty for not being Icelandic, guilty for being stupid enough to walk into the lake at this time of year.

"Well, Amma," Freya chimed in, "you can let me do the worrying. Jess finished her GED under my tutelage, so I think that this summer should be all about getting ready to start university. Don't you, Jess?"

This wasn't really a question at all because in a matter of days Freya would be pulling out her application forms from the University of Winnipeg that she had brought along for my benefit swearing that even though it might be too late to apply, I should try anyway.

I nodded. Amma and Afi climbed the stairs as Freya whispered, "Second room on the left."

I shook my head, the water still sloshing stubbornly in my ear canals.

I watched them disappear up the stairs before I walked through the large doors to the left of the fireplace and found a chair on the far end of the expansive deck. I brought my knees up to my chest and took deep breaths while trying not to cry. I lit a cigarette and felt an all too familiar feeling in my stomach.

A few days previous I had been chopping vegetables and throwing them into a pot. I wasn't sure what I was going to make but decided to let myself be guided by the culinary gods and goddesses. We got a box of food delivered every week from a farm just outside of Winnipeg. I was excited as I took off the lid to reveal what we had to work with.

"What are you cooking?" Freya said as she walked into the kitchen.

"I don't know. I guess whatever's in the box," I said, giving the pot a stir.

"It's just like you to take whatever you can get," Freya said while munching on a carrot. "To not have a plan."

"What's that supposed to mean?" I said, hearing a defeatist tone in my voice.

"You look in the box and take whatever soggy, wilted vegetables those fucking farmers send us." She was smiling and clearly not finished. "You come here without a plan and take whatever you can get—me—when you get off the train. You have to start being a little more intentional with your life, Jess. You have to start thinking about things like university or getting a job. You have to start thinking about what you want, as opposed to what you don't want."

"Don't call them fucking farmers," I said, feeling the steam from the pot on my face.

"That's what you're going to choose to take issue with? Defending farmers? Aren't those the people that you ran away from out of fear for the safety of your sanity and soul?"

I stood motionless, tongue-tied.

"It smells great. You're such a good cook, must be in your genes," she said while pulling my hips toward her. She kissed me on the mouth and left me breathless. "Let me know when supper's ready," she said, and then whispered into my ear, "maybe we could eat in bed," biting the top of my ear before her quick exit from the room.

Maybe Freya was right. Maybe it was time to be more intentional about my life. It was freezing outside. The chill still hadn't left my body, so I stomped out the cigarette and went back inside. I took the metal rod sitting next to fireplace and shuffled the logs around, watching as the fire regained life. It was a small piece of satisfaction in a night of otherwise lost causes.

"Hey, what are you doing? Put that out and come up to bed."

I turned to see Freya on the stairs staring down at me.

"Admit it," Freya said, "you love it here already."

I couldn't hear exactly what she had said, the water still sitting in my ears.

"I love you." I said smiling.

She came down the stairs, wrapped her arms around my neck, and pulled me to the couch and on top of her. "Why don't you come up to bed with me?" she said, kissing me.

I took a deep breath and a moment to recover. "I think that I'm just going to stay down here for a while."

"Come to bed," she said kissing my ear and neck. "You left me alone last night. Do I have to suffer again?"

"No, really, I think that I'd just like to enjoy this fire for a little while longer. Why don't you curl up with me and we could read to each other or something?"

"Fine," she said curtly, detaching herself from me and standing up. "Good night."

And that's the way it was with her—if I wasn't able to pull my desire inline with hers she became cold.

"Are you mad at me Freya?" I said as she started up the stairs.

"No," she said without turning around. "I don't know why you always think that there's something wrong."

After a moment, I went outside to the car where there were a couple of bottles of wine forgotten in the trunk. There was also a box of books, which I brought into the cabin. Opening a bottle of wine, forgoing a glass, I picked-up *The Unbearable Lightness of Being* by Milan Kundera and decided to finish both the bottle of wine and the book by daybreak. I wanted to know what he had to say about women. Freya had come home one day infuriated because she was supposed to read the book for a class. She pronounced him a misogynist and promptly quit the class.

After many hours of reading, as I entered a state beyond tired, I thought I smelled coffee brewing. I was at first mystified and then frightened when I heard the door open. Someone came into the cabin. I thought that I was well hidden in the depths of the recliner when a voice spoke from the kitchen.

"Amma, did I wake you?" It was a deep, resonating male voice.

"Who the hell are you?" I said, still hidden behind the recliner and under my blanket.

"Who the hell are you?" he answered back, sounding equally as shocked.

"Can I have a cup of coffee, too?" I said, hearing the sound of a mug being filled.

"Well, only if you tell me who you are," he said, opening the kitchen cupboard again.

I put my book down beside the chair and swivelled around to see a very tall, broad-shouldered man with blond hair and bright shining blue eyes holding out a cup of coffee to me.

"Jess," I said trying to take in the large-framed man.

Pro-wrestlers have this impossibly large look about them—as hyperbolic as their profession—but this man looked simply like he'd been blessed with the potential for huge muscles.

"Jesus! Were you born or created in a Schwarzenegger factory?" I said, trying to mute my shock.

His face flushed crimson starting at his neckline, up toward the bottom of his beard, and then high on his cheekbones above the hair. His look of stunned horror lasted a little longer than I was comfortable with before a large smile came across his face as he extended his free hand.

"I'm Halfsteinn, and here's your coffee."

Which he pronounced HuFF STain.

"That's the best name that I've ever heard. How did you get it? What does it mean?" I said, taking the cup from his hand.

"It means that I better get onto that lake because I'm losing daylight, so I better tell you the story some other time." He reached for his coat and started to make his way to the door.

"Are you a ghost?" I said, suddenly realizing that I might be only half awake.

"Oh," Halfsteinn said, flashing his big smile again, "I guess we'll have to see tomorrow morning at around the same time." He closed the door gently behind him, careful not to make a sound; he possessed the same quiet movement as Afi.

Sitting back down in the recliner I pulled the blanket up to my chin, leaned back, and immediately fell asleep.

When I finally woke up some time in the late morning, I looked toward the kitchen to see Amma, Afi, and Freya sitting at the table, eating an early lunch and chatting.

I observed them unnoticed for a while. I shook my head, it felt like I had gone a little deaf during the night and I couldn't hear what they were saying. I was surprised by the look on Freya's face; at first I couldn't understand what was different. Then I realized that her lips weren't moving. She was sitting back in her chair with knees up to her chin, sipping contently from her mug. She wasn't dominating the conversation. In fact, no one was dominating the conversation. The words were sparse between the three of them, and they all seemed to be considering each other carefully.

I was stuck in my reverie until I suddenly remembered Halfsteinn. I was about to say something about the strange man brewing coffee in their kitchen, but as I became more conscious I decided I needed to keep it a secret.

Joining them at the table I found myself in the middle of a heated debate regarding local politics. Apparently, when the discussion turned to politics, people spoke freely in that house. I ate in silence, listening attentively while intermittently fetching supplies from the fridge as needed. When lunch was over I started doing the dishes while Afi and Amma sipped tea and Freya picked at the remains on her plate.

"Jess," Amma said, "what are you doing? You're a guest here; you don't need to do the dishes," she looked very stern. I immediately turned the tap off and stopped filling the sink.

"Sit down," Afi said, waving his hand at the chair I had been sitting in.

"Oh no, no, no," Freya said. "When you let her do the dishes it makes her feel connected to her heritage as an oppressed Mennonite woman." She started laughing and tugged at my shirt affectionately. "Come on Jess, sit down."

I felt my shoulders tighten and a quiet anger rising. I had a double standard—I could make those kinds of jokes, but when Freya did, it was mean.

I sat down beside Afi and watched as he poured me a mug of tea.

"Freya tells us that you left your family," Afi said without sounding like he had a need for me to respond.

"Yeah, I guess that's kind of true. I guess it's a bit complicated." I chose my words carefully and spoke slowly, matching Afi's speed. "I didn't run away though," I added quickly.

"Um, I'd call it running way. You're a minor and you left your family without telling them that you were leaving or where you were going," Freya said, listing off the reasons on her fingers. "And you haven't contacted them since you left."

That's not true, I almost yelled, but bit my tongue.

"This does sound complicated," Amma said, pulling her glasses off of her face and perching them on top of her head.

Freya didn't say anything, but looked at me, waiting for me to respond.

"I'm not in any trouble, if that's what you're thinking. My parents and I are just having trouble seeing eye to eye."

Amma nodded, "We're always happy to have visitors."

"Do your parents know where you are?" Afi said, folding his hands together.

I had hoped the conversation was over.

"They don't. I tried to call them, but my mom wouldn't talk to me."

There was a long silence in the kitchen. Freya reached over and rubbed my back. "Her parents are very homophobic, and she felt like she had no choice but to leave."

There was more silence.

Finally, Amma spoke. Looking at Freya she said, "We're going to get the mail. Maybe you would like to show Jess around Gimli a little."

We cleared the table and climbed into the car. When we stopped outside the post office. As Amma made her way inside, Afi stopped and turned to me.

"Here," he said, folding some bills into my hand, "maybe you will need to buy a few things."

Freya ran into friends on the street and I followed the smell of something delicious in the Central Bakery. I wandered into the bakery, clutching the money Afi had given to me. I walked out with a slice of Vinarterta—a layered jam cake that reminded me of my grandma's cookies, which we always called "jam-jams." I wandered toward the beach thinking about the time we took my grandma Klassen to the mineral hot springs in Watrous, Saskatchewan. I had never seen my grandma in a bathing suit before, and, as a seven year old, it changed my world. I had never heard of anyone's grandma going swimming, let alone my grandma. She was well into her dementia at that point, and it was so fantastic to see her smiling and happy as she floated easily, buoyed by the salty water. I raised my Vinarterta in the air, a silent salute to my dead grandmother. I could have sauntered

72

down to the beach, but instead I stayed the course, aiming toward the Gimli harbour. At the end of the pier was a huge ship called the Nammao—a research vessel, I would later find out from Afi. The wind was howling and it was much colder on the edge of the pier than in town. It felt exotic out there staring at the endless lake, surrounded by Icelandic last names and baked goods.

That night, when I went to bed with Freya, my heart felt light and free. The presence of Amma and Afi gave me a sense of safety I hadn't felt for a while and there was something about the town that automatically gave me the feeling of being on vacation.

Freya mumbled something, nearly asleep.

"They are great," I said.

"What?" she said, rousing herself slightly, "Who are you talking about?"

"Amma and Afi. Amma and Afi are great, that's what you said, right? The whole town, really. I had a great day."

"Not even close," she said, pulling my arms into place so that I was spooning her.

After she fell asleep I crept downstairs to take up my post on the recliner. I picked another book from the box and opened another bottle of wine and went outside. Looking out at the lake, in the silence, I heard a buzzing sound as I lit a cigarette. I shook my head again and pressed my palms to my ears. Nothing seemed to help. I felt my lips moving—marching along all on their own without my asking them. I searched in the pockets of my jacket, found a pen, and started writing on the cigarette package.

You are warmer now
You are more silent than I...

"Am I writing poetry now?" I asked the lake.

I shuddered, stomped out my cigarette, and went inside to hide under the covers of words that were not my own. Tonight I would start on *Tipping the Velvet* by Sarah Waters. It was one of the books Freya had highly recommended. When she saw me packing the Kundera next to the Waters, she scoffed, "Why do you want to put that sexist bastard next to her beautiful work of art?" I said nothing in response, turning the offending book to face the other way.

I became conscious again with the smell of coffee brewing and the sound of water being pushed through a drip style coffee maker. I jumped out of the recliner, determined to be sitting at the table, ready for a conversation with the ghostly coffee-drinking fisherman. The door opened moments later. It was Halfsteinn.

"Good morning," he said in what apparently was his attempt at a whisper.

"Will you teach me how to fish?" I said, completely ignoring social graces.

"Not today," he said filling his travel mug with coffee and smiling at me. He sat down at the table with his mug in front of him and pulled out a pouch of tobacco. To my amazement he rolled a perfect cigarette in seconds.

"Will you teach me how to roll cigarettes like that?" I said with genuine admiration.

"All-right," he said patiently, "I've got time to teach you how to roll the perfect cigarette, but you have to promise me one thing."

I nodded silently.

"I want you to promise me that you will pick one small, seemingly insignificant thing in your life that you will care about passionately as a craft. It doesn't matter what it is, but I want me to promise that you'll pick one thing. Whenever you are feeling uninspired about your own life, you will turn to this art that you've chosen and do it with as much passion as you can muster."

I nodded again; I knew it was a promise I could keep.

"First, take out your pouch of tobacco and your papers. Open the pouch and pull out one paper.

"Second, pull out enough tobacco to stretch from end to end, the length of the paper. Make sure to put the tobacco in the fold of the paper, and make sure that the glue is on the outside, on the bottom, and facing toward you.

"Third, cradle the paper with tobacco in between the thumb and forefinger of your non-dominant hand.

"Fourth, tamp down the tobacco with the forefinger of the dominant—free—hand and then slide the paper so that it's resting equally on the middle finger and the thumbs of both hands.

"Fifth, start rolling the paper between middle fingers and thumbs until the paper is almost moulded into the cylinder shape around the tobacco.

"Sixth, lick the glue and roll the cigarette all the way and make sure that it's tight, but not too tight. If it's too tight you can't pull any air through and it wont burn. On the other hand, if it's too loose, it will just crumble in your mouth and be useless."

I licked my cigarette shut and held it up to Halfsteinn for approval. He nodded his head.

"Now all you have to do is pinch and twist the ends to make it nice and neat." He took his pouch and papers from the table and returned them to his breast pocket. "Enjoy that Sarah Waters' book, she's a very gifted writer." He smiled and made his way out the door and into the morning darkness.

How was it that a man who spent most of his time floating around Lake Winnipeg was so well acquainted with the author of a fictional account of a lesbian burlesque star?

For the next few nights I woke up, frustrated that I hadn't made it downstairs for my early morning meeting with Halfsteinn. The next week came and, after catching up with sleep, I stayed awake; but there was no sign of him. Perhaps he was a figment of my imagination.

That morning, he came again.

"So," he said, putting a cup of coffee in front of me. "How are the university applications going? It's getting pretty late. Are you worried that you're not going to hit the cut-off dates?"

"What? How do you know about that?"

He smiled, "I found you asleep in a pile of forms the other morning."

"Oh, yeah, that makes sense. It's been all Freya has been focussed on lately. She's pretty worried about it. Are you guys starting some sort of worrying club?"

"No, I wouldn't say that I'm starting any clubs with Freya." His response was terse, which made me curious.

"Everyone likes Freya. You don't sound so convinced," I said, pouring cream into my coffee.

"Cream today, hey? What's going on?"

"My stomach's been hurting lately," I said, rubbing my stomach gingerly. "Don't change the subject. What's with the hate-on for Freya?"

"Don't you change the subject. How come Freya's worried about university and you're not? She's got you up until all hours trying to fill out these forms and you don't even want to go."

"I didn't say I didn't want to go. She's just trying to help me."

"Then how come you're not worried about deadlines?"

"I don't know," I said, too tired to battle with my ghost friend. "I guess I have some sort of feeling that Freya has already filled them out for me."

"Well, I guess we'll find that out soon enough." He put the lid on his travel mug and headed toward the door. As he grabbed his coat he turned to me. "The poem you wrote last night was very good."

"You were snooping," I said incredulously.

"It was mostly in plain view," he said while closing the door behind him.

I climbed into the recliner again and pulled out my old friend Martha Wiens. I stopped and closed the book before I read anything and instead found my pen and a piece of paper.

I woke up, once again, to the sound of Freya, Afi, and Amma eating lunch. From what I had gathered in my relatively short time at the cabin, Afi and Amma liked to do four things: eat, nap, read and go for walks. I liked that about them.

"Hey you!" Freya called from the kitchen in a jovial tone.

I hadn't heard her at first and was intently staring at the dead ashes in the fireplace.

"Hey!" Freya said, startling me. "Wadda deaf?" She smiled as she bent over to kiss my forehead. "Ewww, go upstairs and take a shower, you stink and your hair is all greasy and gross."

"Oh," I said mumbling. "I'll shower."

I spent the afternoon reading on the couch while dipping in and out of sleep. During one of my short naps I dreamt that I woke up to the smell of coffee and when I turned the recliner toward to kitchen, expecting to see Halfsteinn, I saw him and Freya having sex on the table. I woke up with a gasp and Freya kissing my cheeks.

"Hey, sleepy," Freya said, "what were you dreaming about?"

I felt my face turn red with embarrassment.

"Why are you blushing? Were you cheating on me in your dreams?" She took my book off my chest and lay down on top of me.

"I was thinking that maybe I could walk into town and get groceries and cook dinner for everyone tonight." I said, trying to distract her.

"Jess, you're so thoughtful, but all the relatives are coming over for dinner tonight. Unless you want to cook for everyone, save that plan for another night."

"Oh," I said, shifting my weight slightly, "does that mean that your mom is coming too." I was trying not to sound too enthusiastic.

"You were having a sex dream about my mom, weren't you?"

"No," I said quickly, feeling myself blushing again.

"Oh my God, I can't believe that you have the hots for my mom."

"I don't," I stuttered, unsure as to why I felt so embarrassed, "that's not what the dream was about," I said, shaking my head. "Your mom seems really nice and I like her."

"Well, I don't think that this will count as a pastoral visit, so I highly doubt she will be coming. None of her family members have had a good old-fashioned crises in a while, so I don't think that she'll be interested in seeing us." She looked away, avoiding my eyes.

I sat up, pulling her with me. "Freya, do you feel like your mom doesn't give a shit about you unless you're having some sort of crises?"

"I think my mom doesn't like who I am. I do everything that she would want—I'm a radical leftist queer feminist—she likes all of the things that I do, but she just doesn't like me." She looked like she might cry as she wrapped her arms around herself.

"Oh, Freya," I said, rubbing her back, not knowing what to say and scared in the face of her vulnerability. "I doubt that's true but I also know how that feels—to a certain extent." My heart felt like it might break as I held her hand. My fear in the face of her vulnerability faded into thinking that we'd be all right if we stuck together.

"Yeah, except I choose not to be a victim," she said, abruptly standing up and walking to the kitchen.

I slipped upstairs to the second, more private bathroom and sat on the edge of the tub. I thought about Martha Wiens and wondered if she would consider herself a victim all those years ago being queer in the face of so much hate and fear. Why didn't she just move away? Why stay on the edge of that river in seclusion but still so close to a community that rejected her?

Several hours later relatives started to arrive. Freya gleefully greeted them at the door and then introduced them to me. She was like a six year old during show and tell hour at school. I lost track after the fifth Bjorn, the third Johann, second Erika, and seventeenth Kristjanna. It seemed Freya was related to half of Gimli. I examined all of the middle-aged women who arrived, hoping that one of them would be Freya's mother.

I found a spot in the corner to observe everyone. The cabin was packed with relatives preparing food and sharing wine. I noticed that within an hour of glasses of sherry being passed around, everyone was much more jovial and loud. The men all sat at one end of the table, loudly discussing the same conflict in local politics that I had awoken to the previous day. Something about water stewardship and the lake; all the conversations seemed to lead to the mighty Lake Winnipeg.

Before I knew it, everything was going in reverse with the women washing the dishes and putting the food away. During the supper there had been much discussion about whether I was Icelandic or not. When it was discovered that there was not a drop of Icelandic blood in my veins, an air of disappointment seemed to settle in. I didn't mind though; you get used to discussions such as that from an early age when you're Mennonite. Playing the "Mennonite game" is a national pastime within my community, and the same type of questioning would have occurred had Freya been sitting with my family. Either that or they would have ignored her completely, you never can tell with Mennonites. There's something about finding family when you're such a sparsely populated people that seems urgent, like fixing a leaky roof. In the same breath, Mennonites slip into exclusionary politics with frightening ease.

As I sat in the corner I felt grief. I realized that no one would call me "Schekjbenjel"—errand boy—if I went downstairs to get my mom's canned pickles to add to supper. I knew that in this crowd, not everyone was a devout pacifist or knew the beautiful taste combination of deep fried dough, corn syrup, and watermelon. I knew that no one could see all those things, and yet I felt it all over me like a second skin. When you are seventeen and have, at the age of sixteen, ripped yourself out of the comfortable womb of a small town in Saskatchewan, you feel both a sense of accomplishment and a sense of terror at the thought that you alone can not carry on with the activities usually carried by the collective shoulders. Every homogenous group is rife with contradictions, and sometimes, when you're lucky, you start to recognize them.

I had fallen asleep but was gently woken by Amma. There was still a large crowd in the cabin, but some people were putting on coats and shoes. It was the kind of loud hum that I remember falling asleep to as a child, curled into a pile of jackets.

"The kids are going to the hotel, why don't you go with them," she said. "Here's twenty dollars." She put a neatly folded bill into my sleepy hand. "Go have a good time."

"Come on," Freya said, waving from the door, "we're going out for beer!" She'd clearly had enough alcohol already.

I stared at Amma, not sure whether to take the money but she had let go and was smiling at me. I nodded at her. She removed her glasses and leaned in close to me.

"Jess, there's very little that being scared shitless can't teach you."

I titled my head to the left. Had I heard her right? There was a din of noise in the background—children running around, adults arguing, and dishes being stacked and put away. I wasn't sure if I was fully awake yet.

"I'm not scared," I said.

"What dear?" Amma said, while walking back to the kitchen.

"Oh, OK" was all I could stutter as I stood up from the couch.

We drove to the bar near the highway that leads into town. We all piled out of the two cars and made our way into the bar. There was instant recognition of Freya—she seemed to know everyone there. I sat down with her cousins while she made the rounds, catching up with old friends.

"So," Cousin number one started, "I hear you're Mennonite."

"Yup," I said, unsure how I was expected to respond.

"And from a farm in Saskatchewan."

"No, but close enough."

Silence followed. My eyes rolled over to the bar. I definitely needed to drink some more to get through the stilted conversation that lay ahead. I panicked as I wondered whether they would ask me for ID. And then I saw him. Halfsteinn was sitting at the bar, alone and drinking a beer.

"Excuse me," I said absently, getting up and making my way to the bar. He was sitting at the far end, reading the *Globe and Mail.*

I sat down beside him. "Where did you get that?" I said, pointing to the paper, "I've asked all over town and no one sells the *Globe and Mail.*"

He smiled warmly. "So we meet again," he said, folding up his newspaper. "I went to the city."

"I will buy you a beer—well, more precisely, Amma will buy you a beer—if you tell me the story of your name now."

He laughed, "All right, Fort Garry Dark. Thank you, Amma," he said, saluting her with his beer.

"Nice choice. I like your story already." I ordered the drinks and Halfsteinn began.

"The name Halfsteinn is a very uncommon name. In fact, I've never met anyone else in these parts named Halfsteinn," he said, taking a sip from his beer.

"Have you ever been to the middle of the lake, Jess?"

"This lake? No. I had a little dip at the shore but not to the center."

He nodded. "Well, as you can imagine, I have, and so has my Afi. My Afi used to fish with his best friend, whose name was Halfsteinn. Afi and Halfsteinn were out in all sorts of weather; they were experienced fishermen. They knew the lake and the weather. They felt it in a way that those kind of men can't verbalize. Afi and Halfsteinn spent most of their time together on the boat. Eventually, Afi married Amma and they had kids. Every morning, Halfsteinn would come to the house to get Afi to go fishing." He took a sip of his beer and coughed. "Halfsteinn never married, never had children; he always said that the two loves of his life were fishing and his boat.

"One day, they went out in terrible weather and got pulled out to the middle of the lake. Afi says a big wave pulled Halfsteinn in. He just disappeared. Afi stayed out and tried to find Halfsteinn—he stayed out the whole night waiting for his friend to emerge. I guess he hoped that if he waited long enough he would see Halfsteinn somewhere in the distance holding onto something. The morning came and everything was calm again. In the distance he saw something. He immediately went to it. When he got close enough, he saw that it was a stone, floating in front of him. Before he could reach down to drag it up onto the boat, it sank to the bottom of the lake.

"Seeing this stone gave Afi great comfort because he realized that it was Halfsteinn—Halfsteinn means "sea stone"—and he knew that Halfsteinn had made his journey to the next world and had made peace with his death.

"That is the story of my name."

"But it means more than just sea stone," I said.

He nodded and we were both silence for a moment. I tried to imagine Afi telling a story like that.

"Well, I think that you should tell me the story of your name and I'll buy you a beer," Halfsteinn said.

"What if the love you want is the kind of love that's owed to you?" I said, suddenly feeling like I might cry, knowing my question was off topic and not knowing what it meant.

He considered my question and didn't seem to mind that I had strayed away from the conversation at hand. "I think that love is a gift. Sometimes it's like that pair of underwear you get for Christmas just in the nick of time."

"My parents named me Jess because my mom got to name my two older brothers. It was my dad's turn and he decided to name me after the family cow."

Halfsteinn laughed with a sharp exhalation. "I don't believe you for a second."

I lit another cigarette before feeling a tap on my shoulder. I swivelled around, catching the tapper's hand sharply. I was annoyed to see Freya standing behind me.

"Jesus, Jess, what's your problem?" she said, glaring directly at Halfsteinn. "Why are you ignoring my cousins?" She was still looking at Halfsteinn.

"Isn't Halfsteinn one of your cousins?" I said, my eyes trying to get a lock on hers.

"Jess, can I talk to you alone for a minute." She turned to go outside.

I followed her, smoking down my cigarette quickly.

"Why are you being such a jerk? I don't ask much from you," Freya said through tight lips.

"I don't have a fucking clue what you're talking about Freya," I said, exhaling and becoming less calm, not sure why I was answering her so aggressively.

"Why did you just walk away from my cousins? We came here with them. Are you trying to be an asshole? Because you're doing a really good job of it."

"Freya, I'm not trying to do anything to you. I'm trying to have a conversation with Halfsteinn," I said turning, to go back into the bar. It was the first time I had fired a shot and walked away. It felt good.

I rejoined Halfsteinn at the bar.

"You were saying something about love?" he said, expressionless.

"It seems like you two might have a history. Although she didn't say anything, I've got a good sense about these things sometimes," I said.

Halfsteinn used his toothpick to dislodge something between his two front teeth and then moved the wood to his back molar to chew on. "You may be right about that. But, that does not speak to the question I asked you regarding your name, 'cause I don't believe that bullshit story you just told me."

"I'll tell you a story, but it also may or may not be true." I looked around to see if anyone was listening in before beginning. "When I was a kid my name was Ruth. I was named after my father's mother—

Ruth Klassen—and I was happy enough with that name for a time. You may know Ruth, the biblical character that would not leave her mother-in-law after her husband died."

"Sounds familiar," Halfsteinn offered. "You've got to remember that I was raised vaguely Unitarian."

"Aren't all Unitarians vaguely Unitarian?" I said, hoping to impress Halfsteinn with a clever joke. "I hear that it's the church people attend when they find even the United Church too much church to handle."

He laughed. "Yeah, pretty much everyone's 'vaguely Unitarian' except for Freya's mom."

I stopped in my verbal tracks. "You've got to tell me about her." I knew Halfsteinn would be able to give me information.

"No, not now, we'll put that on the agenda for tonight's meeting of social outcasts, but for now, on to the story of your name."

"Well fine. My name was Ruth but then—I don't remember what age exactly—I found a word to describe many of my thoughts and feelings, and that word was 'feminism.'"

"So you're saying that as a wee child you realized that you were a feminist and called it that?" he said without a hint of sarcasm.

"Yes." I said. "I realized that the Bible was a bunch of patriarchal bullshit and I didn't want to be associated with it."

Halfsteinn stared at me intently, waiting for more of an explanation.

I felt guilty for stretching the truth, so I continued on a slightly different path. "I have realized three things, Halfsteinn. The first was that there is no longer any inherent reason for men to have the buttons of their shirt on one side and women on the other. Gender is largely a construct that we wear. The second is that the Bible was written by real live human men. Men, not women. The third is that God as father above us in heaven does not exist but somehow I still catch myself believing."

"All of this before the age of ten?" Halfsteinn asked, still without sarcasm or a hint of disbelief.

"I think that we're smarter when we're younger."

"And Ruth?" Halfsteinn said, lighting a freshly rolled cigarette. "What have you learned from Ruth?"

"I'm starting to learn that maybe Ruth had a point."

"And what point is that? You'll have to school me here. As I said, I know nothing about the Bible."

"Loyalty has its rewards."

"I already learned that from TV."

We both laughed and then were quiet while we sipped.

"Are you and Freya related?" I said.

"No," he said. "No we are not."

"Well how come she's so upset that I'm talking to you," I said, slurring.

"A good Icelander never gossips, Jess, but I will tell you this, you've got your hands full."

"How do you know so much about my hands and what they're full of?" I said turning toward him defensively.

"Let me buy you another drink," he said.

I nodded and allowed him to keep it at that. Pressing him would get me nowhere. He was only four years my senior—a fact that I had learned from one of the Kristjanna's over dinner—but something made him silent and thoughtful like an old man.

Halfsteinn and I drank our faces off that night. I tried to keep pace with him, but it was impossible. Instead, I tried to smoke him under the table while perfecting my cigarette rolling technique.

"How is it," Halfsteinn slurred, showing the first sign that the alcohol was affecting him, "that you are Mennonite and a lesbian? Isn't that an impossibility?" He stared at his palms and then brought his hands together at his pinkie fingers. "Isn't that a contradiction in terms?"

"That's a good question, Half, and since you are so clearly thoughtful and intelligent I'm going to explain this explicitly." I spit out the ex in explicitly.

"Please do, I've got all night, really."

"Well, Half, if I may call you that," I said, wagging my finger in his face, "my brand of Mennonites are the least conservative of all the Mennonites that you'll find in Canada. You can't get less conservative unless you move on to all the Mennonites who have left the Mennonite church and now are in the United Church. So we, officially, are cool with women behind the pulpit, which might seem very liberal, but just watch the cars drive up on a Sunday morning to see who's behind the wheel, that's where the real test lies. Things like divorce are now OK, too, but the gay thing, well that's another thing. Being gay is not cool with most of the so-called liberals of the Mennonite church. But I know it's OK and do you want to know why I know it's OK?" I said suddenly shouting. "Because their evidence is bullshit."

"It's pretty simple, hey?" Halfsteinn said in a way that made me feel like there was a good chance he had read the Bible cover to cover.

"The ironic thing is that it is the tools given to me by my parents that have dismantled our relationship. It's like they taught me to drive the tractor and cultivate the fields to help feed the family, but then I had to drive over the house." I took another sip from my almost empty bottle of beer.

"It's funny, you know, because from our discussion it would seem that your sect of Mennonites still practises shunning, if only on a subconscious level." He waved his hand at the bar tender and ordered two shots of Jaggermeister. "Here's to," he said, raising his shot glass, "the shunned."

We drank our shots down and slammed the glasses on the bar.

"My only remaining question is this, why do you love her?"

"I love her because she's beautiful and when I'm around her I feel beautiful."

"Now can I have the real answer? Because I don't believe that one," he said.

"Because no else loves me."

"That's not a good enough answer," he said, his voice a little unsteady. Halfsteinn stood up and put some money on the bar. "You need to stop believing that." His voice was angry.

I sat at the bar, trying not to think about anything, distracting myself from my thoughts by trying to remember and recite verses from the Bible that I had been made to memorize as a child. I ordered a shot, threw it back, and felt it all coming up to my throat again. Running outside, I found a corner to hide around.

I threw up and watched the jammy Vinarterta Amma had made for dessert splash onto the side of the building.

"Oh, sorry, Amma."

"Jess, are you talking to yourself?" said Freya, who knew from my swift exit that I was sick. "You always drink too much."

"Yeah."

"Well, if you would listen to me you wouldn't get so sick," Freya said, taking my hand and leading me to the car. She found a bottle of water in the car and handed it to me.

I felt better as she brought me to the passenger seat of the car. "I love you, Freya," I said while crouching into the back seat.

"OK, drunky," Freya said tenderly.

I fell asleep in the back seat of the car. I have no idea how much longer we stayed at the bar. I woke up as we rolled into the driveway of the cabin. I took a shower, brushed my teeth, and headed to bed. When Freya put her hands on me I said nothing and didn't move.

"What's the matter? You always want to have sex," she said, not taking her hands off me.

"Nothing."

"Don't say nothing, because that's a lie."

"I don't want to go to university, Freya." It wasn't the answer, but it was all that I could say.

"That's not true," she said, smoothing my hair.

I said nothing.

"Hmm, looks like you need a haircut," she said sounding worried. "I should probably take you into town tomorrow." She brushed her fingers through my hair thoughtfully. "You don't mean that. You're so smart, why would you not want to go to university?"

"You've never said that to me before," I said, still facing away from her. I was slurring a bit.

"What are you talking about? I always tell you that I think that you're thoughtful and intelligent," she said while rubbing my back. "I think that you've read every book in our house."

The truth is that I don't remember if she told me that all the time. She might have, or maybe it was something she said to everyone but me.

That night, as she lay sleeping and the wind rolled across the house, my words came. I slipped out of bed and found a pen.

I could learn to greet you in any language
But I lost myself in translation—
Forgot to bring my dictionary

Half of this is memorization
A basic adherence to an agreement
And there's a finite way
To describe what we don't know
So why doesn't everyone just speak English?

And I feel hard
Like dry soil
Under the plough too many times

A grammar easily learned
To juxtapose love and lies

(I buy it every time)
And I know that your landscape comments are subjective
And narration is filtered
But the vast nothingness
Calls me to attentiveness
(the scariest kind)

After, I went outside for a cigarette. It seemed like a good idea not to let Freya see any of my writing, because she might want to make me into a writer.

After my night with Halfsteinn, I started meeting with him during the day when he returned from fishing. He would come over to the house and sit with Amma and Afi for hours, talking about the books they were reading or what they had seen on the news the night before. Sometimes I would find all three on the deck, sitting in the sun reading. He would stay for supper, clean the house, and smoke on the deck with me. Or we would just sit in silence together. Halfsteinn wasn't always there. His house was a small shack of a cabin on the far side of the island, which Freya referred to as "the eyesore." It was ironic coming from Freya considering that's what the neighbours on Walnut Street said about our house. His house didn't have electricity or a phone or heat. It never occurred to me that it might only be his summer home. Halfsteinn seemed tough enough to live through any conditions.

Halfsteinn's parents weren't fishers. His father, like Freya's, was a lawyer, and his mother was a financial planner. Both parents had never quite given their opinion of his being a fisherman. Their only comments were about whether the fishing was good, and how his boat was running and the monthly care package from his mom who was concerned that he wasn't eating properly. It showed a certain ignorance of her son's life given the fact that he often cooked meals at Afi and Amma's that were nothing short of spectacular. Halfsteinn was never proud of being a fisherman, he just was one, and other people did other things. He didn't seem to have any friends other than Afi and Amma and me, but he didn't seem unhappy about that.

The closer I got to Halfsteinn, the more Freya hated him. Her hostility usually surfaced around issues of the environment, questioning the ethical nature of fishing and how his boat polluted the water. He would counter by saying that his small operation was the most sustainable way of fishing. I started seeing him in private.

When Freya was away or asleep, I would spend time with him, or I would carefully steer him out of the house when she was around so we could spend time without her comments. He never said anything about Freya's behaviour or comments; he continued to talk to her in the same manner that he spoke to everyone—calm, thoughtful, and respectful. I don't know how he kept his cool. Maybe out on the water when he was alone, he would scream curses at her, who knows.

One day, we sat on the deck basking in the warmth of the afternoon—he was taking the day off because the factory was processing a backlog of fish and couldn't accept anymore, or something like that. We were drinking coffee that afternoon and I was talking about the latest book I was reading. It was the *Edible Woman* by Margaret Atwood, and as I turned toward Halfsteinn to make a point about the significance of the woman eating her cake at the end of the book I saw he was staring at me in a new and odd way.

"What I just said wasn't that brilliant, Half, stop looking at me like that." I looked for a fresh cigarette.

"Are you going to apply for university?"

"No," I said.

"Is that because Freya probably already did for you?"

"Maybe." I scrunched my up face and looked toward the lake. "Maybe I did and got a letter back already," I said, lighting a cigarette. "But it's not exactly the situation that Freya has set up in her mind." I swivelled my head around to see if anyone was listening in.

"I think Freya is under the impression that she knows what's going on," Halfsteinn said, pulling out his pouch of tobacco. "I heard her say the other day that she's so excited to be in classes together with you."

I was silent.

"I don't know what you have up your sleeve or what you mean by a different situation, but I would suggest you have a conversation with Freya and tell her exactly what's going on. She needs a dose of someone else's reality once and awhile."

"I think it would be bad for our relationship. I'm happy the way it is."

"No, you're not." Halfsteinn was looking at me, but I could not face him. "You're a kept woman. She tells you what to do and expects you to fall inline."

"Now, Halfsteinn, I think you're jealous," I said, throwing out the most absurd comment I could come up with to deflect his. I felt, for the first time, that I disgusted him. I swung my legs around the edge of the chair, ready to get up and walk away.

"When I was a child," Halfsteinn said slowly, stopping me in my tracks, "my mom used to tell me that I felt too much—as though feeling was something you could do too much of—so I stopped having feelings for a long time. I walked around like a little robot and didn't say anything; I just watched my parents to figure out how I was supposed to react. There was only person in my life that I could truly be myself around, because he wouldn't accept anything less from me. My parents were so proud of me for getting myself 'under control.' From my friend I learned that acceptance is not something I can live without." Halfsteinn paused for a moment, he was looking out to the lake, away from me. "From him I also learned that we need to feel our feelings even when they are not returned in the way you want them."

"Fuck you, Halfsteinn," I said, regretting the words as soon as they came out of my mouth. I stood up and walked to the door.

"That's not what I meant," I heard Halfsteinn say, his voice cracking slightly.

.....

That night, after Freya and I had sex, I wrapped my arms around her and tried to feel the way I had felt for her when we met on the train and I thought that I did.

"Have you ever thought about just moving away from here?" I said to the back of her neck.

"Oh yeah, I'll likely go away for grad school for a few years and then after that, I'm not sure."

"What about leaving after the summer is over?"

"What about scratching my back for a little while."

I obliged in silence for a few minutes. "I have something to tell you," I said finally.

"Wait," she said, rolling over to face me, "there's something I need to tell you first."

"Ah, OK." I couldn't imagine what she might need to confess but I wasn't looking forward to it.

"I sent in an application for the U of W on your behalf. Don't get mad, I just didn't want to see you sit around and do nothing while your opportunities pass you by."

"You pretended to be me and forged my signature?"

"Yeah, but it was for the greater good." She smiled.

"That's really sweet of you," I said. Inside, I was completely horrified.

"Oh, babe, I thought you'd be all mad. I'm so glad you're not." She curled herself closer to me and kissed my neck.

.....

The next day, I went for a long walk along the shore. When I got back to the cabin, Freya was waiting for me. She excitedly kissed me.

"I have a surprise for you," she said kissing my cheek close to my ear. "But first, come upstairs with me."

I had a bad feeling about the surprise—that maybe she had heard back from the university regarding her application for my enrolment. I was still horrified that she had applied for me, but also distracted by her kisses.

"Guess what" she said again, kissing my shoulder. "Your letter of acceptance arrived today; you're going to school with me!"

I smiled in an effort to camouflage any real emotion, but my efforts were futile.

"What's wrong? This is amazing news," she said, still smiling. She was convinced that I was just afraid to succeed.

"Umm," I said, hesitating until a sudden clarity of vision took over. Looking at her smiling face I decided to take a chance. I decided to believe that she was excited because our lives could be parallel—that we could plan a future together. "I applied to the University of Waterloo and I want you to move there with me if I get accepted." It was a bit of a lie because I had already been accepted, but I felt the need to hold some cards close to my chest.

"What?" she said, laughing.

"I'm serious."

"Why would you want to go there if you've been accepted here," she said, her tone now cutting and much too calm.

"I want us to go somewhere together," I said optimistically, "a place where we're both new. I'm sure you could transfer."

"That's the stupidest fucking thing that has ever come out of your mouth. Why would I want to move away from Winnipeg?"

"But you said the other day that you would want to move someday. Why not now, with me?"

Her brow furrowed and her mouth was slightly agape. "Jess, that's ridiculous, we are independent of each other, I am an autonomous being and I don't do things for you, and you don't do things for me." She tilted her head disapprovingly. "Go if you want, I don't care, maybe you need to learn to live on your own anyway." She turned and faced the other way. "Maybe I need to remind you that you don't have any family except for me."

I lay there, staring at her back.

"No, you don't have to remind me of that, Freya, it's my life, I'm pretty fucking aware of that." I heard my tone and didn't like how angry I sounded but couldn't stop.

"Did Halfsteinn tell you that it was a good idea to go somewhere where you have no friends or family?" she said with a softer tone.

"No, Freya, I told myself that eight months ago when I decided to leave my family," I was shouting at her now.

"OK, ssshhhh, it's OK," she said, putting her arms around me, "I know that this is hard for you, it's going to be OK." She kissed my forehead again. "I'm sorry, I didn't mean that family comment to sound so mean."

I cried as she wrapped her arms around me. I struggled away from her.

"First you tell me that we're autonomous beings and then you tell me that you're the only family I have." I was still crying but now perched on my haunches on the mattress looking down at her.

"You're making yourself crazy," she said in a half-whisper. "I'm just trying to help you make good decisions."

I shook my head, trying to figure out if that's what she had actually said. My stomach turned to acid. I put on pants and a T-shirt and left the room.

That night, I stayed up waiting for him to come for his early morning coffee. When he arrived I was sitting at the table with a cup for both of us. He smiled when he saw me and sat down.

"Something on your mind, Jess?" he said. "Anything I can help you with?"

"Not unless you know someone in Waterloo that I can live with."

Halfsteinn nodded, "Actually, I do." He wrote something on a piece of paper, folded it neatly, and handed it to me.

"Am I doing the right thing, Half? By leaving before I'm left."

"I don't quite follow you."

"I think it's pretty obvious. She's going to get tired of me not doing what she tells me to do and then break up with me; not that we're even officially in a relationship."

"Jess," he said stirring cream into the black coffee, "I don't know if that's ever a good reason to leave, but maybe sometimes it's better to do the right thing for the wrong reasons then doing nothing at all."

He left, as usual, after one cup of coffee.

I had no money, I knew no one in Waterloo. I was aware of what I didn't have. I made a mental list to combat the feeling of nothing.

What I have:
1) *A good sleeping bag.*
2) *Extensive experience with dumpster diving (thank Freya and her friends for that).*
3) *An ironclad belief that everything will work out.*
4) *I have read* On the Road *by Jack Kerouac.*
5) *A piece of paper with someone's name on it from Halfsteinn.*

I crawled back into bed with Freya after Halfsteinn left. I kissed the back of her neck and started rubbing her breasts. She wasn't awake but made tiny groaning noises from the depth of her sleep. It was the middle of summer and there was no relief from the blistering heat that night, not even a cooling breeze coming off the lake. Freya was completely naked. When I went down on her she woke up laughing.

"You dirty little fucker." She was still giggling.

I stopped and looked up at her to gauge her reaction.

"Don't stop," she said, her voice thick. "Don't stop."

As I continued I thought about sitting on the deck smoking and watching her swim in lake, the sun gleaming off of her wet, blond hair. I thought about her finding me on the train and wondered if I would ever find someone as beautiful as her. With my every movement I bid her body goodbye because I knew that I wouldn't be able to say it.

As she came, I thought about how much I loved her perfume. I had no idea that I had just sentenced myself to an emotional lashing, because the subtle sweet and woody smell would buckle my knees for many years to come. Even now, mid-sentence, I'll catch the smell of her and my mind will blank, my eyes will stare absently, I'll stop breathing for just a moment, and the air will stop moving in the room. Then, I shake my head, focus again, and breathe normally. Scent is a powerful memory because it has no words, just a scent image of someone or something that can unceremoniously rip you out of your present, pushing you far back into your past.

Later that morning, I woke up with Freya and went downstairs for breakfast with her, Afi, and Amma. As I sat down for coffee I smiled at Amma, saying nothing.

"Even when you smile you look like you're sad," Amma said, reaching across the table to pat my hand. "Like when you're happy you can only allow yourself to be half-happy."

"How could she be happy, Amma," Freya said kissing my cheek, "she spent the entire summer at the lake and she evidently hates it."

"How did you come to that conclusion?" I asked, hurt. "That's pretty random."

"Because you haven't so much as dipped a toe in the lake after your first night here and the summer's almost over," she said accusingly.

"Well, first of all, I think that my first night in the lake was enough and second of all, don't you know that Mennonites don't swim?" I took another sip of my coffee and leaned back in my chair. "It's just not a part of our heritage; we've never had to swim."

"I don't know anything about Mennonites, you never talk about it," Freya said sarcastically, wagging her index finger in my face. "And one would think that now that the water's actually warm enough you'd want to jump in."

"Well, we're not allowed to dance, drink, play cards, or have fun, so talking about ourselves is the only thing left to do, except that's not being humble, which is also sinful." I said, stretching my sleepy neck from side to side.

"Ha," she said, reaching over to kiss me again, "I think that the real entertainment lies in your collective masochism."

I shook my head, saying nothing as I stood up to fill my cup with more coffee. I couldn't tell by her tone whether she was annoyed or just teasing me.

"Well," Afi said, coming to my defence, "I've very much enjoyed our conversations regarding your faith and cultural history."

"When have you had conversations regarding Jess' faith and cultural history, Afi?" Freya said incredulously. "I've never heard you guys talking about that."

"That's because you weren't listening," I said, heading outside for a cigarette, taking my cup of coffee with me.

Freya followed me, also lighting up. I put my elbows on the deck railing and inhaled while looking out to the lake. It was a sunny morning, and I was already sweating. Freya faced me, one arm leaning on the deck. She still had her robe on and the sun was shining through the shear cloth from behind.

"We're going to be leaving soon, Jess, are you going to miss it here?" she said exhaling. "You do know that you're going to have to pick your classes in the next week or so, right?"

"Yeah," was all I said, staring at her.

She laughed, "I know that look, Jess, and I don't have time right now because I promised Amma that I would go grocery shopping." Before going back into the cabin she leaned over and kissed me. Flicking her tongue gently into my mouth, she pulled me closer.

I pulled away and laughed. "You're trying to kill me, aren't you? Just a tease, hey?"

"Yeah, but you like it," she said, letting go of me. She closed the deck door with the sole of her foot as if her hands were too full to pull it shut.

A bunch of boats floated on the water that sunny morning, and I thought that I spotted Halfsteinn's boat but knew it was impossible to tell one dot from another.

"Fuck," I said to myself. I paced around the deck, smoking cigarette after cigarette. *Why do you love her?* I heard Halfsteinn asking me over and over again.

The next morning, I waited downstairs for Halfsteinn at our regular time. He had no idea that my bags were packed as we sat and talked. Then again, maybe he did. He tossed me a pouch of tobacco.

"Here, I bought two by accident. Why don't you take this before they both dry out on me."

It was a sketchy statement at best, considering the fact that Halfsteinn smoked enough to ensure that an extra pouch wouldn't go dry.

I stared at him, blinking and trying not to cry.

He pointed at my packed bags, "You need a ride somewhere?"

Halfsteinn's truck idled on the shoulder of the highway as I tried to figure out how to say goodbye to him.

"Thanks, Half." I leaned over and hugged him. "I'll come and see you again one day."

He nodded silently.

"Don't you have any sage words of advice for me?"

"No, I think that you're going to have to figure it out for yourself. But you know where to find me if you need me."

I stared at him as my fingers trembled. I said nothing as I tried to prevent a seismic event from taking over my body.

I dragged my things to the side of the highway and promptly threw up as Halfsteinn drove away. I sat down in the ditch with my head between my legs trying to recover. I ached all over and shivered despite the warm weather. I couldn't stand to look at the town, so I kept my back to the ditch, took a sip of water, lit a cigarette, stuck my thumb out, and hoped for the best.

LOUISE AND THOM

"You must be Jess," Thom said, opening the door. "We've been expecting you, but weren't sure if you would actually show."

"My phone call from Kenora wasn't clear?" I smiled in spite of the hunger and lack of sleep.

"You come highly recommended, or at the very least you're in need of some rescuing," Thom said nonchalantly.

"I don't need to be rescued," I said. "In fact, I think I've had enough of that."

"Well, you did walk away from Freya, so I'll give you credit," Thom said without much expression. "I'll let Louise know you're here."

Louise and Thom were grad students with a long friendship. After completing their BAs at the University of Victoria they had made a pact to apply to all the same grad schools. Whichever one they both got into was the one they would attend. Out of seven programs they applied to, Waterloo was the only one that accepted them both.

I was replacing a recently departed housemate who left after a disagreement about dishwashing schedules and too much noise in what she described as her "scheduled sleep time."

It was just as well that the old roommate left; her "schedules" were getting on Louise and Thom's nerves, especially after the newly made "check the mailbox for mail" schedule. For some reason the housemate daily interrogated Thom and Louise as to whether they had checked the mailbox, which led Thom and Louise to purposely and as studiously as possible, avoid the mailbox. Sometimes the recently departed housemate would call in the middle of the day to inquire as to whether the mailbox had been checked. Her fixation on mailbox checking was one that Thom and Louise could never figure out. Both Louise and Thom contemplated asking but could never summon the energy to care enough.

I found Thom's comment regarding Freya surprising; it made me feel like I was unwillingly entangled in a network of people. "I don't think that we should talk about Freya," I said, still not sure what to make of my feelings for her.

"I have a feeling that we're not going to talk about much," Thom said, smirking. "Come in, I'll show you your room." He led me with my bag and box down the hall and bowed as he opened the door to my new room. "I'm making lunch and you're probably hungry. I imagine that you haven't eaten since you left Winnipeg?"

I thought for a second. "I guess not really."

"Oh my God, I was joking. You're serious, aren't you?"

"It's really not that long of a ride," I said, relaxing a little bit, "especially if you're drunk or sleeping."

Thom and I went outside to the porch for a cigarette after lunch. I had finally worked up the courage to talk to him about Halfsteinn.

"What's your relationship with Halfsteinn?" I said, lighting a cigarette while we stood on the porch.

He was clearly caught off guard while being equally guarded. "Why, what did he tell you?"

"Something about being cousins."

Thom looked down and let out a "hmm" through his nose.

"You're not cousins." I said, sitting down on the porch couch.

"Nope, not even close." He took off the ring he was wearing and spun it in the palm of his hand.

"But you grew up with him, you know him, right?" I was anxious to have anyone other than Freya to discuss Halfsteinn with.

"Yup."

"You don't want to talk about this," I said, ashing my cigarette.

"I just haven't before." Thom turned his head toward me, looking as though he might cry. "We grew up together—did everything together—we were best friends. When we were sixteen someone—likely your *wonderful* ex-lover—told our friends that I was in love with him and tried to kiss him while we were watching a movie." Thom took a deep breath and swallowed hard. "It wasn't true, I mean, I did love him. He was my best friend. I wasn't in love with him. Before the rumour was spread it hadn't even occurred to me that I might interested in boys, I just kept thinking that I hadn't found the right girl yet. Anyway, Halfsteinn stopped talking to me. Well, he basically stopped talking to anyone. My life was absolute hell at our high school after that. I managed to graduate early and then got out of there."

"You haven't spoken to Half since?" I said, as gently as possible.

"Not until he called last week."

"I'm sorry." I felt guilty for having hurt him before even meeting him. He had his hair parted and combed over to one side just as Half liked to wear his. They hadn't seen each other as men, and I wondered how many hours Halfsteinn had spent on his boat punishing himself in isolation for his past silence.

"There's no need to apologize," Thom said finally, "sometimes it's good to be forced to think about shit you don't want to think about."

We stood on the porch, staring at each other. I was not looking forward to trying to sleep in my new surroundings.

The first night in the house was strange. Thom and Louise had dragged a discarded mattress in from a nearby curb during the annual swapping season that happens between semesters on the sidewalks of Waterloo. My room was the largest, because the former roommate was insistent that she needed the most space. The space was very clean—the walls were washed, the ceiling had no cobwebs, the windowsills were dust free.

"Here you go," Thom said, throwing me a blanket, "the sheets are on the bed. Louise and I are going for breakfast tomorrow morning—I told her to wake you up and bring you along. See you there at 10:30?"

I nodded, feeling tired for the first time in many days. I had spent about half an hour unpacking my backpack and hanging clothes. When I put my small collection of books on my bookshelf, I felt a sense of peace. I sat on the porch most of that afternoon smoking and reading over my package of information for new students, trying to decide whether I had chosen the right classes. I had made the choices so fleetingly and secretively—as though it was only a dream that I might one day actually be in them.

When I crawled under the covers, book in hand, I snapped on the small bedside lamp and read for several hours. When I finally turned off the light, I felt somewhat comfortable in my new surroundings. I closed my eyes.

What the...

My brain felt like it was about to explode and I couldn't figure out if I was awake or not. I sat up sharply, looking around furiously while trying to get my breathing back to normal.

Am I breathing? Am I breathing? Am I breathing?

I swallowed hard and my ears popped sharply, as though I had just gotten off an airplane. Tears stung my eyes and I started panting like a dog, the pain was so incredible and unreachable. It felt like it was jutting down directly into my jawbone. I put my palms against my ears and rocked back and forth gently.

"Fuck," I said as my breathing relaxed and became more even.

When I removed my palms from my ears I no longer felt water inside. Everything was sharp and crisp.

I celebrated my newfound hearing by going outside for a cigarette. The wind was coming in from the north. I heard the house shift, like it was trying to find a good spot to fall asleep. I kept thinking I heard whispering and would look down the street, waiting for people who never came. I couldn't sleep that night—I could hear too well, and the noise from the traffic and barking dogs and the wind through the trees kept me awake.

I woke up in the morning, very groggy, but followed Louise to the restaurant just off campus to meet Thom for breakfast.

Louise and I sat down in a booth at the same time. Sliding toward the wall, I looked at the clock on the diner's wall; Thom was supposed to be there already. I was nervous about making polite conversation with my new housemate.

I snapped out of my zombie-like state as the waitress came round in her pseudo 1950s shirt and enthusiasm, dispensing menus with an exaggerated arm movement. After fifteen minutes, it appeared that Thom was not going to show up, and I was having difficulty developing a conversation due to the early hour and my general inability to socialize; everyone at Freya's house had been content to let me be the silent observe,r and this was an adjustment. I came to find out that Thom believed, with religious fever, that one must always be fashionably late, which was why Louise told him to be there fifteen minutes early. Out of the corner of my eye I spotted the waitress coming to the table, undoubtedly to ask, once again, if we were ready to order. I was hungry. With the waitress coming closer to the table, Louise lunged across the table and grabbed my sleeve near the wrist with a terrified grip.

"You have to order for me," Louise said with an urgency that came from nowhere. There was a look in her eye that I dared not question. Somehow I understood, but couldn't commit to the knowledge, so I forged ahead cautiously,

"What, do you have to go to the bathroom or something?" I asked.

"No, I just...I can't order breakfast. I can't. I can't do it, I get mixed up with the way I like my eggs. Nothing comes out right. I thought Thom would be here to help, but now you have to. That stupid bastard, he knows that I can't order without him," she said in a way that made it unclear who she was talking to. "I get so confused and then they become impatient and there's so much pressure, you've got to help me. I hate the pressure, you've got to help me," Louise said, not letting go of my sleeve.

"OK, well, what do you want?" I said, looking directly into Louise's panicked eyes.

"I want two eggs cooked so that they've still got the runny stuff, but not too much."

"So you want them over easy?" I said nodding my head.

"Yes, yes, you've got it!" Louise said with enthusiasm. "And toast, I want toast," she continued, "two pieces, two brown pieces and pan fries. And I need vinegar. Can you do it?" Louise finished, still clinging to my sleeve.

"Got it," I said with a sideways, yet solemn nod. The waitress approached and addressing Louise, asked if she was ready to order.

I jumped in. "Yeah, I'll have two eggs over easy, brown toast, and pan fries."

The waitress wrote the order down while nodding her silent approval. "And for you?" the waitress said, looked directly at Louise again.

"She'll have the same." I said, mixing as much indifference and authority in my voice as I could.

"The same?" the waitress said with a little apprehension, still looking at Louise.

"The same," I said firmly without moving my gaze from the waitress, "and we'll need some vinegar, too."

Louise stared at me in amazement. It was as though I had just disarmed a nuclear bomb. She nodded her head in approval.

I would soon find out that Louise was finding her way back from the edge of death when we met. Hanging on with her last ounce of hope and strength, Louise had wandered through most of the previous year with nothing more than sleeping pills and the complete collection of Walt Whitman's poetry.

Exactly one month before her first year of university was to begin, Louise's father succumbed to the cancer that was eating into his liver and stomach. There was no love lost between him and Louise; they were mortal enemies, literally. Louise's father believed she was creating "useless garbage." He was the head of a large advertising firm in Toronto and could never understand why she "wasted" her talents. Louise dealt with loss by not sleeping.

Louise stayed awake, as if to prove she was still alive. But she wasn't alive; she wasn't even close to being alive. When I first arrived, everything she would attempt to cook was tasteless. It wasn't that the food would be horrible, just tasteless. Spices recoiled from her touch; it was a culinary rebellion. It had been months since she had painted. Empty canvases accosted her when she walked into the studio. The brushes weakened in their perpetual state of soaking, and her hands lost their paint stain. Her supervisor was starting to ask questions, and Louise had no answers.

After breakfast, Louise walked me to my first class.

I was both confused and grateful as she sat down beside me. "Are you in this class too?" After the incident at breakfast I suspected that Louise wasn't able to do much on her own.

"Yeah, I don't really feel like going to the studio, so I'm just going to cuddle up for some..." she trailed off, leaning over to look at my list of classes, "Introduction to Feminist Literature."

"Won't that be boring for you?" I said, slightly concerned for her sanity.

"No, I'm just going to find you a good rebound woman," she said, scanned my classmates as they filtered into the room.

"Louise," I said, trying to use the same voice I had used ordering breakfast for her, "I left Freya less than a week ago. Seventy-two hours ago, or something like that," time was confused for me, "I was still in a cabin north of Winnipeg with the woman that I love."

Louise leaned over and said, a little too loudly for my comfort level, "I'm not liking any of your options, Jess, I think we should leave."

"The class hasn't even started," I said.

"So?" Louise replied, genuinely confused.

"I signed up for the class because I'm actually interested in the topic," I said.

"All right, suit yourself," she said while signing one of the sheets the professor was handing out.

When the class was over, Louise brought me to my next class and sat down next to me again.

"What's this one, Jess? Is it Women's Studies or something like that, because your chances are definitely better in one of those."

"It's Introduction to Literary Criticism," I said, looking down at my sheet and narrowly avoiding a collision in the hallway.

"What is with all these literature classes?"

"I'm thinking that I want to be an English major."

"Yeah, you should switch to Women's Studies, way more ladies," she said, nodding her head quickly.

"But I want to study literature."

I looked over with what I imagine was a look of exasperation to see a tiny smile in her eyes. Even now, I'm never really certain when Louise is serious or not but I'm always happy to see that hint of mischief in her eyes. It reminded me of what I loved in Freya's eyes.

"This is a disaster," she said, sitting down next to me in the next class. "Where are all the sexy ladies?"

Just then the professor walked in and said, "How would you all feel about starting this semester off by heading to the pub for a pint? It's on me, come on."

There was a general round of enthusiastic nods as people gathered their bags up again and piled out of the classroom.

"I think we have a winner," Louise said, whistling and shaking her head.

"What?" I said incredulously.

"Yeah, she's hot and young; bag 'er kid. She's probably still a PhD student or something, so it doesn't even matter," Louise said, utterly unselfconsciously.

"She's my prof, she's not going to sleep with me. I'm sure that she has no interest in sleeping with her stupid undergrad students," I said, rejecting the idea, however intrigued I was.

"You're eighteen, right?"

I nodded. I was almost eighteen.

"No problem, all you gotta do is drink your classmates under the table," Louise said as we followed the herd out the door. "And just remember, this isn't about sleeping with that woman, it's about not sleeping with Freya. Good luck," she said, heading in the opposite direction, "and call home if you get lost; Thom and I will come and get you."

We headed down to the bar in the student centre, where the professor ordered several pitchers of beer and sat down at the table and introduced herself, which was followed by a round of introductions. After she outlined the semester for us we were free to go. A few of the students left, some went to the bar for more drinks and I headed to the patio for a cigarette.

"Hey, Jess," I heard behind me. I turned around to see that it was the professor. "Do you mind if I bum a smoke?" she said, smiling.

"No, not at all," I said, smiling back, "but only if its going to influence my grade positively."

She laughed and took the cigarette I was holding out for her.

"And only if it means that you'll pull out some Kristeva during the semester," I added.

She laughed again. "You have the wrong class. The French feminist linguists course is only being taught next semester, just after hell freezes over."

"Well, as long as you promise to fill the quota of white European male thought, because that seems in danger of being phased out these days at the post-secondary level. It's a concern of mine," I said, inhaling carefully, "so I'm thinking of starting a club that will lobby the university to make sure it stays on the curriculum."

She laughed reaching for a random bottle of beer on the table.

"Is that yours?" I said, laughing.

"Yeah, I don't think so. But all the beer they serve here is swill anyway, so who cares." She drank it down, and I smiled at her.

"What are you doing?" I heard a voice behind.

I twirled around, convinced that my dad was standing behind me. How did he find me? It turned out to be a colleague of the professor I was sharing a cigarette with.

They engaged in some friendly conversation as the colour drained from my face. I found myself overwhelmed with a memory of when I was fourteen and at school with my dad. It was guest lecture season in the university calendar and I was asked my opinion of the lecture by one of my dad's PhD students. Before I knew it, I was holding court with a few of my father's colleagues. Someone challenged something that I had said and I was mid-sentence in defence of my opinion when I heard my father behind me. "Jess, that's enough" was all he said. I stopped speaking and felt my face turn crimson. "Your mother needs your help cleaning up the food." It wasn't the first time that he had told me to stop talking but usually

I had some warning that the commandment was forthcoming. He had snuck up, heard what I was saying, and obviously didn't approve it or who I was saying it to. Often, our suppertime arguments led to me being sent to my room and being told to do my homework before I tried to argue with him. That time, I had no idea I was even arguing with him.

"Do you want to go somewhere else?" She touched my elbow.

I came back to the conversation and took a drag of my cigarette, feeling certain I had just been talking to myself.

"You OK?" she said.

"Yeah, I just was suddenly hit with a weird memory."

"Why don't we get out of here?" she said. "Let's go to a non-university bar."

"I don't think that exists in this town, from what little I know. Anywhere but here sounds good to me." I smiled broadly, hoping that she wouldn't think that I was insane.

"You're very astute," she said, exhaling. "Why don't you hop the fence and meet me out front. I'll go back inside and excuse myself." She handed me her cigarette, "I'll be right there."

She walked back into the bar and I knew that I was looking for trouble.

We walked toward the bar and I regaled her with stories of my upbringing in rural Saskatchewan, hoping that I sounded older than I was. We spotted a corner table on the covered patio and made our way past the pool tables and people crowed around the TV watching a football game.

"I'm not sure about this bar," I said as I followed her, "it seems kind of like a sports bar."

"Yeah, I know, but just trust me, it's not. It's really a hipster bar disguised as a sport's bar."

"Brilliant disguise," I said as a waitress approached us.

We ordered drinks and I lit a cigarette. "So," I said offering her my pack, "have you slept with any of your students before." I couldn't believe those words had just come out of my mouth. I diverted my eyes, pretending to look at people walking by to prevent her from looking into my eyes.

I looked back as she smiled and raised an eyebrow. "Can I borrow your light?" She lit the cigarette. As she leaned over to put the lighter back she touched my knee underneath the table and said, "No, but I've never really had students before."

"Hold that thought," I said as I got up. I felt my heart race. "I've just got to go to the bathroom." I went to the bar, ordered a shot of Jaggermeister, threw it back, and walked to the bathroom.

I was about to go into a stall when I felt a hand on my hip. I turned around. It was the professor. She pushed me against the wall and kissed me.

"Do you want to go back to my place?" she asked.

I was nodding quickly, "Yes, yes. Definitely," I said, feeling my brain and my ability to form full sentences migrate to a warm spot between my legs.

After we had sex she kissed my neck and said, "I think you are going to have to drop my class."

"I'll just take it next year," I said. I smiled, but all I could think about was how I was going to leave as soon as possible.

"Because," she said, purring into my ear and biting my ear lobe, "I think that I may be slightly biased when marking your work."

"I think I've got a night class in a few minutes," I said. It was the only excuse I could think of to get out of there.

"Call me." She kissed me again before releasing me out of her arms.

I got dressed quickly and realized that the sun had not set yet. "Can I borrow these sunglasses?" I said, reaching for the pair that was on the kitchen table. I suddenly felt the need for anonymity, despite being in a city composed entirely of strangers to me.

"Yeah, yeah," she said, waving her arm from the bed, "take them, I don't care."

I walked into my house and tried to walk past Louise and Thom, who were in the living room, without them noticing, but it didn't work. They were preparing their bong and looked very engrossed in their work.

"Wait a second," Louise said, "where did you get those sunglasses? And where have you been?"

I said nothing, staring at her from behind the sunglasses.

"Holy shit, it worked. You slept with her, didn't you?"

"I'm feeling a little shitty about this, Louise," I said, biting my bottom lip. "I don't know what came over me; I've never done that before. It was so easy. She wants to see me again." I stopped short and thought of Freya, wondering if somehow I should consider her in all of that. "But now I'm thinking that there's plenty of fish in the sea," I said, more to myself than Louise or Thom.

"Well, Jess," Louise said, taking a hoot, "you know what they say, the best way to get over a woman is to get under one. Think of it as therapy." She exhaled. "It sounds like you got some sort of monkey off your back tonight."

"Yeah, I guess so. I think she really likes me," I said, wincing. "What do you mean by monkey?"

"That's just what you needed," Thom said, taking the bong from Louise. "Make yourself happy Jess; no one's going to do it for you."

"What about Freya?" I said, not sure what I was asking.

"She's the monkey," Thom said enthusiastically.

"I don't know, " I suddenly felt panicked. "What if Freya still wants to be with me? Fuck." Thom and Louise stared at me incredulously. "I'm still in love with her," I said, trying to explain.

"Of course you are," Louise said, "but that doesn't mean it's a healthy thing. From what I've heard about this Freya woman, she's just a wee bit controlling." Louise held her thumb and forefinger about an inch apart.

"Maybe I should try calling Freya," I said, and then thought about the call I had tried to make home while living with Freya.

Thom crossed his arms and shook his head, "No, you will not. This professor of yours, however, definitely call her."

I turned around to leave the room.

"Wait a second," Thom said, exhaling, "didn't you say at breakfast that your dad is some kind of president of a Menno college in Saskatoon?"

"Yeah," I said suspiciously. "Why?"

"Interesting," was all Thom said.

"What do you mean by that?" I said a little too defensively.

"Some sort of Freudian thing, is that what you're thinking, Thom," Louise said, not looking at me.

Thom was nodding, "Yeah, yeah, I just haven't figured it out exactly yet, it might take me a few days. I've got to give it time to percolate," he said, nodding and pointing at his head.

"Oh no, no," Louise said passing the bong back to Thom, "I think that this is a pastor's kid phenomena, except for Jess, it's a child of a Mennonite academic thing." She stopped smiling and nodded enthusiastically. Thom did the same.

"Go on, Louise, I really think that you're on to something," Thom said, shouting for no apparent reason.

I stood there, thinking that maybe I was still drunk, while two virtual strangers picked at my psyche like a bowl of warm noodles.

"Oh yeah," Louise continued, "this is so classic and obvious, Jess, you've got to get your sin on because you're a good Mennonite farm girl, but there's a twist," she said, violently pointing her index finger at the ceiling and standing up. She walked toward me, took my shoulders, and shook me. "The twist is that your dad is a Mennonite academic, so you have to fuck a prof even if she teaches a boring class like Introduction to Literary Criticism."

"Oh God," was all I said as I left the room and promptly threw up.

MEET ME IN MY OFFICE TUESDAY, 9:00 AM SHARP
(THREE YEARS LATER)

"Ms. Klassen."

"Don't call me that, Rob, Jesus Christ almighty, don't call me that."

"You know why I asked you to visit me this afternoon, correct?"

"First of all Rob, it's the morning, it's nine-o-fucking-clock in the morning. Second of all, yes, I know why you called me in here and the answer is no. No, I have not yet interviewed anyone who gives a fuck about Martha Wiens, nor have I found anyone else who has done critical work about her. No, I have not found any material that Martha Wiens has produced other than *In the Wilderness*. No, I have not talked to Martha Wiens other than in my head."

"You do understand that you must produce a thesis."

"Yes, I understand that. You know what else I understand? That I'm making you look bad with this shoddy bullshit workmanship. I understand that, Rob, but I also understand that this is just a fucking undergrad thesis. Who cares? No one cares."

"I care. I care a lot. And you know what else, I don't care that this is an undergrad thesis, that's irrelevant. It's work that you believe in; it has value, you just need to do it."

"I think I've proved that I'm not lazy."

"Jess, there's no need to get defensive. I'm not saying that you're lazy. I know you're not lazy. God, that's not the point at all—you do more research and tutoring in this department than I've ever seen from an undergrad, maybe even from a grad student. Anyway, that's not my point. My point is that the problem is something I can't help you with."

"And what exactly is that, Rob?"

"I think that this is no longer about Martha Wiens. This is no longer about your undergrad thesis. This is about your life. This is about working through some psychological barrier that you need to get past, and I don't know how to help you with that. I probably shouldn't, even if I could."

"Well, thank you so very much for that stunning insight, Rob. So now, if you'll excuse me, I have some fucking first years to attend to who couldn't string together complete sentences if their lives depended on it."

"One more thing."

'Yes."

"Besides your thesis, you need another elective to graduate. And I'm thinking you should kill two birds with one stone."

"Ah, pardon me?"

"There's a Bible as literature course that a friend of mine just developed—it's a religion course, so that would satisfy your requirements—and it's literature, so I thought you might be interested."

"I am not interested."

"It might be a good idea to just go to the first class, just test it out, see how it feels."

"How on God's green earth did I allow you to know me this well?"

"You're welcome."

A CALCULATED CHANCE MEETING

It was the Wednesday night killer at one of those small Christian colleges on campus. "The Bible as Literature" was the unoriginal name of the course, and we were the only two who smoked. We were also the only two not caught up in the mucky business of feeling defensive about subject matter discussed in class, at least that's what I was desperately trying to convince myself when I walked up to the class that night. I felt that Rob had thrown down the gauntlet, and I had no choice but to answer the call.

After three years of studying modern-Canadian writers and beat era poets from the States, I had to diversify my course choices or risk not graduating.

Old English classes were out of the question—I had gone to one class and it was like speaking Low German. After I left the first class mid-way through to throw up, I knew I couldn't do that for an entire semester.

The professor started talking about pieces of literature that were influenced by the Bible. He was not one of those professors that simply hands out a syllabus on the first day and dismisses the class. We went over the outline for the semester. As I scanned the required textbooks section I saw that the Bible was listed. My stomach went numb, as if it had been pulled right out of me, and I had to grip the desk for support. It shouldn't have been a surprise, but it hadn't occurred to me that we might need to actually read the Bible. Just as I was recovering from the shock, a young man put up his hand. He wore a shirt that featured stick figures of a man and a woman having sex. A second picture featured two stick-figure women having sex with the stick-figure man watching.

"Is this class only about the Bible? Are we going to talk about all the religions and their influence on literature?"

It was an earnest question and I tried to stifle a giggle as I looked down at my syllabus and read the course title again. The Bible as Literature. "We're all idiots," I said under my breath.

"Because when it says 'The Bible' on the syllabus," I heard a hushed voice behind me say, "it really means 'all religions.' Jesus Christ almighty."

I turned around to respond to my cheeky neighbour, "I'm constantly amazed at..." I was stopped short by a row of big square teeth with a slit between the two front ones, gleaming blue eyes, and brown hair with that messed-up look that I could never accomplish, purposely or accidentally.

"You were saying," she said after what seemed like five minutes of me staring at her.

I regained my composure, if only externally, "...at the fact that we have yet to make those two globally synonymous." I ended the sentence with a big smile and we locked eyes for a second. I sat up a little straighter as I estimated that she had a good four inches on me.

"Well, I think that if the Church of Shea was sending out missionaries, you'd be my first pick." She turned her head away to look as though she was paying attention while moving her eyes back in my direction, still smirking.

"Oh no, I'm sorry, I would have to decline. I don't want my children to become MKs." As soon as it came out, I realized that it was a term that only churchy types might be familiar with and that I shouldn't assume an understanding.

She didn't blink twice. "Oh, those poor missionary kids, I certainly wouldn't want to be responsible for creating that."

I turned and faced forward, also pretending to pay attention to what was happening in the class. Then I leaned back and whispered over my shoulder. "Those kids were either way too twitchy from living in constant fear of being kidnapped or wouldn't shut up about having fresh goat milk yogurt made for them every morning by their maid."

In her effort to stifle her laughter she ended up spitting on the back of my neck. I wiped the saliva off. I felt her desk shaking as she attempted to suppress her laughter.

"Stop it," I said, whispering again as I noticed the nasty look we were getting from the professor. "You're making me feel like I'm a comedic genius which will ruin my sense of humility and put me in danger of being a very bad Mennonite." I did the best impression of earnestness I could muster.

She stopped laughing, leaned closer to me, and whispered, "Well, I'm just trying to give you something to feel guilty about. I'm doing you a favour."

The professor was talking. People were engaged in some sort of discussion or were scribbling notes. My back was on fire as I was keenly aware of the body behind me. I willed her to touch me, sending all of my energy out toward her. I closed my eyes and pushed against my cell walls, trying to get every part of me closer to her.

The professor finally set us free at break time and I found myself, very much on purpose, standing outside borrowing a light from the woman behind me.

"Jesus, what a hard-ass, keeping us there for that long. I always take that as a sign of ego," I said.

"Yeah, the guy's kind of an asshole, I've had him before," she said, taking her lighter back from me, brushing my outstretched fingers gently.

Just then the professor came outside and walked toward us, "You want a ride home, Shea?"

"No, I'm not going home," she said.

"Do you know when you're going to be home?" he said, sounding concerned.

"Dad," she said, exasperated but still good-humoured, "remember how I'm an adult now."

"Right," he said, zipping up his coat and heading in the opposite direction.

"Oh fuck," I said when he was out of earshot, "that's embarrassing."

"For me or for you?" she laughed.

"Definitely for me," I said, trying my best to relax as I felt all of my muscles contracting.

"I don't think so. I'm the loser taking a class from my dad for the sake of some twisted, lame, psychological self-testing." She exhaled through her nose, sending a long stream of smoke into the insistently cold fall night. "Plus, I moved back to my hometown from Montreal and am living with my dad. Weird, I know."

I smiled, thinking that I might die. "Speaking of psychological self-testing, why is it that the children of academics seem to be almost as fucked up as children of ministers and missionary kids?"

"Hmmm," she said, looking down at the ground, "I'm pretty sure you're going to have to buy me a beer to get a good answer." She smiled and looked into my eyes.

"Can't," I said, shaking my head, suddenly filled with terror. I handed her a piece of paper and ran in the opposite direction and didn't stop running until I got home. When I got home I was breathing hard and barely made it to the bushes in our front yard before throwing up.

.....

"What did you expect?" Thom said without looking away from the screen where he was guiding Mario through the series of obstacles. "In case you haven't noticed, there's about a billion Mennonites in the K W area. They were the first farmers here, they moved here following the British army after the American Civil War."

"Yes, yes, I am well aware of my Mennonite history, thank you, Thom," I snapped at him. "And when's the last time you've been in the studio? Speaking of history."

"Just calm down, Jess," he said, pausing the game and putting the controller down on the coffee table. "First of all, do not criticize my work habits, it's not attractive. Now, let me get this straight, it was love at first sight and then you realized that the prof is her dad and now you're freaking out. How do you even know that they're Mennonites?"

"Because" I yelled, barely breathing, "their last name is Driedger and he teaches at the Mennonite college on campus, it doesn't get much more Menno than that." I pulled a cigarette out of my pack.

"All right, she's a Menno, that still doesn't mean you can smoke that in here," he said pointing at my cigarette, "so let's go outside and think about this."

We went outside. Thom took the porch recliner while I stretched out on the couch and felt my body starting to cool down. He pulled his glasses down low on his nose and crossed his legs. Just then Louise arrived home and took her perch on the railing.

"What's going on here?" she said.

"Well, it appears that Jess is in love."

"Not in love. Don't use that word," I said, cutting Thom off. I had never spoken about love after Freya.

"But in a cruel twist the object of her affection is not only a Mennonite, but also the daughter of a Mennonite academic, so we're just breaking this down for her." Thom said, while Louise nodded knowingly. "Now, Jess, let me get this straight, she's the most attractive person that you've ever laid your eyes on?"

"It's not that simple," I said.

"And we've deduced that she is of genuine prairie Mennonite stock?"

"Yes," I said. "I mean, who knows about her mother. But father, yes."

"And she was not only incredibly physically attractive, but she also made snide remarks about church and missionaries and said something about getting you into the missionary position?" Thom said, rubbing the scruff on his chin.

"Yes to the first part but no, she didn't say anything about getting me into the missionary position," I said, getting agitated again.

"But she did invite you out for beer which, after watching you in action for the past three years, means you're going to get laid."

"And," Louise said, ready to jump into the conversation, "usually means that you will never see or speak to this woman again, leaving us to field phone calls from said broken-hearted woman. Now, you've run away before you even slept with her. Interesting."

"Very interesting," Thom added. "Is our Saskatchewan prairie ice-princess melting?"

"And more importantly," Louise said, "is she finding her heart melting? Definitely interesting."

"That's not interesting," I said defensively.

"Oh, I think all the people on this porch know that's very interesting," Thom said, getting up and going inside. Louise followed him, leaving me alone, lying on the couch, listening to intermittent roars of approval coming up from the university football stadium.

I got up and paced. I wanted to find her. Maybe she'll walk by, I thought.

"Shit, shit, shit," I said to no one.

I kept pacing and lit another cigarette. I felt angry and agitated and I couldn't stop moving. I wasn't completely cut off from the world of Mennonites; I was surrounded by them in Waterloo County. I generally chose to avoid them, but it felt like everything was unravelling with Rob's comments, the new class, and the woman whose name I didn't even know and the fact that I couldn't avoid myself very well. Why was I so afraid of this woman, I wondered, yet also so desperately wanted her to happen by the porch that night? I inhaled very deliberately as a memory punched at my stomach. Finally, I sat down on the railing and hung my head.

When I was twelve and my brother John was eighteen and had a year of university under his belt, he asked mom if he could bring a lady-friend home for dinner. Mom asked if the woman was someone from the college, in other words, was she a Mennonite woman that mom knew. John tried to avoid the question by asking if Tuesday night would be good for her. Mom responded with silence, her back was still turned to him while she was doing the dishes. "She's Catholic mom," John said, "that's what you wanted to know, isn't it mom? And she's from the city," his voice was raised. He exhaled through his nose like a bull ready to charge. "I really like her and she's excited to meet my family."

Mom turned around and dried her hands on her apron. She looked at me and said, "Tuesday doesn't work because you promised to take your sister to a movie that night and she's been looking forward to that for a week now."

"Yeah, John, you promised," I said quickly and then saw the angry devastation in his eyes. I assumed that he was angry with me for ruining his plans. I felt torn because I really was excited about spending time alone with my big brother and I really was excited to see a movie. The thought of some woman interfering with our plans didn't appeal to me at all, but I could see he was disappointed. He turned and walked out of the room without another word. While mom finished preparing supper, I walked in circles in my small bedroom until I couldn't stand the pain in my stomach. I went to the washroom and threw up as quietly as possible; I didn't want mom thinking that there was anything wrong. I went downstairs and tried to talk to John, but all he said was, "Forget it, Jess, this has nothing to do with you."

After all those years, I still blamed myself for ruining that relationship—we never heard about her again. If only I hadn't been so selfish, he might be happily married, I had always thought. I allowed the memory and a little emotional housekeeping, realizing that it hadn't been my fault.

I started crying. It had been a very long time since my last cry. I curled up into a ball on the porch couch and let myself shake and cry until I fell asleep.

OVER FOR COFFEE

Two days later, the doorbell rang at a little after midnight. I jumped out of my chair. It could have been anyone, but not really. None of the regular house friends rang the doorbell and it was too late for sales or solicitations. I took a deep breath and made my way to the door but stopped halfway through the kitchen to take a seat on one of the chairs. Thirty seconds later, the doorbell rang again. My movements and the lighted house were enough to make the ringer believe that someone was home. I stood up and completed my journey to the door. Turning the knob, I took a deep breath again and opened the door.

"Du bist spat," I said with a look of indifference, pulling out my High German.

"Pardon me?" the guest said as I moved aside to allow her through the door.

I reached into the pocket of my sweater, producing a pack of cigarettes.

"I'm going out for a cigarette, make yourself comfortable."

The guest put her jacket back on. "I'll go with you."

"That would be fine."

She followed me to the backyard where a lone tree covered the small patch of land with its branches. I went into a dilapidated with doors that didn't appear to close anymore. My guest followed me in. We couldn't sit on the porch with Louise and Thom in the living room watching us; that was out of the question.

"Don't sit there," I said, "that's my spot. The guest-smoker seat is there," I said, pointing to the lawn chair set up against the back of the shed.

The guest frowned, "I don't think it's load-bearing anymore."

The chair used to be yellow but had faded into benign white, looking to be woven together with strips of printer paper.

"Oh, I assure you that *that* chair is load-bearing, but I do have an outstanding guarantee for all past, present and future guest smokers that, if it breaks while you're sitting on it, I will quit smoking for the remainder of the guest smoker's life."

She laughed and shifted around in the chair.

"No shifting, you're cheating."

The wind picked up slightly, making the shed wobble.

"Believe me, I have nothing to gain from your quitting smoking for the remainder of my life," the guest said, ashing her own cigarette.

"I think you do."

The guest laughed again revealing the perfect thin slit between her two front teeth. I estimated that the slit was big enough for two pieces of paper to slide between.

"So what brings you by at such a late hour?" I said.

"Other than your invitation and specific instructions to come at this late hour?" She said exhaling through her nose.

"Yes, other than those two factors," I said nodding.

"Coffee." The woman sat with her hands folded on her lap and legs crossed.

I wanted to reach down and brush the tiny strand of hair touching the edge of her chin but I resisted.

"Well, I should get onto that then shouldn't I?" I said.

"Suit yourself."

"I will." I stood up and put my half-finished cigarette out on the cement floor. When we got to the door I stopped and turned toward Shea. "You're welcomed to come in, if you like."

Shea shrugged her shoulders and pushed her way past me into the house.

"This is my house and this is the kitchen where I'll be making the coffee."

"Is there a guest coffee-drinker seat?" Shea said, trying to keep a straight face.

"No, but there is a coffee-making observer guest seat which is the left-hand side of the couch when facing it." I said opening cupboards.

With silent obedience, Shea made her way behind the table to the kitchen couch.

While I was growing up it was easier for my grandparents to fit many children on a bench rather than buy extra chairs for the dining room set. The bench in my not-so-distant past was white and backless and referred to as the "schlop bank"—the sleep bench. The kitchen couch in this kitchen was a whorish red with fake leather covering that was coming apart at that seams.

"Are you comfortable?" I inquired.

"Yes, quite."

"Well, now you must observe carefully as I demonstrate the fine art of making coffee with the French press. Were you aware that it's a fine art?" I couldn't help but smirk. I was losing my mind. Although I had a very specific ritual for making coffee, I had never once verbalized it, let alone explicitly demonstrated it for anyone.

"I believe your invitation made a veiled reference to that fact. I have to tell you, though, I have personally participated in the making of coffee with a French press, so I'm not sure you have anything to teach me."

"Oh, I think I do. If making coffee was an Olympic sport I would most certainly qualify to represent Canada," I said while gathering the tools of my amateur trade. Within moments I had lined up on the counter a French press, toaster-oven tray, the kettle, a coffee canister, a wooden spoon, and the coffee grinder. "I'm self-taught, by the way."

She laughed, "But what inspired you to this level of passion?"

"Well, that's a long story involving a pouch of tobacco and a friend that I haven't seen in quite some time." I paused, putting away my feelings of missing Halfsteinn as quickly as possible.

"I have a feeling that you have a lot of long stories that you could share with me that involve cigarettes," she said, nodding her head.

"I do and I will, gladly, but right now on to the business at hand."

Step One:
   Line up above mentioned items on the counter.

Step Two:
   Put raw, unroasted beans on cookie sheet and set oven to 450 degrees. When oven reaches 450 degrees place cookie sheet in oven, stirring beans occasionally to achieve an even roast.

Step Three:
   Set kettle to boil.

Step Four:
> *Wash French press without using detergent.*

"Why no detergent?"
"It will sully the taste. I thought I had nothing to teach you?"

Step Five:
> *Fill thermos with hot water.*

"Why are you going to put the coffee in the thermos?"
"So it doesn't get cold."
"Aren't we going to drink it right away?"

Step Five:
> *After fifteen minutes of roasting, remove beans.*

Step Six:
> *Put desired amount of beans in grinder (usually more than you think). While pressing down grinder button, shake up and down like a martini to insure even grind. Deposit into French press.*

> *Note, if you do not have fair-trade organic coffee, you should buy some. Anything less is evil.*

"So it's OK to smoke like a fiend, but if you drink coffee that's not fair trade and organic you're evil?"
"Yes. Are you going to let me continue?"
"Please continue."

Step Seven:
> *Diligently watch the kettle so that it doesn't boil. It is imperative that the water does not boil.*

"Why is it important that the water doesn't boil? Isn't that what water is supposed to do when one puts the kettle to boil?"
"First of all, I said imperative, not important; there is a difference. Second of all, when one pours boiling water over coffee grinds it burns them, and one doesn't want burnt coffee."
"I think you're talking out of your ass."
"No. No I am not."
"All right."

Step Eight:
> *Add almost boiling water to French press, making sure to stir with wooden spoon while pouring water in. Why wooden spoon, you ask? Well, I'll tell you why. Wood is imperative in that it will not add an undesired metallic taste to the coffee.*

"Undesired metallic taste? Are you on crack?" she said laughing.
"The guest will kindly restrict her comments to questions only."
"I hate to pay attention to detail, but those were questions."

Step Nine:
> *Place plunger into French press but DO NOT FULLY PLUNGE YET. Plunge only a quarter of the way down and let rest for at least three minutes. Continue to plunge down in quarter plunges with rests in between, allowing flavour to fully find its way into water.*

Step Nine:
> *Heat a gulp of soy milk on the stove. You better heat it or that shit will curdle.*

Step Ten:
> *Empty hot water from thermos. Fill thermos with coffee, but do not fill thermos entirely with coffee.*

Step Eleven:
> *Add two tablespoons of sugar and a gulp of milk to every half litre of coffee made. Put lid on and, once again, shake like a martini. Serve in lid cup, passing it between as many people as present, refilling lid cup until all are satisfied.*

"You don't strike me as the sugar and cream type. I'm shocked."
"It's much easier on the digestive system." I said, picking up the thermos of coffee and motioning to Shea to follow me. Leading her down the hall and into my room, I gestured in the direction of the mattress on the floor. "You sit there," I said, "and I'll be right back."

I walked into the living room where Louise and Thom were engaged in intense head-to-head Super Mario Kart action. Eyes glued to the screen, Thom and Louise, in an uncharacteristic move, instantly paused the game. Louise was the first to speak.

"What the hell are you doing in here?"

I stared silently out the window with my back to them.

Thom was the next to chime in. "Yeah, what the hell are you doing in here? Get back into your room with her."

Louise and Thom were clearly focused on delivering their message.

"Jess, look at me. Turn around and look at me."

I complied silently.

119

"This is not the time to let your brain fuck with you, get back into that room. It's time to be open to the possibility of loving someone enough to let them hurt you as much as Freya did."

"Fuck you," I said without much enthusiasm.

Thom continued with a less subtle approach. "Jess, she's hot, and she makes you nervous; I'm not sure why you're in the living room right now. Get back in there or I'm going in," Thom said, changing his tone to threatening at the end of his last sentence.

"Yeah, I'm going in there in thirty seconds if you don't," Louise said, backing up Thom.

I remained silent, standing in front of the window, looking at her shadow. Louise and Thom looked at each other and stood up, making their way toward me. I didn't notice their movement.

"We have no choice," Thom said, "now we must have a group hug."

"OK, OK, I'm going, there's no need to get up off the couch or anything, no need to do anything like hug."

Having clearly scored a victory, there was no need for Thom and Louise to rub it in; they made their way back to the couch and resumed their game.

"Jess," Thom said before letting her leave the room, "what's her name?"

"What?" I said.

"Oh, don't give me that crap, Jess, have you or have you not asked for her name yet?" Thom said, still watching his character navigate the Super Mario Kart course.

I exhaled loudly and cleared my throat. "Shea."

There was no response from Thom and Louise, so I left them to their video game.

She looked up as I entered the room again.

"Did you think that I had abandoned you?"

"It wouldn't have surprised me, frankly."

I walked toward her and picked up the thermos. "Do you want some coffee?"

She nodded her head, "Yup."

Unscrewing the top, I poured the first cup and handed it to her. Shea took the cup and inhaled. Again, she cracked a wide grin as she looked up at me and took a sip. "You make a fine cup of coffee," she said, having fully swallowed.

"Thank you. Now, do you mind if I ask you a personal question?"

"I've been waiting all night for you to ask me a personal question," Shea answered while sipping her coffee.

"As you read this story, do you see any signs of a narrator you cannot trust?"

"I see no initial signs. But Literary Criticism 100A was a long time ago," she paused. "Was that the personal question?"

"Now you're just terrorizing my narrative—steering it in a certain direction, attempting to project onto it."

She smiled, "All readers do, it's unavoidable. But what I'm really wanting is a story, true or not, because I tend not to put much stock into historical accuracy."

"There once was a girl who…is that what you're waiting for?" I said, taking the cup from her hands and sipping.

"I'm surprised," she said, taking the cup back from me and stretching her legs out, "I mean, I wouldn't expect that sort of thing from you on a first date."

"Is this a date?"

"Well," she said, reaching over to move my big toe back and forth a few times, "I think that when I tell this story, I'll say it was a date."

"And who am I to choose your words," I said shrugging.

"Where are you from?" Shea said quietly.

"Oh, you know, somewhere else—not here, nowhere. Does it matter? I'm sitting here with you in this room. Isn't that all that matters?"

"Yes, and no," she said thoughtfully. "Yes, in that I have no desire to be anywhere else right now or with anyone else. No, in that the beauty and mystery of life is all those little moments that accumulate and bring us into moments like this. I am a naturally curious person."

I started biting my nail but then became conscious of it and stopped. "Have you ever heard of a poet named Martha Wiens?"

"No, but she sounds of good Russian Mennonite stock. Is she a contemporary?"

"She is of good Russian Mennonite stock, but whether she is a good Russian Mennonite remains a mystery. I kind of think not." I reached over and examined the CD sitting next to my pillow. I gave it a polish and put it in the player. "Her poetry is the subject of my thesis project, but I know nothing about her, I've been asking everyone for the past couple of years if they've heard of her and no one has."

She took the cup back from me. "How is it that you know her poetry but she's so ghost like?"

"I was rummaging through my father's private belongings when I discovered her chapbook."

She laughed, "Well, mystery solved, or rather, the mystery can be easily solved. Surely enough time has passed since this transgression. Why don't you just ask your dad?"

The window was cracked open and the smell of a wood fire wafted through. I could still hear the hum of Super Mario Kart coming from the living room. One of my housemates slammed the fridge door shut. Everything was normal in the house. Everything was normal except sitting on my bed a stranger who didn't feel like a stranger, drinking coffee and speaking about our feelings. The scary part was how strange it didn't feel.

"That's not an option."

"Why?" she said, unflinching in the face of my icy response.

"It just ain't."

"Why?"

"I'm ready for another cigarette. This time I'll introduce you to the front porch smoking area." I tried to smile. I didn't want her to hate me, I just couldn't respond.

"That sounds good to me."

She stood up and extended her hand. She pulled me up with a good deal of force.

"You're short," she said, as my face nearly collided with her collarbone.

"Well, you know what they say about short women?" I didn't wait for a response. "They're all liars."

"Well, maybe I want to hear your lies."

We walked out onto the porch and sat side-by-side on the couch. The coffee was finished and my hands were shaking.

"How come I've never seen you in any of my classes before?" I said accusingly, "You're not a Lit major, are you?"

"I am, in fact," she said while lighting her cigarette, "but I just transferred here from Concordia. I was starting to feel guilty about spending so much time away from my father."

"Isn't he an adult who can take care of himself?"

"Yes, but my mom left us when I was very little and we don't live close to any family. I guess I'm just trying to be a good daughter. And I do have a lot of childhood friends here." She sounded a little defensive and exasperated.

"Are you still a Mennonite?" I said exhaling into the wind.

She exhaled, puffing out her cheeks and then rubbed her eyes with her palm. "Nobody told me that was an option," she said with fake shock.

I laughed.

She laughed, too.

"I know that's not very funny," she said, still laughing, "a very lame joke to be sure, but Jesus, I've been living in Montreal for some time now and I've missed a bit of that unspokeness amongst our people."

"You know, for me, it's all kind of just faded, leaving me like an illness that you forget once you're over it."

"You're a lucky one, then."

"Shall we?" I said, motioning with my head to the door.

I looked around at my bedroom and tried to imagine what Shea's looked like. There was very little to show that I had made it my home for so long. I was deathly afraid of accumulating things.

That was a lie though; things hadn't faded at all. Everything hurt all the time. My stomach wouldn't allow food in it, my legs ached at night when I tried to fall asleep, and my eyes felt like I'd been punched.

"Tell me about one tradition that your family has." I said. This time my eyes met hers easily. A car passed on the street below my window, and I could hear kids yelling.

"Well, when my mom left, my dad and I decided that we had to make up all new traditions for Christmas and summer and Saturday mornings, you know, those kinds of things. So, I guess the first one was…"

I cut her off abruptly. "No, I want to hear about the oldest ones, the ones with your mom, when everybody was all together."

Shea's face set to stone; I noticed the change immediately. For some reason I needed to push those buttons, needed to see what they were and how she reacted.

"It's funny," Shea said, finally interrupting the silence, "now I realize that even when we were together, we were never really together. My parents are the poorest match I can think of. My dad just has this sense of 'dad' about him. You know, he tells really lame jokes and asks me if I've eaten that day when he's trying to get me to talk about my feelings and avoiding talking about his. On Saturday afternoons he washes the car. All that stuff. But my mom just seems like a wanted criminal on the run."

I laughed; thinking of my mom in those terms was the most absurd thing I could imagine.

Shea continued, "Before my mom left us she would put me to bed and she would sing this hymn to me. 'In the Rifted Rock.' Do you know it?"

I nodded.

"Well, it was the only remotely religious thing that I remember her doing. She left when I was eight."

I pulled both feet toward me. Removing my socks, I asked a question. "Will you love me?"

"Am I allowed to?" she replied softly.

I studied my naked feet feeling my stomach heave. Instinctively, I felt the need to smoke or vomit. My eyes fixed on the bottom quarter of my body.

I contemplated the question. No one had ever asked permission to love me and I had never asked. My life had been filled with something called love foisted on me like the hand-me-downs from my older brothers. I searched my memory and could only recall of being told to accept love, but not being asked.

"No answer, hey? Just as well, I have to go to the bathroom anyway."

I stared at Shea's knees for a moment, saying nothing. I thought about the bathroom, how it probably hadn't been cleaned in a good four months and how the mould in the shower was starting to look like wallpaper. I avoided the walls when I took showers, gingerly reaching for the soap and shampoo without touching the shelves they were on. It had, in fact, been four months since the bathroom had been cleaned. It had been the weekend that Louise's mother came to visit her daughter.

Mrs. Owen had come for the weekend, laden with cleaning agents. She spent a good twenty minutes examining every part of the washroom, as if planning her attack. The whole time her mother was in the washroom, Louise sat on the couch with her knees curled up into her chest, saying things like "This isn't good, Jess, this isn't good." I didn't understand, but apparently it was the first time they had seen each other since her dad's funeral. When Louise had opened the door, all her mother had said was, "You've got his eyes," before marching straight to the washroom and launching her assault. An hour later, when she was finished her cleaning, Mrs. Owen walked back into the living room and said, "Now we're going for a sensible meal," and then, pointing at me, she said, "you're coming, too, and you're driving." I looked at Louise and for the first time since her mother arrived, she smiled.

"I think that I need a cigarette," I said, putting my socks back on and standing up when Shea had re-entered the room, still in a state of reverie.

"So you're not allowed to smoke in the house?" Shea seemed genuinely shocked.

"Oh, heavens no. It's strictly verboten."

"Your housemates smoke weed in the house, but you can't smoke cigarettes? That doesn't seem fair to me," Shea said sympathetically.

"Yeah, that doesn't seem quite right," I said, making my way out to the living room. Louise and Thom had finished their video game and were watching TV. "You guys," I said trying not to get distracted by the TV, "how come you can smoke weed in the house, but I can't smoke cigarettes?"

A roar of approval came from Louise and Thom; they were watching one of their favourite shows. It was on the outdoor channel and featured dogs running through an obstacle course.

"Molly just kicked that weave pole's ass!" Thom said approvingly, just as the program went to commercial.

"First of all," Louise started, "don't say 'you' when you really mean 'us.' We all smoke weed and don't try to deny that you don't just for the sake of your guest."

Thom picked up from the second point. "Second of all, cigarettes stink," he finished.

"Thirdly," Louise continued, "getting high and watching these dogs run the course is one of your favourite pastimes, too, so why don't you sit down, smoke a bowl, pass it to your guest, and help us cheer Bounder on to victory." She muted the TV. "He's up after the commercial."

I turned toward Shea, shrugged, and sat down, forgoing my need for a cigarette. Shea sat down beside me and smiled. I turned toward the TV screen. Shea slipped her hand into mine.

When the show was over, Louise and Thom took their leave, finally giving the TV a rest. I thought I heard it sigh when they clicked it off. Shea and I sat side by side in silence for a long time, looking out of the bay window into the darkness. Finally, Shea stood up and took my hand, leading the way back to my bedroom.

The house was quiet save for the sound of Louise closing her closet and opening dresser drawers. I heard Thom flush the toilet.

"I think that you should go," I said quietly, still refusing to look Shea in the eye.

She kissed me and I felt everything untangle inside. "I think I'm just going to stay here with you."

"I don't think you want to do that," I said, feeling tears way down in the pit of my stomach.

"I know exactly what I want."

Her face hovered close to mine. I looked for something familiar in her eyes—terror, disgust, lust, an alcohol-induced haze. What I saw was unfamiliar, but I recognized it like puzzle pieces coming together.

I crawled into her arms and woke up in the middle of the night sobbing.

"Why are you crying?" she said, wiping a tear away from my cheek.

I couldn't respond. I just kept crying and crying until it finally stopped.

I sat up, sitting crossed legged, and blew my nose. "I haven't had that dream for a long time, almost five years."

"What dream?"

"This dream that I used to have before I ran away from my family," I said, wiping my wet nose with the back of my hand. "An invading army comes to my town and rounds us all up into a ghetto, except I escape and hide. I don't want to kill anyone—I'm always conscious of the fact that I'm a pacifist—but I feel forced to and then I do, with this efficiency…and the whole time while I'm slaughtering the enemy I keep thinking, 'I'm a Mennonite, I can't do this,' but I do. I kill them all."

Shea offered her hand and I took it.

"I haven't cried since I left my parents."

"Really?"

"No, that's not true. But my crying is different now."

"Why and how?"

"That's a long story."

"I've got time."

126

FEMININE HYGIENE PRODUCTS

Do you wake up in love? Is it like waking up with the realization that overnight you've started menstruating and now your bed is one bloody mess that will never come clean again? You always knew you would start menstruating eventually, but in your own good time. There were always horror stories of messy beds in the morning. You didn't want it to happen to you, and there was no way of preparing for it. What could you have done? Wear a feminine hygiene product for one or two dry years?

No matter how much you scrub that stain will never come out of the sheets or the mattress, it's there forever, diminishing only slightly in the years to come—a constant reminder that we have very little control.

When Shea woke up I was reading Martha while jotting notes.

"What are you writing?" Shea said as she rubbed her sleepy eyes.

"More importantly, what am I reading?"

"No," she said sitting up, "more importantly, what are you writing?"

"I don't really know," I said, lifting the paper from my lap. "Maybe a poem."

"Why maybe?"

"I'm going for a smoke." I folded the paper and put it into my housecoat pocket.

When I returned there was a note from her. "Had to leave, sorry for not saying goodbye but I realized that I am going to be late for class."

.....

When I walked in the door of Ethel's Bar more than a week later, it was packed. My favourite spot at the bar was taken by someone typing messages on her cellphone. I was annoyed about having to sit at a big empty table by myself because it invited people to sit down and converse with me. I liked being able to approach, not be approached.

As I got my pint a few women friends of mine approached the table, one of whom was an ex-lover/ex-love-interest who was in the company of our Menno friends, as I liked to call them. I had been drawn to them through forces beyond my control and had met the woman through them. I couldn't help but admit to myself that I was happy to see them; general hilarity ensued when I was in their company. They especially liked my embellished country-kid stories. I was mid-way through recounting some tale when I saw Shea standing over us and smiling. I stopped while the rest of the group greeted her enthusiastically. They all seemed to be very familiar with each other, including the ex-lover.

"Do you two know each other?" my friend Julia said. I could see a slight smile, which indicated that Julia knew damn well that Shea and I had met before.

This presented the type of moment that Julia was fond of. She called it her "exploiting Jess' exploits" moments. Over the years I had become the subject of many jabs, particularly from this group of friends, because according to them I was quite the player. They may have had a point. But instead of despising or judging me, they simply made fun of me, which suited me quite well. I felt like their younger sister, which was comfortable to me, despite our all being about the same age.

"Jess, this is Shea. She's just moved back from Montreal. I'm guessing you two probably haven't met." She continued grinning and nodding at me, savouring the chance to make me squirm.

I did squirm, not knowing exactly why. "Actually, we just met in a class the other day," I said as Shea sat down and got the attention of the server. I looked at Shea, expecting rage in her eyes or something close to tears, and I realized that she wasn't reacting to my not calling her for a week the way I thought she would. I suddenly felt powerless. The truth is that I had wanted to call her and everyday I waited for the phone to ring or for her to suddenly appear at my door but she didn't call and she didn't arrive. I sat motionless by the phone for hours feeling messed up about the fact that I desperately wanted to call her while not wanting to appear desperate the whole while feeling scared shitless by the feeling that were arising inside of me.

"Oh, which class was that, Jess Klassen?" Julia was fond of calling me by both my first and last name.

"What? Pardon me?" I said, taking my eyes off of Shea for a second.

"Which class did you meet in?" Julia repeated her non-question question.

"Does it really matter?" I said, hoping she would drop the issue all together.

The ex-lover shook her head, smiled, and chimed in. "Jess, you have a way of meeting all the pretty ladies without fail."

"Oh, you are so complimentary, Dana," Shea said, feigning a southern belle accent and then burst into laughter.

"It's just that this town is so damn small. You two," I paused for dramatic effect and took another sip from my pint, "seem to already be acquainted with each other."

"You could say that," Shea cackled. Dana joined her and I had no way of knowing what was meant by it. "But probably not half as acquainted as you seem to be with the female population of this city." Shea lit a cigarette and started waving her smoking hand in my face, "I've been doing some checking, Jess Klassen," she said, taking on Julia's habit, "and you have yourself a reputation."

The others at the table started chiming in when we were approached by a young man, obviously drunk and attracted to the sound of young women enjoying themselves in their own company.

"Hey, ladies," he said, nodding his head in that way that invites people to agree with anything he's saying.

Someone responded with a hello.

"So where are the men tonight? You ladies leave your boyfriends at home?"

He was over-colonged, with a neat white shirt tucked into his black flat dress pants. His cellphone was clipped to his belt and flashing like a strobe light. The lights of the pub were bouncing off his gelled hair.

"I'm just kidding, I'm just kidding," he said, flashing white teeth. "But seriously, where are your boyfriends?" He laughed again, which made it impossible to tell whether he was making fun of guys who ask questions like that or trying to disguise his question by making fun of guys who ask questions like that.

The group collectively ignored him as he crouched down to speak to me. I think that the group had faith that I could dispatch him quickly, so they left me to it.

"So are you guys meeting up with your boys later on or what?" he said, teetering beside me and hanging onto the chair for support. He was way too close. "Maybe we should all go find a party?" His head was bobbing up and down again.

"I do not know what these ladies are doing later, we don't move as a pack." I lit a cigarette and exhaled.

"Well maybe you should move into my pack," he said, slurring considerably while putting his hand on my inner thigh.

"Take your hand off of me," I said sharply, not wanting to allow any fear in my tone.

"Oh, come on, what are you, a lesbo or something?" he said, removing his hand. Violence came into his eyes. He teetered a little closer to me and smiled again.

"Yes." I wouldn't move an inch. I wanted to force him out of my space. I put my cigarette in the ashtray. "I am."

He was still crouched beside me; his eyes glazed when he took my hand and started pulling it toward his crotch.

"Maybe you just need the right cock." He laughed, still not letting go of my hand. He seemed to be under the impression that because he thought he was being funny, I did too.

My free hand was clenched into a fist underneath the table and without thinking I drove it into his midsection as hard as possible.

The bar moved in slow motion as he fell backward. His glass of beer went flying into the wall behind him, shattering into pieces, showering onto the table closest to us. Suddenly, everyone was on their feet.

"You fucking bitch," he sputtered, trying to stand up and come toward me.

He stumbled forward but was stopped quickly by the bartender who had hopped over the bar, a baseball bat in hand. To my great surprise he put the bat to the throat of the man writhing around in pain and started pulling him, with a help of a few others, out of the bar.

I sat motionless and took another drag of my cigarette. The rest of my table was on their feet and had rushed to stand in front of me.

"Jess," I heard in the distance but couldn't locate where the sound was coming from. My fist was still tightly curled into a ball.

"Jess," I heard again and looked to my left where Shea was standing. She tapped me on the shoulder, "Come on, let's get out of here."

She disappeared to my left as I remained staring at the beer trickling down the wall. I said nothing as a waitress swept the boozy glass into a garbage can. My friends were busy telling people that we were fine and that there was "nothing to see here."

Finally, Shea got my attention. She crouched down in front of me. "I talked to the bartender and he said you don't have to pay your tab and he's going to walk us out to the car just in case the guy stays out there. All right? I've got your coat, let's go."

I followed Shea out to the car.

When we reached my house, Shea shut off the engine and sat in silence with me for a few minutes.

"Dude," she said finally.

We both burst out laughing.

"Jess," Shea said, wiping away tears of laughter.

"Shea," I said, cutting her off, my tone serious, "there is something seriously wrong with me."

"That's the problem, you keep thinking that there's something wrong with you."

I said nothing and got out of the car.

She opened her door, got out, and stood in front of me. "I know that we just met but I think it's clear to both of us that there's something real here," she said, waving her hand between her chest and mine. "And I know that you're not going to say it, but I'd like to see you again." She reached over and gently put her palm on my cheek and kissed me on the lips.

I felt short of breath.

"But tonight, I gotta go."

A LITTLE WAY DOWN THE ROAD

We saw each other almost every night after the incident at the bar but we never called "us" anything. She was as skittish as I. We were like two kids playing knock knock ginger on each other's relationship doors. We would arrive separately, if we were going to the same place, but would always leave at the same time. One night, when we were both at Ethel's but sitting at the opposite ends of the tables, she gave me a nod and I started to get up and leave.

"Oh my God, you guys just gave each other an 'it's time to leave' look," Julia smirked, "you have a girlfriend, Jess," she said, astonished. "I never thought I'd see the day."

"I don't have a girlfriend," I replied, as stone-faced as possible. Something prevented me from admitting that all I wanted to do was talk about Shea and for her to be my official girlfriend. There was nothing I wanted more, but I just couldn't. "I think that we're just going to the same party or something. Some English party, you know," I said without much enthusiasm.

"One day you're going to get over yourself," Julia said as I stood up, "and admit that you're dating her. Not only that, you're falling in love with her. And when you do, I'll be sitting right here."

I shook my head, "Look, I had a girlfriend one time and it didn't work out. I think that I'd like this to work out." I walked out of the bar knowing that Shea would be close behind me.

"Well that's something," Julia said to my back.

Shea and I stood outside the house party, smoking a cigarette before going in.

"Did you tell him that we were dating or something?" I said incredulously when she passed along a dinner party invitation from her father. I couldn't imagine a different reason for him wanting me to join them for such an occasion.

"No, of course not. He just thinks that you're smart and knows that we spend a lot of time together."

"Um, and by spend so much time together, did he mean dating?"

"I don't really talk to him about my personal life." She looked away and waved at someone walking by.

"Are you ashamed of me?" I said sharply but not really sure why I was so upset—I certainly hadn't been ready to discuss the fact that we were in a relationship. My response was foreign to me and I was surprised with the words coming out of my mouth.

"Of course I'm ashamed of you—you're a foul-mouthed alcoholic in the making who smokes too many cigarettes and has no social graces."

"I take issue with the 'social graces' part of that." I looked down to the ground for a second. "Look, I've never wanted someone to think that we're dating before, well, at least not for a very long time."

"Please," she said, more serious, "I've never been one to discuss my personal life with him. I care about you, it's just that it's complicated."

I didn't like that answer, but I was firmly established in a pattern of non-relationships and wasn't about to trust my desire to actually be in one.

The table was filled with professor Driedger's colleagues, a few friends from church—some of whom were also colleagues—along with the prized dinner guest of the evening, the president of the college. And, for some reason, me.

In a seating arrangement gone horribly wrong, I ended up seated next to the president with whom I was acquainting myself through the aid of many glasses of red wine. There was discussion regarding the upcoming national church conference being held in town and how that might affect funding for the college. There was some discussion about having to compete with the college in Saskatoon for national funding. I felt my guts melt as someone talked about Dr. Klassen in Saskatoon.

"The last time I travelled to Saskatoon to meet with him he was forty-five minutes late for the meeting and he'd definitely been drinking before he got there," said a bearded man whose glasses kept slipping down his nose. "I just thought to myself, come on, Dave, you're on the edge of losing it. I mean, we've been friends forever, but what am I supposed to say to a guy like that?"

I went to open a second bottle of wine.

When I came back the gossip was still raging. I could hardly keep upright. Shea was at the far end of the table completely unaware of my state of sobriety and what was being discussed at our end. I started getting angry. Angry that they were discussing my father like that. Angry that they didn't have the decency to confront my father about his problem. Angry that my father had become a drunk. Angry that Shea was seated at the end of the table in a blissful conversation with her father and his friends. Angry that instead of telling the gossipers to shut the fuck up I politely answered the president of the college when he asked what my connection to the host was.

"I didn't think Glen had another daughter," he chuckled, "are you marking for him this semester?"

"Oh, heavens no," I said, slurring.

The president kept a brave face with his well-practiced perma-grin as he waited for me to answer his question. A look of horror came across his face, as though it occurred to him that I might be professor Driedger's new love interest.

"Oh, I'm not Glen's daughter, Edgar," I said, addressing the president by his first name. And then, cupping my hands around my mouth, bullhorn style, I said, "I'm his daughter's lover." And then I deepened the tone of my voice trying to imitate the narrator of some sort of horrible instructional video I said, "But not to worry, fellow Christians," I boomed, "it's OK because I'm actually in love with Shea," which I punctuated by pointing down the table at Shea just in case people weren't sure who I was talking about.

Everyone stopped talking.

The president could not conceal his surprise. "Oh," he said as he sent his wine glass smashing to the floor.

I think "bastard child" or "Glen's new fuck bunny" would have been a better answer. Anything but what came out of my mouth.

The silence was broken by the host (and father) "Oh my God," he groaned in a voice that suggested he had just died inside.

This was followed by the quick and efficient exit from the room by Shea. As I watched her leave, my own shock was disrupted by the smell of a cigarette, which I noticed I had lit and was now smoking. My first thought was, I shouldn't be smoking in the house. Calmly, I dipped my cigarette in my wine and left, following in the steps of Shea.

When I arrived outside, Shea had just slipped the car into reverse, backing over my bicycle and out into the street. The car came to a screeching halt. Shea rolled down the window and yelled, "Your bike's broken, I better drive you home."

Except Shea didn't drive me home. She drove past my house out into the country, past the giant Zehrs, past the dump, eventually exiting onto the highway going north to the lake.

I could barely prevent myself from throwing up as she sped along. The realization of what I had said and the news of my father was mixing with the red wine in my stomach.

Shea stared straight ahead, and I could see the white of her knuckles despite the low light.

"Shea," I said, trying to get her to acknowledge my presence.

"Don't you fucking talk to me," she hissed without looking at me.

"Shea," I tried again. But it was to no avail; I was met with the stoniest silence I had ever experienced.

We finally arrived at a beach on Lake Huron in the middle of the night; we were both freezing cold. The waves relentlessly smacked the sand, and I wondered how anyone could find the beach a relaxing place to spend their time with all the noise. We were alone on the sand. In fact, for the first time I felt completely alone with her; no one was going walk to in on us or interrupt our conversation, and it scared the shit out of me. We were standing apart, not touching, and Shea was crying—weeping. I stood two feet away, hundreds of feet away, wondering if she would speak.

"I hate her for leaving. I know that if she were here this would be OK. She would talk to him," Shea said, still looking at the waves coming in. "Back there," she said pointing behind her, presumably in the direction of her dad's house, "you murdered him in front of everyone important in his life. Jesus Christ almighty, do you know what you did? How dare you," she screamed. "How dare you bring something into his life that he did not ask for. How dare you tell him about us when it's none of your god damn business. Do you know what you've done? To me, to him—professionally? What the fuck is he going to do when he walks into his office on Monday."

She started circling me and waving her hands wildly. "He teaches at a Mennonite college for Christ's sake, do you know what kind of Pandora's box you've opened? There were people there from his church, what's he supposed to say to them. He could get kicked out of his church. He could lose his job."

"You think I don't know that?' I screeched at the top of my lungs. "Me, of all people," I said, pounding my chest, "you think I don't fucking know that? You think I just packed up my bags and walked away—that's why I ran away from my family, Shea."

"How am I supposed to know that?" she screamed back, still circling me. "How am I supposed to know anything about you? You say you love me, but since we met you've been nothing but a brick wall. I know everything about your relationship with Martha Wiens mystery poet and nothing about your relationship with your family."

"You want to know something about my family? Why don't you just ask some of your dad's friends." My throat was starting to hurt from screaming. "I sat at the end of the table tonight, while your dad's friends—those people same who professed tonight to being my dad's friends—shit talked my dad."

"What are you talking about Jess?" Shea said, finally stopping her circle around me.

"My dad," I said as tears started to roll down my cheek.

"Oh my God," Shea said before I could continue, "David Klassen is your father."

I nodded silently.

She wiped the tears from her cheek with the back of her hand.

Suddenly I was angry again. "Do you always hide your women from your dad? Why am I your dirty fucking secret, Shea?" I said accusingly.

"What?" she spit out. "You don't know a god damn thing about my dad. You don't know what he's been through. You don't know what I've been through after my mom left."

I had heard a version of the story of how her mother had left, but it was usually portrayed as funny, like a legend a family tells about a drunken, yet loveable, uncle who long ago ran away to join the circus.

"What kind of mother leaves her eight-year-old daughter for no reason?" Shea said, not really addressing me.

I knew that after fourteen years of Glen sheltering Shea and subtly badmouthing his ex-wife, Shea was further away now from healing than when her mother first left. Now it was not a scar, but a disease that racked her body. Like a sunburn turned to skin cancer, Shea was now suffering far more than need be and maybe the doctor was to blame.

But it wasn't entirely Glen's fault. The woman that he loved had left him for reasons that were never made entirely clear to him, and his heart was shattered. Shea had told me that there had been rumours of infidelity on his part, which had resulted in the church treating him like a pariah for the first couple of years. After that, he chose his daughter, eschewing relationships with any other women. He had always told his friends that he could wait for love until Shea was ready for another mother in her life. It would have been perverse had it not been so utterly pathetic.

"I used to cry myself to sleep every night. I would speak to her, pretending that she was sitting at the end of my bed like some kind of fucking angel. I thought she would come back. Dad was almost sick with anguish at seeing his daughter almost hysterical so he told me clearly, calmly, 'Your mom is never coming back.'"

"He was right, she didn't come back." She paused, remembering what came next.

"I used to get letters, but then I wrote her back, 'Dear mom, please fuck off permanently. Sincerely, the person who used to be your daughter.' The only thing I respect her for is the fact that she respected that," Shea said, pushing through tears. "My dad never asked why the letters stopped coming. He's not even officially divorced because she disappeared after that and he can't serve her papers. He thinks it's immoral to date anyone until he's officially divorced."

I felt hurt and angry about the night's proceedings and felt that I had the right to keep shouting at Shea. But I stopped myself as a thought migrated from the back of my brain and then revealed itself as words. *This isn't about me right now.*

I knew that I loved her. What do you do? So helpless to heal someone else's pain, yet so invested in it.

"Stop being a fucking victim," Shea said, but I wasn't sure if she was addressing herself or me.

"Thinking about how the words 'queer Mennonite' are an oxymoron," I started, "I was convinced that my family would have to choose between their church and me, convinced that my dad would have to choose between his job and me, knowing that I'm only one person against thousands—it's all become so second nature that

137

talking to you about it is like telling you that I'm breathing. And now…" I trailed off, looking out to the dark lake over Shea's shoulder, "it all seems so trite; bullshit that no one cares about."

"I care," Shea said, stepping away from me, "but your excuses are bullshit."

"You need to talk to your dad."

"Jess," she said, "just hold me."

I complied. We held our shivering bodies against the cold wind coming off the lake. ,

We walked back to the car and I sank behind the wheel. Shea curled up in the passenger seat and was almost immediately consumed by sleep.

The drive back was hard. I should have stopped the car and slept. Instead, I put cigarette after cigarette into my mouth, feeding off a constant nicotine high to stay awake. A styrofoam cup of coffee, which was a few days old, was perched between the two front seats on the e-brake. I thanked God for it.

It occurred to me that proclaiming my love during the dinner party was not the best idea. Then again, it wasn't my idea to say anything of the sort that night, or any night for that matter. It was an action that revealed something I didn't know. I couldn't help the smile that came across my face, which I directed to Shea who was curled up against the door of the car. I felt like our bodies were no longer solid units but hovered inside the car, mixing freely, looking for a way to reconfigure themselves.

Maybe love is something we fall asleep to. Like the CD you put on before bed. As you cross the line between consciousness and unconsciousness, it plays on as the soundtrack to your dreams. Maybe love is forgetting as you lay awake, back turned to the night, completely unprepared for your uterus to complete its exercise of rejection. Maybe love is like something we're offered every month—like a fresh start.

ELEVATOR SONGS

"Plunging to the depths with a perceived lack of oxygen."

That was the last thing I remember thinking before passing out a few days later.

When Shea arrived home, she was more than a little surprised to find me lying face up on her father's kitchen floor.

"What are you doing here?"

"I don't know," I said, speaking into the bottom of the refrigerator, which was humming along quietly.

"Yes, you know exactly what you're doing. Why the hell are you in my house lying on my kitchen floor?" Shea was standing overhead, refusing to look down at me.

"It's warm, especially right here beside the fridge," I said, slurring.

"Jess, get off the floor," Shea whispered as loudly as possible, looking over her shoulder as though someone might be overhearing her.

I popped to my feet instantly. I felt like I towered above Shea, although I'm at least four inches shorter. With a full sweep of my arm I took all of the fridge magnets off the door of the fridge.

"Where have you been? You haven't called me in a week. You disappeared. I thought that since you were avoiding me, I would arrive at your house." I reached my hand closest to the fridge out trying to lean on it for support but somehow missed it and stumbled into Shea's arms.

"So you've been drinking," Shea said, sarcasm thick in her voice. "Did you even go to class today?"

"I'm feeling a little bit vulnerable. I have to go now," was all I could say.

Shea grabbed me by the arm before I could make it to the door. She swung me around, dizzyingly. I dropped to my knees and vomited onto her shoes.

Wiping my mouth, perfectly humiliated, I got up to take my leave but she stood between me and the door.

"Can we talk about this later, Jess, I think that my dad will be coming home soon. Please, he's barely looked at me all week." She was standing in a puddle of my vomit.

"I should probably sleep here tonight," I said in a surge of nausea. I headed toward the basement where her room was and stopped. "What about the puke? I should probably clean it up."

"I'll blame it on the cat."

Shea took my hand and led me downstairs.

Maybe it was five minutes, maybe it was an hour before Shea came down to join me. I gasped and opened my eyes, apparently I had blacked out.

"You could use a shower, maybe a little toothpaste, perhaps a litre or two of water," Shea whispered, perhaps in an effort to hide my presence from her dad. If that was the reason why she was whispering she nonetheless had a look of trying to stifle laughter.

"Sleeping, can't," I said, keeping my eyes firmly shut. My movement has set in motion a good amount of drool I had deposited onto the pillow and was now pushing against my cheek.

"You're not sleeping in my bed if you do not comply."

Shea started helping me out of my clothes. Cradling me in her arms, she stroked my hair and took four deep inhalations.

"You're very compassionate; you must get it from your mother," I said.

"I doubt that I get compassion from my mother. The only thing I get from my mother is a dislike of tomato juice and a yet untested ability to haul ass at times deemed appropriate." Shea was still working at removing my clothes.

"Why don't you just make your dad talk?" I said, starting to help myself undress.

Shea shook her head. "I don't understand how you can sit here and say that while in five years you haven't so much as let your parents know you're still alive."

"I think," I said, getting up out of bed and walking toward the bathroom, "you have a distinct advantage. You're his only kid, the only one in his immediate family."

"Is this some sort of competition?" Shea called from the bedroom.

I walked back into the room to speak to Shea face to face, "I don't know how many times I need to make this clear to you, but I'm not avoiding them, I'm helping them."

After the arduous journey from bedroom to shower to bedroom again, I flopped down into bed, closed my eyes, and tried to be as still as possible. Shea lay down beside me. Soon there was the sound of the door opening and footsteps above us. The night pressed on. I felt a tingle in my throat. I wanted a cigarette but knew that we were trapped downstairs, hidden away from the footsteps above us. I refused to give up my silence but as I lay with closed eyes I felt my eyeballs moving rapidly underneath their eyelid blankets.

.....

"Say my name."

Silence.

"Jess, say my name."

Silence.

"I want to hear you say my name."

"My mouth has been moving this whole time, didn't you hear me?"

"No."

"You have to close your eyes. You have to be ready to hear."

I opened my eyes to see the moon shadowing the room. The furnace turned on again.

The act of naming, always an Adamesque practice. To name, to own—to form a conclusion. I knew I couldn't do it. My body convulsed. I opened my mouth.

"I can't," I admitted finally.

"Why?" Shea was looking at the ceiling.

"You're trying to force me to exclude you before you have to do it yourself. I won't do that dirty work for you." I turned toward Shea and curled a strand of her hair around my index finger.

Shea rolled onto her side. "Jess."

"Nice try."

I heard a piece of paper crumple in Shea's hands as she read aloud.

And now you bury me
Deep under the willow trees

141

You brought me to the river
Revealing ripe saskatoons
Congealed blood under your thick spade
I am grave maker you made

"I don't think it's appropriate to quote Martha to me."

"Oh yeah, well here's another quote I thought you might like: 'Polsemy—the text is made up of words, many words, and those words have many meanings. I couldn't bring my text out of life because without the text my body lay lifeless. My body is a page with ink being thrown onto it like a blast from a firehose putting out a false alarm.'"

"Who wrote that?" I said.

"You know damn well that you left that as a note underneath my windshield wipers today."

"I suppose I do."

"Even when you're not around you leave pieces of yourself all over me. It's not good enough for you to leave pieces of yourself airborne all around me, you leave it on me and in me," Shea said, grabbing my pack of cigarettes.

"You just take, take, take and then blame it on me. You're incredible." I couldn't convince myself to of the seriousness of my own words.

"Can I have a cigarette?"

I nodded silently.

"I'm not blaming you for anything, Jess, I'm not even saying all of this is a bad thing." She lit her cigarette. "It's not like I didn't spend the whole week thinking about you. You force me to be honest with myself, even when I can't speak it to you."

"How hard was that to admit?" I said, a smile tightly roped across my face.

"Not hard at all," Shea said, kissing me.

"Liar."

She smoked silently.

"You know what I hate the most about you?" I said, taking the cigarette from her fingers.

"No, I don't know, but with a sentence as romantic and tender as that, I'm intrigued."

"The fact that you don't need to smoke. You just do. There's no part of your body that controls you, moves your fingers toward a pack of cigarettes without your even being conscious of it. You always make the conscious decision to smoke and your not smoking is unconscious."

"So what you really mean is that you hate the fact that I'm not the same as you?"

"No, no, that's not it at all. It is through our difference that meaning arises, however subtle."

"That is the cheapest and most unimaginative rip off of Jacques Derrida I've ever heard."

"I'm just jealous that you don't have an actual addiction to cigarettes and can stop whenever you want to."

"Kiss me," Shea said, pulling my chin with gentle momentum toward her.

.....

When I woke up she had left. "I knew it, she was never here, this is all a dream," I said to myself. But she was not gone and I was not dreaming, Shea was upstairs getting me breakfast. Breakfast? When's the last time someone got me breakfast?

"Do you want some coffee?" she whispered, coming back into the bedroom.

Who says that coffee doesn't constitute breakfast?

"I don't actually drink coffee in the morning," I said, trying to remember my geographical location. The question of me sleeping at her house had never come up before. "I always make it at my house because you want it."

"I woke up early just to make you a cup of coffee, now you're not going to drink it?" Her morning belligerence suited her.

"Well, thank you for your unwavering devotion to my nutritional needs, but I will throw up if I drink that."

"Why do acts of kindness cause you to throw up?"

"Jo, daut weet de Hund nich."

She laughed, "Don't try to distract me with the Mother Tongue. Why do you refuse to answer simple questions?"

"I did answer."

"Your mind, your heart, how your brain works, some personal history." She looked genuinely concerned. I should have taken her up on her offer. I should have poured out my heart into her waiting hands, but something inside me couldn't move.

"That even the dog doesn't know," I said repeating myself in English.

"I don't care about the dog, I care about you."

"I think we're just arguing about semantics, let's go back to sleep." I rolled over and closed my eyes, convinced that she would leave it at that.

"Good, you're sleeping," she said. "Maybe now you'll listen to me. You show up at my house, pronounce your undying love for me in front of my father, his friends, not to mention the president of the college, and now you're refusing to provide pertinent information which could save this titanic of a relationship, not to mention life." Her head was cocked to one side and I noticed that her eyes still had a tiny bit of sleep in each.

"First, let's be clear. You invited me for dinner. Second, I don't know what pertinent information you're referring to. And third of all, and most importantly, please don't say things like 'this titanic of a relationship,' because honestly, references to the Titanic can no longer be subject to nuance, so I have no use for them."

Shea looked at her watch and terror came across her face out of nowhere. "Fuck, we have to get out of this house before my dad wakes up; he'll want a ride. Shit." She looked around the room, as if it could provide some answer to her concern. "Shit, shit, I think I hear him upstairs," her tone turned frantic as she pulled me out of bed and pushed me up the stairs to the side exit. "Shit, shit, shit, dad's awake" she said, her panic making her voice an octave higher.

Shea had me out the door and into the car swiftly. We sat in the car for a minute before the inertia finally broke. By then I had already lit a cigarette.

"Don't smoke in my car," she said with a surprising amount of conviction for someone barely awake.

"When have I ever been asked to butt out in your car before? And may I remind you that you and your dad both smoke in your house and car," I said, continuing to inhale.

"My dad doesn't smoke," she snorted.

"Has your sense of smell and grip on reality escaped you?" I said in my pseudo-British accent attempting to match the insanity of the moment.

"Can you just bike home please?"

"I'm not sure if you remember, but you drove over my bike, rendering it dead. Its lonely carcass lies in the side hedge," I said pointing to the offending hedge.

"Fine, I'll drive you." She reached over and took the cigarette out of my, mouth, extinguishing it in the car's ashtray. "Fuck that was close. What if he would have seen you?" By now she was inches from my face, speaking very loudly and with perfect annunciation.

I pulled out another cigarette. "Um, have you lost your mind? Did you see yourself pulling me out of your house?" I lit the new cigarette. "Why are you so afraid to disappoint him? Because your mother disappointed him and now you and your dad have a no-disappoint pact. But one thing has yet to be decided: What's 'disappointing'? So now the two of you are trying not to disappoint each other with no idea of what that means. Oh wait, let me correct myself, you're walking around trying not to disappoint him. Why don't you pull the car out of the driveway?" I said, to which she batted my cigarette out of my mouth.

She was still inches away from my face and didn't appear to be backing up at any time in the near future.

"Well, we're agreed then," I said looking out the passenger window.

"Is this what love is, Jess?" Shea said in what I thought to be a complete change of topic while pulling the car out of the driveway and down the street. At that point she was a strange concoction of catatonic and explosive.

"Are you referring to me or your dad?"

"Fuck you," Shea said. It sounded like a question rather than an insult.

"This is insane, Shea, the jig is up. Why are you going to so much effort to make reality different than it is?"

We drove to school and found a parking spot.

"I have a class," she said and slammed the car door.

While I didn't have a class, I also didn't have clothes. "I don't know if you noticed but I'm wearing the housecoat you threw on top of me on our way out." I sat in the car for an hour and a half smoking cigarette after cigarette, waiting. I went through the same thoughts I always did whenever my mind was not stimulated or numbed.

You should go home.
I can't go home.
Why is that?
Because then they have to choose.

Finally I heard the key in the door.

"So, you want a ride home?" she said, closing the door and putting the key into the ignition.

"That would be lovely."

"It would be my pleasure. What have you been up to since I left?" She was much calmer now and seemed to be laughing at herself.

"I've been obsessing over how my parents would react if I went home to talk to them. What did you learn at school today dear?"

"We discussed the picture view of language." She reached over and pulled on the cord of my housecoat, exposing my bare legs.

When we got to my house she killed the engine and followed me up the stairs. Sticking my key into the door, I stopped. Turning around, I summoned all of my energy. "If you're coming in for sex— which is what I'm assuming by your trying to take my housecoat off—well, then, you should probably leave, because I'm not sure if you noticed but you acted like a crazy person this morning."

"Can I have sex with someone else in the house?"

"No."

"Well, unfortunately, I know you too well already, and your idea of a conversation is not a real conversation anyway, so why don't we just have sex."

"Fuck you," I said.

She responded exactly as I had expected. Turning to go she said, "Start talking, Jess. Stop being such a hypocrite."

"I'm not a hypocrite, it's not my fault, it was *her*, the Icelandic goddess, there's not much more to explain than that fact."

"Oh yes, I've heard all about it and guess what? That's not even remotely good enough, Klassen."

Nobody tells me what to do, least of all the people I love the most. Nobody tells me what to do, least of all the people who have a better idea than I do of what I should do. I let her leave, as I always did, but I hated myself for doing it.

It was around noon and I was exhausted. I melted into the couch. It offered me sleep. I probably should have gone to class instead. I never miss class, I'm not that kind of student. But things were crumbling, and my theory is that if your mind is going to crumble you should at least prevent your body from crumbling too.

I woke up and it was dark. My neck seemed irreversibly bent backward and my feet were asleep (I had neglected to remove my shoes). Coming into consciousness I realized a glow in the room was coming from the TV. Cross-legged, my two housemates were engaged in vigorous Super Mario Kart head-to-head action. I thought they would take no notice of me, but they were immediately aware of my presence.

"Good, you're awake, now we can turn music on," said Thom.

"Your grandma called," said Louise.

"That's impossible," I said, "both of my grandmas are dead. I think."

"Maybe they called from the grave begging you to wake up and do some fucking dishes." Despite her lack of subtlety Louise, nonetheless, remained charming whether she was telling me to "do some fucking dishes" or reminding me that she had paid for beer last time.

"You might just have a point there, Louise," Thom said without taking his eyes off the screen.

"Or, perhaps your grandmas were calling from the grave imploring you to take a fucking shower," Louise said, her charm continuing.

"Wow, you guys, it's shocking that our friendship never seems to stop gaining depth and honesty."

"What's going on, Jess," Thom said, "you never skip class and I know that you did because you're always gone at this time on this day." Thom paused the game to let me know that he wasn't shitting around.

"Nothing's wrong, Thom," I said, rubbing the back of my neck, "everything's fine. I'm just really tired because we were doing it all night long."

"Huh!" Thom exclaimed, "You and who? You can't even say her name."

It was an astute observation, or maybe just a lucky shot in the dark.

"No," Louise chimed in, "no need for blatant lies and the inability to say people's names. What's going on? Why do you continue being an asshole to her? After your dinner party shenanigans you should be happy that she's still talking to you. Have you ever thought that she might need a little time to come out to her dad, that maybe it's not as easy for her as you think it is? That maybe she's legitimately freaking out right now and you need to support her?" Louise was pointing at her temple with her forefinger, encouraging me to think.

Louise has a knack for simple questions; simple, pointed questions that I never seem to want to answer.

"You Mennonites are almost as bad as Icelanders—never say a goddamn thing about anything inside," Thom said to my silence.

"We don't talk about Icelanders in this house," I said in an angry tone that surprised me.

"You're talking to an Icelander, Jess. But what I think you meant to say is, 'Let's not talk about one Icelander in particular,' and to that I couldn't agree more," Thom said hitting the continue button on the game. "*Freya broke my heart. Freya bossed me around. My parents hate me*," Thom said in a high-pitched whine. "Boo fucking hoo. That's old news, Jess. Here's a news flash, of all the women that have paraded through our house since you moved in, this one is the best. It will not get better than her."

"So you're the picture of getting over a heart broken by an Icelander?" I said.

Thom and Louise refused to answer as a team. I had gone way too far.

I realized the extent to which I had fucked up my neck while sleeping. Neck aching, eyes adjusting to the bathroom light, I thought it odd that someone had called posing as my grandma. Peeking my head out of the bathroom, I yelled down the hall to Louise, "Did my grandma leave a message?" It was a non sequitur at best and elicited no reply from either Thom or Louise.

It spooked me to think that maybe my grandmother had called. I considered three options. One, she was calling me from the dead. Two, she had somehow tracked me down and desperately wanted to speak to me, her favourite grandchild. Three, Thom and Louise had been mistaken.

Showers are the Bermuda Triangle of time for me, they always have been. It starts when I take my clothes off. Naked in front of the mirror, immersed in the cycle of recognition and disassociation. Who is that person standing there? We so rarely see ourselves, or anyone else for that matter, naked, it is the clothed body that dominates our perception of our physical being. And the perception of what's beneath that haunts us.

That is stability: warm water pouring over the body—object blurs into subject, subject into object, body into water, water into body. Quantum mechanics has shown light to behave as both particle and wave depending on the experiment. This would suggest that the person setting up the experiment ceases to be subject exclusively and crosses into the world of object. Scientist and experiment become one, inextricably enmeshed in each other's arms. Time exists whether we humans exist or not (as Alice Fulton asks, how did people think of measuring particles if they only exist in their being measured?). Time exists when we wear our watches.

Language is not stable or constant. It is completely arbitrary (how come a French cat makes different sounds than an English cat?) and it's only a matter of memorization to speak a language. We jumped into language just as we jumped into time; in relationship with others where someone is there to say "Why one and not the other?"

You are involved in this experiment of language and time: you (object) are in the arms of your lover (subject). Waves or particles, this language and time, this experiment of life, you are involved in.

I turned the water off and stood there while goose bumps formed. The fog in the bathroom was so thick that I could barely see the door. Groping around I found my towel. A voice started reading in the fog,

A state of mind
Like a space heater
Kill the warmth
Pull the plug
I'll throw anything out of this brain
Bring it curbside and hope your eyes will walk by

You think it's easy?
    This nothing of a nothing
    This dumpster diving for clues
Carefully selected refuse reclaimed

A shallow grave surely
I've got the blank look to prove it
Waiting outside, right on the border of my state of mind
Sits my ignorance, not going anywhere fast
Is everything in the meantime while I wait for brains?

"Where did you get that?" I reached up to dry my hair.

"Well, I'll give you a hint of where I didn't get. I did not get it from your precious Martha Wiens. In fact, I think, maybe, that I got it from you."

"You didn't *get* that from me, you snooped in my room and found it."

"I could have killed you. I could have been a murderer waiting for you. You should be more alert. But I guess after twenty-five minutes under the hot water it's a miracle that you're still conscious," she said without answering my question.

"I've been in here for that long?" The walls played witness to my length in the shower; it looked as though the paint was peeling.

"Yeah, I was waiting in the living room but I thought that watching you shower would be more entertaining than watching Thom and Louise play Super Mario Kart. I did have time to go through your personal effects before coming to stare at you."

"Yes, well, I think we've already established that." I said again already knowing that she had gotten it from my bedroom where it was sitting on my pillow.

"You could stand to do some laundry," was all she said.

We gathered up all the laundry on my floor and headed to her house to wash it. Clean laundry—it made sense at the time. I stuffed the laundry into the machine and sat down on it. She took up a seat across from me on the dryer. This time, she seemed devoid of her previous concerns about her father coming home and seeing us together.

"Someone claiming to be my grandma phoned today."

"What did grandma say?"

The machine was filled with water and started to agitate.

"I don't know. Louise took the call."

"Are you sure it was your grandma? Louise and Thom appeared to be in fine form when I came over." A smile crept across her face.

"Really? I guess I didn't notice." She started to shake and tremble. "Why are you shaking?"

"I'm not, you are." I had filled the washing machine too full, causing it to threaten a trip across the laundry room floor.

"I guess that's just a matter of semantics."

"You and your god damn semantics," she said, smile erased from her face.

"What about you and your god damn semantics?"

I guessed it wasn't worth replying because she didn't. We looked at each other for a few silent minutes.

"I guess I have an interest in language," I offered.

"I think your laundry is done."

"I guess I have an interest in what comes out of people's mouths and how it's perceived by others."

She slid from the dryer and shoved me off the washing machine. "Laundry's done."

Her attempt to launder was pissing me off. "You're trying to deny my existence. Why can't you talk to him?" I shouted at her. "It's so typical, the Mennonite way, just pretend that it never happened, and then, after a couple of weeks, it just goes away."

After listening to my father's raised voice telling me that he was "not shouting" I had vowed never to shout at anyone, but had since determined that shouting itself was fine. I just didn't want to make people feel the way I did—didn't want to make people throw up.

I rarely shouted, but she seemed to bring it out of me.

She started shouting too. "I don't really to say anything to him since you professed your undying love for me at the dinner party."

"You keep bringing that up. Why are you so fixated on that? And I didn't say 'undying.'"

I couldn't hold it in. I smiled. I started laughing. She started laughing, too. When she laughs, I have to kiss her. She motioned with her head to go downstairs to her bedroom. I followed her.

STOP STOP STOP

I'm tired of description, metaphor, simile. I'm tired of analogy. They all fall short, they all refer to something else. Finding difference finds...what? Where's ontology? Where's purity? Which word is it that stands in place—is the purest sign—of my mouth following the curve of your body? Which word stands in place of what I say to you—the words that find no place in alphabetic vocabulary?

START START

START?

"Yes, Jess."

"How did you know I was going to say something?"

"I was hoping you wouldn't speak, actually." She wasn't joking.

"You don't like it when I speak?" I wasn't joking either.

"I love it when you speak. I had this feeling, though, that just as you allowed pleasure to build you would start to pull things down."

"I wanted to tell you how I refer to you in my head."

"I would like to know how you refer to me in your head."

"I refer to you as *The Object of My Love*." My stomach sank. I knew that I had thrown a rock at her head. In my effort not to name her I had named her. And it wasn't the truth anyway. I waited for a reaction. She made me wait just a minute more than I was prepared to.

"Jess" she said, "We both know that there is no separation between object and subject. Love is pretty god damn scary."

"The 'subject' is not something given, it is something added and invented and projected behind what there is. Nietzsche, *The Will to Power*," I replied.

.....

Later on, as my fingers gravitated toward my pack of cigarettes, she said, "Don't ever quote Nietzsche again while we're naked together. There's something dishonest about it."

"But is it OK if I smoke in your bed?"

She kissed my cheek and took my cigarette, lighting it for herself. There was a long silence broken only by rhythmic inhalation and exhalation. Soon our breathing was in sync. I was on my side looking at her, the distance between our bodies was substantial, but I could still feel the warmth of hers. We had a mug between us that we were using for an ashtray. It said "World's Greatest Mom" and featured a robust female cartoon character in an apron with a smile suggesting lunacy. Shea noticed the picture just as I did and laughed.

"My mom, the world's greatest mom, that's laughable at best."

But it wasn't laughable. She put her cigarette out and lay back on her pillow. I took one more drag, put my cigarette out, and placed the offending mug on the floor. I kept my silence; I knew better than to interfere with her thoughts. I felt her anguish leak out of a place that was far away from me. Her hands were shaking as she ashed her cigarette. Our body can betray our mind's effort to hide pain. Is this the "unbearable lightness of being?" Does our spirit reject this world until it reaches the limit of its escape?

In one motion she turned toward me, crawling into my arms pressing her eyes to my neck, she started crying softly. I relaxed my muscles, allowing myself to reach down through every nerve ending that was touching her. No one had ever cried in my arms before.

Her breathing relaxed and slowed. I felt her hand unclench and open up. As she fell asleep, her palm brushed against my cheek and rested silent on the pillow beside my head. I heard what sounded like her soul attempting to break with its past. I heard her hair growing and her eyelashes becoming longer. I heard her fingernails lengthening and her pores opening up to let the sweat out. I heard her living, and it was beautiful.

I held her close. Between us was the alto and soprano parts of the hymn "Praise God from Whom all Blessings Flow," a detailed map of guilt and longing, a refined pallet for smoked sausage, an uncanny ability to remember names, a God-given (however wasted) talent for playing volleyball, internal grappling hooks, a history of martyrdom (both near and distant), and a belief, which hung on like a bur in the middle of your back that your arm can't reach, that conditional love from parents is somehow biblically justified.

BANK NOTICES AND DEATH CARDS

Many days later.

"What the hell are you doing?" Thom said, peeking his head through my half-cracked bedroom door.

"Packing, I'm sure you're familiar with the practice."

"Jess, it's three o'clock in the morning. Where are you going?"

"Sorry. I didn't think I'd wake you. You usually sleep like a rock." I scratched my head, a little unsure as to where I was.

"I just got home. Didn't you hear me walk in the door about ten minutes ago?"

"Damn it."

"What?"

"You woke me up?"

"Yeah, I guess so. I'm sorry. Are you actually awake right now, Jess?"

"No."

So it wasn't you, you weren't calling me. It was just Thom wasn't it? Now I'm talking to myself.

I woke up the next morning lying face down, backpack strapped to my torso with nothing in it. My muscles felt like I had been wrestling for eight hours previous.

I heard a shattering sound; I thought that my body had finally broken.

Calling in the glue of my soul, I waited for a gathering so that piece by piece it could reconstruct itself. The mending had begun, but how long would the glue hold? The bed held me still; it was my cocoon that morning until it dropped into nothing.

Rehearse your lines, I said to myself. Get ready for death today.

What will you say when death comes to you? When you go to death?

Grandma Loewen always told me that death was a black envelope in the mail. One day you go to get the mail and among the bills, bank notices, and Eaton's catalogue, there it is—the black envelope waiting to be opened. Waiting to explain that a terrible accident had happened, or that the delivery didn't go well, or the body was just finished living.

Grandma Loewen was wrong, though, the black envelope arrives in the mailboxes of the living.

I can feel the wonder of a newborn child
I can stand in awe while looking at a blade of grass
I can forget my past

But I couldn't. The words I had written the night before stopped there, as if they had staggered in drunk, attempting to make sense but saying nothing. The words were on a piece of paper lying on the floor among other pieces of paper, mounds of clothes, stacks of books, dirty socks, and not quite dirty shirts. Yesterday's laundry was yesterday's laundry. It wasn't that my room was dirty or messy, but more nest-like than anything. I was like a crow picking shiny things off the ground and bringing them home. When I would lie alone in my nest and look up at the ceiling, when the lights were out and the world was quiet outside, I pulled the blankets up to my chin, cocooning myself into place. Then, and only then, did I have a feeling of home. Thom didn't see the nest-like qualities of the room, though, and he requested that the door be shut at all times because it offended his aesthetic sensibility during the walk to his room. With the old futon on the floor the things that were important ended up closer to the centre of the nest, eventually creeping into the bed.

In the morning, I thought it best to just stay there.

POKER FACES

I was on my way home from school, armed with headphones, wallet, journal, and file folder filled with scraps of paper covered in vaguely poetic scrawl. I had an extra shirt—the usual school fare.

As I walked up the steps to the student centre I noticed the shuttle van opening its doors, waiting for students who needed a ride to the airport. I got in, handed over my credit card, and buckled up.

Highway 8 was clogged up all the way to the 401. "Fuck I hate the traffic in southern Ontario," I said to no one in particular. I worried about missing my flight even though I didn't have a ticket yet and I wasn't entirely convinced that I was going anywhere.

IN THE AIR NOW

Near the back of the plane, I was seated next to a man who looked to be in his late forties and smelled like he'd had a couple of drinks in the airport bar. As the aircraft began its ascent, I kept my eyes glued on Toronto. We made our way west. The sun was going down and the streetlights clicked on throughout the city.

"Sure is gorgeous isn't it?" It was the man next to me, leaning over to share my view of the city.

"Yeah, from up here it's quiet."

The stewardess was at our seats. The man took the opportunity to order another drink. He was a sad-looking spectacle—hair grown too long since its last cut, jeans a little too tight and short, cowboy boots, trucker moustache in need of a trim, a shirt that was probably manufactured in the late 70s. One got the impression that he was once at the height of fashion in his particular social group, but was obviously more comfortable in settings where cleanliness was not highly valued. He reached for his can of beer. As the stewardess started to walk away he said, "Wait," and turned to me. "Can I buy you a drink?"

"No, thank you. I'm not much of a drinker," I said, trying not to look at him. With a nod of acceptance the man opened his beer and took a long drink. Since he had the flight attendant's attention, I decided to order two cups of coffee. I've always found that one aeroplane size was never enough to last. It's safe to say that the man sitting next to me was of no interest at all. I would have preferred sitting next to a screaming baby or an eager Christian ready to spread the gospel, anyone but that man. A drunken white man old enough to be my father who, at any minute, was probably going to ask me about my boyfriend was not an appealing seatmate.

"Where are you going?" he said, sipping his beer.

"Home," I said curtly, then decided quickly that the only way to avoid the conversation was to be in control of it. "How about you? What puts you on this flight today?"

He took a long drink and then a deep breath, looking away for just a moment and then back at her directly he said, "I'm going to Winnipeg. My brother was piloting a two-seater airplane and they crashed. His wife was with him; they both died." He said it simply and then took another drink from his can.

I looked away hoping he wouldn't see the shame come across my face. The man had obviously not expressed any kind of deep emotion for some time. His hands were still on his lap like he was sitting nicely in church. His mouth was stuck, so he took another drink to unstick it.

"I don't usually drink this much, but when I'm sober I just can't speak, and if I don't speak I'll never say anything, and if I don't say anything I think I might die too." He coughed violently and continued. "I frame houses for a living in Northern Ontario, mostly cabins. Been doing it for twenty years. Never had an accident." He took another sip, "I'm just really sad about this."

"I'm really sad about this too," I said, thinking that I might cry.

"Do you believe in God?" the man said.

"I keep trying not to." I joined him in a long drink.

"You're an angel sent to comfort me."

"Yes, I am."

"Are we going to land?"

"Absolutely."

The man finished the last of his beer and handed the can to the passing stewardess.

"Thank you," he said in a whisper. Then he tilted his seat back, closed his eyes, and fell asleep.

I gazed out the window. There was no angel to comfort me and I decided for the first time in a long time, that alcohol was not an option.

My thoughts turned into a list; they were easier to manage that way. It wasn't a list of things to do; it was a list of things not to do as represented by people. A good friend of mine had always told me to write lists.

1) Mom and dad: do not expect them to be happy to see me after five years of unexplained absence.

2) John and Francis: do not expect them to recognize me after five years of unexplained absence.

3) Grandpa Klassen: do not expect him to register that I've been gone for five years.

4) Freya: do not expect jilted ex-lover to be happy to see me after four years.

5) Thom and Louise: do not expect housemates/best friends to keep their mouths shut about where I've gone.

6) LOVE: do not expect her to be happy for leaving without explaining myself.

I looked down to catch a spectacular view of the thousands of little lakes that lay below us. I couldn't help but wonder if they had all been explored—had human feet touched every inch of that land? The plane had leather seats and TV consoles for each passenger, which contrasted starkly with the rock and water below us. The contrast made me feel like I was in more than one place at a time. I was nowhere and everywhere at once and I decided that I'd take the train back. The thought struck me that, despite taking five years to return, travelling back this quickly was unhealthy.

I looked out my window and threw words into the water below the plane, "I'm afraid," I said.

"Don't be afraid," a woman's voice said.

I turned around to see that a stewardess had heard me and thought I was afraid of flying.

"Thank you," I said, trying to be casual. "Do you by chance know what the time is in Saskatchewan?"

"Just set your watch back two hours," the woman said with a smile.

I wasn't wearing a watch but I felt better with that information.

I resisted the urge to pour music into my ears. No, I thought, this is a time for focus. I closed my eyes and listened to my seatmate and thanked God as every breath he took signalled that he was still alive.

COLD CONCRETE AND RESOLUTE DEFIANCE (A REUNION)

Suddenly the door of the stall gave way to the force of her arm. Even though it was locked, it popped open nicely.

"What the fuck are you doing here?" She towered over me. I was sitting on the toilet.

"Apparently, being made to participate in a social taboo."

Above us was the faint sound of music. It was in between sets at the Blue Note Café and the music was turned down just enough for boothmates to have a conversation.

The world ground to a halt. I could hear the lights, almost life-like, humming above us and the toilet tank in the next stall filling. My legs were beginning to numb. I looked down at my blue jeans and wondered when I had last washed them.

"Freya, I'd be more than happy to answer any and all questions if you'll just give me a minute to finish peeing in private."

Freya's expression turned from anger to disgust.

It made me stop peeing. "You're the one who walked in," I said in my defence.

Freya turned around sharply. She was dressed in black from head-to-toe. She was smoke drifting through the night. Something elusive, something camouflaged. I thought I might cry. It was a stiff drink gone down the wrong way. I sputtered. It was what I had wanted, just not as I had planned. Then again, I hadn't really planned it.

Back in the café, I took a seat opposite Freya. "I have a boy-friend," she said, calmer now.

"Oh yeah," I said without surprise. "Isn't it really hard to be a lesbian in charge of the LGBT Centre when you have a boyfriend? Or is he a lesbian-identified man?"

"Funny. And that was four years ago. Or did you lose track of time when you stepped out to get a pack of cigarettes?" Freya said, her blond hair constrasting sharply with her dark clothes. I felt like asking her to go home and change; it was so unlike her.

Jesus, what happened to hippie anarchist punk Freya? What happened to Freya?

"I guess boys are easier to control," I snarled. "That is what you do best."

The ketchup bottle between us, keeping our gazes occupied.

"You know, Jess, you're quite the hypocrite considering you controlled a man for an entire summer." She lit a cigarette. "He was devastated when you left." She exhaled a cloud of smoke. "We found some common ground."

"What do you mean you found common ground? You didn't find any common ground with Halfsteinn, you hate him." I leaned back, my heart started racing and I tried to keep my tone as calm as possible. I didn't want to believe that she was being civil to Halfsteinn, let alone anything else.

"What are you doing here, Jess?"

"You're lying." I wanted to punch her.

"What are you doing here, Jess?"

I clasped my hands together as the cigarette smouldered between the fingers of my right hand. "What do you think?" I said finally.

"I think that you look a lot different then the last time I saw you, but then again, I was half asleep, curled up in bed with you, not thinking that it would be the last time I ever saw you so it makes sense. I offered you my home, my bed, my family, my love and support—all of which you took—and you left without so much as a note saying goodbye." She looked around the café as a couple walked in and took a seat. She got up and approached their table while I stayed seated and smoking.

When Freya was done taking their orders and delivering beer to the new customers she returned to my table and sat down again. "I don't know where you've been or what the fuck you're doing here. I don't care. How dare you just walk in here looking for a reunion. You can't come in here again."

"I won't," I said, ashing my cigarette on the floor beside the booth.

"Where have you been?" Freya asked, this time not able to hide a slight hint of pleading in her voice.

"You knew me—where I had come from—I thought you would have been happy to see me go."

"Fuck you," Freya said sharply.

"You did. A million times." It was a catty high school comment and I knew it. There was something about Freya that brought out the worst in me, but I wasn't prepared for this behaviour to rear its ugly head. The band started playing again as I stood up to leave.

.....

Masochism run amuck, like too many Christians in the same room; nothing to celebrate, just something to give up. Each one in their quest to be chaste and holy, making themselves burn bright with the ungodly bonfire of their individual vanity. Vilification hand in hand with blindness made acute by looking directly into their own fire, seeking their own sun to manipulate through the day's points in the sky.

I wasn't prepared for Freya to be vulnerable, or to be anything other than in control of the situation.

Why did I get on a plane just to have a conversation I knew wouldn't go well? Because I needed to. I didn't consider that maybe she didn't need to have that conversation.

.....

One thing I learned while living in Winnipeg was that intense heat and cold wave at each other from opposite sides of the calendar like two old friends who have never met. Trees never look real, especially on Walnut Street in the middle of June. But it wasn't the middle of June, it was early spring and the snow still clung to the edges of the road, and I was happy for that. I didn't want Winnipeg to appeal to me in any way because I knew that it would only lead to heartbreak.

There had been too many times in the course of the past week that I had woken up to the sensation of both of my arms asleep. Somehow, as if in act of defiance, my arms would seek out places that guaranteed a numbing reaction. I worried that I was praying in my sleep.

Flashes of memories followed me as I had walked into the café and slid into the same booth I had sat in during my time living with Freya. It was that time of night when management turned the lights down hoping to dupe people already on their way to being drunk to drink more.

It was not a place one goes to while the sun is still up. I had tried that before and it was a mistake. Not that it was *that* dingy or *that* sleazy, but a keen awareness that something was lost in daylight.

I had spent many hours reading books at the café. It was a time when I was soaking in everything. Freya's friends would regularly join me while I was reading, and I would listen intently to their conversations about existentialism, modern architecture, world religions, veganism, and the merits of reading all of James Joyce's books in order. It was where I had studied for her GED exam, and it was where we celebrated my passing grade with rounds of drinks. It was also the place where I learned to confidently order a beer as though I was legal.

I never really had a name when Freya's friends were around; I was simply referred to as "girlfriend," which was later shortened to "G." It was then that I learned that to name something is an act of power and I couldn't help but think that the nickname was lame.

I remembered allowing Freya to peel back my layers, slowly revealing the truth in carefully crafted stories. As I walked through Vimy Park I remembered telling Freya about the origins of my name. Freya had been looking at my driver's licence.

"I don't believe a word of that story. Besides, I thought you said you never learned to drive. How is it that you have a driver's licence?"

"I didn't learn how to drive, I just knew how when I took the test."

"Bullshit."

How had we started talking about that?

"My parents have never been ones to force their opinions on their kids, which made naming their children especially difficult for them. Occasionally though, my father is struck by a sudden flare of practicality. When I was born his thoughts were on getting baby and mom home and back to normal life as soon as possible. He marched down to register his new daughter's name legally. Not having picked a name yet, or even consulted with my mother, he was taken aback by the blank space on the form. Undeterred, he asked the clerk what her name was. 'Jessica Moor, sir,' she said.

"'That's too long, people will just shorten it anyway,' my father said.

"So in the blank for first name he put 'Jess' and in the blank for surname he put 'Moor,' without ever giving a thought to the fact

that neither he nor my mother had the surname of Moor. Shortly after, the mistake was found out by my mother. But she and dad were
never ones to tell each other what to do and if that's what he wanted
that was fine with her."

"That also sounds like bullshit to me." Freya had been smiling
though. She let me tell her stories.

The park was not the safest place to walk through, but I did
anyway. Funny how nature is labelled with experience and given a
persona by humans. It's unfair how we blame nature for being evil,
unsafe. Funny how in a city of 750,000 one could feel so utterly
alone and vulnerable—half a million people and no one to protect
you. It's partially the nature of the location of Winnipeg. Alone in
the Prairies, in the middle of the country, where the wind blows hard
and the snow can pile up around your feet while you wait to cross
the street.

The traffic had lightened on Portage, giving the city the capac-
ity for silence. I felt like I might start crying. I thought about going
back to the café to apologize, to try to make amends, to make her
like me again. I started walking toward the café but stopped and sat
down on a bench in the park.

"Aren't you done with this? Are you finished with this?" I said
to myself.

"OK," I said out loud, standing up.

I crossed the park, approached my former residence on Walnut Street, and walked up the steps. Reaching for the doorknob, I
stopped myself.

"This is not a good idea," I said to myself. "I don't live here
anymore."

I was struck by the possibility that Freya still lived there with her
gang of anarchist friends and that I could probably walk right in and
be welcomed. I retreated from the house and headed back down the
street, two blocks up Westminster to Halfsteinn's house where I had
stashed my backpack in the front porch.

When does a pattern become a pattern? Does a pattern represent
truth? In science it would seem so. Do the same thing over and over
again and get the same result—then something is true? A good scientist will never accept the results though—always expecting to be
proven wrong. My brother John had taught me that.

Maybe the trees were only beautiful because I thought they
were—the Oscar Wilde view of life. Maybe the sum of her plus an

unknown made that beauty. Maybe beauty was part of the equation and the result—the effect was life.

When I got to Halfsteinn's house I was surprised that there was a light on in the living room. "Shit," I said. I sat down on the front steps, lit a cigarette, and tried to decide whether to go into the house and see Halfsteinn, or to take my bag and leave. I thought that if I waited long enough Halfsteinn would go to bed and the decision would be made for me, or possibly I would freeze to death. I wrapped my jacket a little tighter around me and put my hood on.

I wanted to knock on the door but I was afraid because of what Freya had said about comforting each other. My mind raced as I turned the thought over in my mind and finally came to a wild and horrific conclusion—Freya and Halfsteinn were a couple. Lighting my third cigarette, I heard the door open behind me but didn't turn around, thinking that maybe he didn't see me.

"You know, Jess," Halfsteinn said, his voice without emotion, "you can smoke inside." He stood in the doorway, his great frame casting a shadow over me. "Just for you, I'll make an exception."

I stood up and faced him. He was smiling and his arms were outstretched. I walked into his embrace silently and received a bear hug.

"I ran a bath while you were sitting out there," he said, ushering me inside the house.

"Halfsteinn, I..."

He cut me off. "Jess, don't be mad, but Thom called and let me know that he thought you'd be coming. I put a glass of wine beside the tub. Just have a bath before you say anything." He took me in his arms again and squeezed me hard before releasing me up the stairs.

As I dipped my toes in the warm water I felt them tingle and spring back to life. The bathroom was painted a bright blue with nothing decorating the walls. There was a small pile of stones in the corner near the sink. I heard the cracking and popping of wood burning and Halfsteinn fussing around in the kitchen and then a kettle whistling. The house shifted with the wind, but I felt solid and safe in the tub. Finally, I pulled myself out of the warm water and wandered downstairs to find Halfsteinn sipping a cup of tea and reading the newspaper in front of the fire.

He stood up and pointed to a seat beside him. "Sit down. I've got a cup of tea and a bowl of soup for you. If I know you at all, you haven't eaten today."

He set the tea and soup on the end table beside me and then resumed his reading while I ate. When I was finished he put his newspaper down.

"It's really good to see you, Jess, tell me everything." He smiled broadly. His feet were resting on an old ottoman in front of him. He handed me a blanket as I reclined.

"I missed you." I didn't know where to start.

"What brings you into town?" Halfsteinn said quietly.

"I don't know exactly. I just somehow found myself on a plane today, or I guess technically yesterday," I said, looking at my imaginary watch.

"Spoken to your parents?"

"Not a word." I said, looking at the fire.

Halfsteinn let out a muted whistle between his teeth. "That's a...that's a hell of a long time, Jess."

I bowed my head and remained quiet. I couldn't hear anything he was saying and needed to know immediately. "Half, are you and Freya together?" I said, turning my eyes to him.

"What?" Halfsteinn shook his head. "What are you talking about?"

"I saw her tonight and she implied that you two were together," I seethed.

He laughed and shook his head. "I've seen Freya twice since you left. It was at Afi and Amma's funerals and both times she didn't so much as look at me. So no, we're not together, not to mention that we're first cousins." He stared into the fire.

"Amma and Afi are dead?" I wrapped the blanket around me a little tighter and pushed my eyes into my palms.

"Amma died of breast cancer three years ago. Afi had a heart attack about nine months later. It turned out that Amma had breast cancer the summer that you were there, but she didn't tell anyone." Sitting up, he reached over and poked at the fire, adding another log. He sat back down again and rolled a cigarette. "Some people can't live or die without each other."

I was in a trance watching him methodically remove the pouch from his breast pocket, pull a paper out, pack the tobacco, and lick it shut.

"You mind if I roll one of those?" I said.

"Not at all—I can see if my lessons have stayed with you." He tossed me the pouch and then lit his cigarette.

165

He watched me intently without making a move or saying a word. He just nodded when I finished and returned the pouch and papers to him.

"I can't believe you actually think that Freya and I would be lovers; that's just insulting," he said as he lit his cigarette.

"First of all, you lied about your being related to her. Second of all, yes, I guess I should just assume that you're without friends or a girlfriend for that matter. Heaven forbid you allow yourself the pleasure."

"I have friends," he said, his tone defensive and slightly high pitched.

"Your parents and old guys at the bar in Gimli don't count," I said, starting to enjoy the verbal sparring. "Why did you lie about being cousins with Freya?"

He breathed out of his nose and stared intently at the fire. "I don't know," he said finally. "I don't know."

Considering I was uncertain what put me on that plane, I could accept that answer.

"Are you going all the way home tonight, speaking of parents."

"I'm going somewhere," I said, barely audible.

"You can't stay just a little while?"

"No."

"I had to ask."

"I'm glad you did."

Halfsteinn got up and reached for his teacup. He went into the kitchen and grabbed the teakettle with a tea towel hanging on the stove. I could have sat there all night and watched him move around his house, going from chair to kitchen to fireplace to bathroom to bed. I equally felt like throwing the blankets off and bolting out the door.

"So why now?" Halfsteinn said, examining the cherry on the end of his cigarette. He blew on it slightly and ashed it into his empty cup of tea.

"I went far away, I mean, not that far geographically, I didn't go to the ends of the earth, but I tried as hard as possible to erase the person who came from Saskatchewan; I've been trying to live without a history."

"And why has that been unsuccessful?" Halfsteinn combed his right hand through his hair, attempting to keep his mop to one side and out of his eyes.

"It has been successful."

Halfsteinn remained silent, as though he knew I would amend my sentence. I did.

"Well, I guess it was successful for a time and then things changed."

"It's funny," Halfsteinn said as he got up and went to the cupboard beside the fridge. He produced a bottle with amber liquid in it. From the cupboard next to that one he grabbed two small tumblers. He set the glasses and bottle down beside him and poured.

"I don't think I'm going to drink that," I said as held a glass up to me.

"I think you should."

I smiled, "Why?"

He laced his fingers together, "Because," he started and then stopped, picking his words carefully, "this amber elixir is no ordinary drink. It is special and is the appropriate thing to bring out in the face of a special occasion."

I wanted to interrupt him to ask what the special occasion was, but let him continue without interruption.

"You see, this is bourbon, and there are rules that govern it. You can't just call anything bourbon. It has to be made with at least fifty-one percent corn. It has to be aged for a minimum of two years in new, white, America oak barrels that have been charred. Most importantly, when the bourbon is finished aging, nothing can be added to it to—that means nothing to enhance the flavour, nothing to make it a different colour, or smell differently—nothing. That's why I love bourbon—when it's ready, it's ready. There's no cheating."

I drank the bourbon down slowly and in silence. Halfsteinn stared at the fire and finally spoke again.

"Here's a secret, Jess, I'm afraid of the water."

I snorted, "What? No you're not, you're a fisherman. How could you possibly be afraid of the water?"

"Every morning that I get into the boat I'm scared shitless that I'm going to drown."

I put my drink down and faced him. "You're serious, aren't you?"

"Yes," he took a sip from his nearly empty tumbler, "but life is so much better out on the lake that I fight through it. When I can't, I just say that I've caught my limit for the day."

When I got up and announced that it was time to go, he stood and walked me to the door. He pulled me into his arms and put some money into my jacket pocket, which made me smile into his sweater.

"I could drive you there," he said, still holding me. "I'm not fishing just yet."

"You don't even know where I'm going; I could be driving to Mexico for all you know."

"I think I know where you're going."

"I know," I said, closing my eyes and stepping out of his embrace.

"I'm really proud of you," he said, stuffing his hands into his pockets, his big frame towering over me and a long strand of hair dipping into his left eye.

"Well, I'm not there yet."

"You will be," he said, opening the door for me. "Now get the hell out of here because it only makes sense for you to be leaving in the middle of the night during a sleet storm." He poked a hand out of the door, trying to catch whatever was falling from the sky. "Tell me you have a bus or plane ticket or something."

"Yes, I've got a bus or plane ticket or something," I said, smiling. As I stared at him in the doorway I thought about John and felt my stomach shift. "I miss my brother, John," I said before stepping away from the shelter of the porch.

"He misses you, too," Halfsteinn boomed from the house.

DIRECTIONS HOME

Go west down Portage Avenue, turn right onto the Yellowhead Highway. Allow yourself to embrace the spirit of the Happy Rock in Gladstone. Stop at the Dairy Queen in Neepawa to share a Blizzard with the ghost of Margaret Laurence. Bow down to the aging rock gods on your way past Minnedosa while your ears pop. In Russell, go to the drive-through beer vendor and pick up a six of Fort Garry Dark, just for the hell of it. In Kandahar, Saskatchewan, you might be worried that you've taken a wrong turn and ended up in Afghanistan but fear not, you're in still in Canada.

When I travelled southeast on the train to Winnipeg I couldn't see the little towns, the drive-through beer vendor in Russell, or the sign outside of Minnedosa proclaiming the presence of rock gods. All I saw in the darkness were vague outlines of trees, vast fields, a few main streets, and, of course, Freya. I wasn't really paying attention to the details; those small bits of bread that would lead me back had long ago been eaten by the birds.

After years in the Golden Horseshoe surrounded by the majestic smog-trapping escarpment, traffic congestion, maple stands and apple orchards, small towns that melt into each other, unabashed suburbs, and the mighty 401, what I saw out the window was cinematic.

I got into the semi somewhere outside of Headingly. It had taken a surprisingly long time to walk to from Arlington and Portage Avenue, so when the truck stopped I gladly hopped in. The sun was up but it didn't make me feel any warmer. After hours out in the sleet and dark I was shaking. The driver had a neatly trimmed beard and suspenders over his plaid shirt. In the passenger seat was his daughter, a young girl of about eight who introduced herself as Chloe.

"I'm Thane," the man said as I climbed into the cab, "and it looks like we got you just in time. You look like you're about to freeze to death. Why don't you get into the bunk and get into some dry clothes." He jerked his thumb behind him.

I closed the curtain separating the sleeper from front of cab and followed the instructions, putting on the dry shirt in my bag. Pulling off my pants, I drew a blanket over me and curled up. I was too cold to think that the driver might be a serial killer.

I lay in the sleeper of the semi for twenty-four hours in a fever. When I woke up it was the middle of the night, we had already gone to Calgary to drop off the load. We were barrelling down on Blaurock, and my heart was thumping. In my fever I had mumbled about going home, going to Blaurock, and that's where they were taking me. As the truck geared down, my heart slowed.

"Is this the place?" Thane said, looking back at me.

The sweet hum of a trucker's deep voice was coming through the CB, letting Thane know that there were Mounties with a radar gun about six miles up the road. Chloe sat quietly in the passenger seat staring straight ahead. She pointed ahead toward a spot in the pitch black. "Up there, dad, I think you can pull into that side road up there."

"Yeah, there's a road there. How can you see that?" I said, amazed, looking into the darkness.

"Oh, she's got eagle eyes this one," Thane said, cupping his daughter's chin playfully before grabbing the gearshift and pulling it down and to the left.

The truck came to a stop and Thane put the hazard lights on. I pulled my bag onto my shoulders and stopped.

I took a deep breath. "I don't know why I'm here," I said.

"Are you sure? It's all you mumbled about while you were asleep." Thane said quietly while nodding.

"I've never met someone who could sleep as much as you. Are you going to your mom and dad's to sleep some more?" She was bouncing up and down on her seat.

"I hope not," I replied.

My foot touched the pavement and it felt like a lunar landing.

MANIFESTATION OF A FOUR-HUNDRED-YEAR-OLD GHOST

Thane and Chloe's truck disappeared into the night and I wonder if maybe I'm dreaming. How is it that I'm standing on Highway 11, staring at Blaurock?

Asleep for only another four or five hours, how is it that I used to rise and rest in this place? There's a car coming down the highway, making it necessary for me to get off the road into what seems like a greater risk—inside town limits. When I was a kid we used to hide at night, turning the whole town into one giant hide-and-go-seek game. We'd run around for hours until the horn on top of the town-hall went off at nine o'clock, telling us to get home. We still played when I was into my teens, there was nothing else to do.

One night, through sheer luck, we tried the door of the school. To our amazement it was open. We crept in, on our bellies, as though we were storming enemy lines. I acted as the front scout, making sure that there wasn't someone in authority lurking in the shadows, ready to alert those behind me if we were walking into a trap. There was none. We spent the night lounging on the high-jump mat daring each other to kiss one another. I was the only one not at the receiving end of a dare, although no one seemed to notice but me.

Blaurock. It means "blue dress" in German. Named after one of the founding fathers of Anabaptism, George Blaurock. Despite being built on the rail line, by some miracle the town founders were able to convince the government that they did not wish to live in a town named after a politician in Ottawa or executive at the rail company.

The roads are still the same—a soft asphalt made by spraying a thick, heavy tar on the gravel roads. There's no pavement in this town, no stoplights or much in the way of sidewalks. I see immediately that there's a tooth missing in the mouth of this town. The grain elevator has been torn down. All that stands in its place is an uninterrupted view of the western sky. The town is becoming a bedroom community—there's a new subdivision on the edge of town where my parent's house used to stand alone. A familiar smell drifts over the town, a distinct mixture of cow shit, silage, and straw bales. It comes from the dairy farm just north of town. I remember that people complained about the smell. It seeps into a base part of my brain that has no words. It is simply home.

Home. I'm surprised I've used that word. The word punches me in the stomach and I feel like I'm in grade five again. Sitting in the middle of my elementary school playground brings me back to the time that my best friend actually did punch me in the stomach for telling someone that we were best friends; apparently, I was under a misapprehension. I never used the words "best friends" to describe my relationship with anyone again. Some other kids were making fun of me for the short, cropped haircut I had just received and I had informed them that I just wanted to match with my best friend Allan. The group started jeering him, saying he had a girl haircut and telling me I had a boy haircut. It was all very confusing until Allan punched me hard in the stomach, dropping me to my knees. The crowd immediately dispersed, and Allan never talked to me again. Quite the feat considering we were in a class of only twenty-four for nine years before moving on to high school.

The town is flanked by fields ready to be planted as soon as the ground thaws. I walk into the field across from the schoolyard and bend down to touch the hard ground. I feel incredibly lost, like I no longer fit in this landscape; there's something garish about me. I feel like a stiff drink could strip the feeling away.

My thoughts bring me to my parent's front door. Touching the doorknob I stop, afraid that it will be locked. It's not, so I step through the threshold into the dark silence of the house I grew up in. The smell hits me first. It's the same smell I washed out of my hair and clothes years ago. I half expect mom to be sitting at the kitchen table, doing a crossword puzzle, waiting for me to come home, extremely pissed because I'm really late for my curfew. Without turning on the lights, I make my way to the fridge.

A bag of pre-washed salad mix.

One container of yoghurt.

A two-litre bottle of Pepsi.

A tub of deli-style potato salad.

172

A fridge door filled with salad dressings, a jar of pickles, pasta sauce, olives, and a can of what appears to be bacon fat.

A block of Gouda, a package of Camembert, and a package of Brie.

One litre low-fat skim milk.

Who the hell are these people? This is not the fridge I remember. It's like mom doesn't cook anymore. This is not the fridge of the Mennonite mom that I grew up with. The only packaged goods we had were things we couldn't make ourselves, such as milk and cheese. I grew up with my mom making butter, bread, yoghurt, every manner of canned goods, and even ketchup for goodness' sake. As my paradigm shifts like someone backing a car over my legs, there's a noise behind me.

A plant has been sent flying. I see my dad trying feebly, after the fact, to prevent the crash. His eyes are impossibly large as they meet mine.

He looks haggard in his dress shirt, which is untucked and unbuttoned at the bottom where his belly is the largest. Dad has put on a lot of weight in five years, and it doesn't look good on him. The weight is in his hands and his neck—he looks bloated. For a second I imagine him at every reception congratulating new graduates or celebrating the launch of some book published by the college or hosting a gala fundraising event. I see the weight of an entire community's eyes on him, expecting more, not allowing for mistakes.

"Vot da..." he says trailing off. I'm not sure if it means he's happy to see me. Or maybe he doesn't recognize me—thinks that he's dreaming.

We stare at each other. I was so sure of our history, so sure of our future. I had been so sure of what needed to be done and now I can't choose to leave at sixteen again. I can't have the alternate version of this story. This had been a choose-your-own-adventure novel, but I can't thumb the pages to bring my character back a couple of chapters. I can't put my pen down because I will always be the author. I stare at my father thinking about how I've been telling myself the story of this moment for so long that although I have tried out alternative versions, it all comes out the same way.

"Who are you?" he says, partially regaining his composure.

Does he really not know who I am? And then I realize that he's drunk.

"Dad, it's me, Jess." I don't know what to say. I've played out this moment for so long, but it's just been a picture without dialogue. I thought I had scripted everything so wonderfully, but it appears life set me up for improv.

"I don't want it to be you."

"It is me."

"You left us."

"I didn't have a choice."

"No, you always have a choice."

"Then what's your excuse?"

You can't jam the expectations of a community into a teacup, not in a town with the size and make-up of Blaurock. You cannot speak rationally to God. You're lucky if you can speak rationally to one or two of his followers.

So you make a path of least resistance and stick to it. Except I didn't. I'm back and I'm staring at my father, wishing he was happy to see me. Instead, he's in denial about the fact that we've met.

I'm a bomb that won't stop dropping, and he lets me fall.

"Well I guess you did a bad job of raising me."

He shakes his head, "You never listened. So smart but not smart enough to listen."

"You were never worth listening to." I don't mean it, but it's out now. "I saved you a lot of trouble by leaving."

He says nothing—doesn't move an inch. But I see it in his eyes.

I don't want it to be true. I was hoping he'd say "No, life's been hell since you left" But the hell was all his own. I wonder if he noticed that I was gone.

I thought I had a bulletproof jacket on but I was wrong. No amount of years could have prepared me. No wall built big enough to protect me. No knife sharp enough to cut away biology and longing. His eyes are glassy and unfocussed.

He walks toward me, his eyes full of rage. I smell the ounces of liquor he's guzzled back tonight. This is repression gone horribly wrong (as if repression can go horribly right). His mouth moves, but he's not saying anything. Suddenly, his jaw steels shut. I don't think that I've grown an inch since leaving, but I remember looking up to see his eyes gazing down on me. As though he's noticed the same thing, he points to a chair at the dinner table. He thinks I will sit on command, but I remain standing.

There are unreasonable expectations and then there are Mennonite expectations. Fall in line with military precision while denouncing all forms of violence.

There is beauty in our chaotic inability to be assured of our lives after death—no one will say for sure that they're heaven bound after they die, "in" and "out" we pronounce, contradicting ourselves while as we choke on the theology of our "just to be safe" exclusion. I understand that you have to be defined by something or you risk being nothing at all.

He turns and stumbles toward the bedroom away from the broken plant and me. Something overcomes me and I rush toward him.

"Don't turn your back on me, dad," I plead. And then angry, "Is this it? You just throw me outside with your silence and hope you'll find me dead on the front porch in the morning?" I grab his arm.

As he tries to resist me, his arm pops loose, landing the back of his fist squarely on my high cheekbone below my left eye. I stumble backward in shock but try not to show any reaction. His momentum slams him against the wall, but he doesn't seem to notice as he continues to stagger into the bedroom, shutting the door behind him loudly.

I'm breathing heavily. I will not throw up. I will not throw up. I've got to get out of here.

I'm waiting for everything to sink in. I'm waiting for tears to come, but I am beyond the tears and vomit. My fists are clenched, hard as stone. A memory of shattered drywall crosses my mind.

I let myself into the study and use the letter opener to pop the lock on the top drawer of dad's desk. Opening the drawer confirms that he now has a liquor stash that mom probably doesn't know about or doesn't want to know about. I grab three mickies of vodka, one of which is three-quarters empty.

Walking down the hall, I found the keys to dad's car—the latest clue that is slipping into something unrecognizable—a brand new BMW sports car.

Who the hell drives a BMW in Blaurock?

Shifting the car into reverse, I creep out of the driveway and through the four-way stop, taking a right at the service road and a left onto the end of the main street.

I'm sitting at the stop sign in front of Highway 11. Maybe I should just go to Saskatoon to see John. But the thought of John makes me cry, and I don't want to cry. Instead, I pull the car onto the highway going north, peeling away from Blaurock at top speed. Shifting into fifth, I open the window and throw the bottles out, smashing them into the ditch on the other side of the single-lane highway. I look to the right and see the steep banks of the river.

COLD ROCKS AND LOUD TEARS

Gearing down quickly I almost bring the car to a full-stop. I've driven north of town about forty-five minutes to the North Saskatchewan River, and although it is a stupid idea to bring a small, expensive sports car down a winding narrow dirt road, it's the least of my problems. Killing the headlights, I let the moon illuminate my path and hope to God that I'm recalling how to get here correctly. Although I grew up between the two rivers in the Saskatchewan River Valley, it's the South Saskatchewan that had been a daily sight.

The two rivers have one-hundred-foot riverbanks that never, ever threaten to spill over. It was something, after living in Winnipeg, that I appreciated. Many miles downstream is the summer camp I attended every year as a child. I have a brief flash of happiness thinking about my summers there. I learned to canoe, swim, fish, and make fires. There were Bible lessons, too, which I enjoyed in my childhood, but which made less sense as I got older.

Before the road can lead me down to the river's edge, I stop the car and get out. My face, however swollen, is not allowed into my thoughts. I focus on the riverbank and the open patch of cliff I see ahead of me. The world around me is starting to wake, but there are still patches of snow within the tree line. There is a silence that I have not experienced in since I moved to Ontario, and I'm pleasantly surprised to find that I'm not scared of it. After tonight, maybe I'll never be afraid again.

Just beyond a willow bluff to my right, I can see a clearing. I blink a couple of times, thinking that I see something illuminated. The bottom of my left eye is swelling, but I do not acknowledge it openly as I walk toward the illumination. The wind picks up for a moment and blows through the willow bluff, making a sound like sand falling on metal.

The ground is wet in places, and the grass too high to see the puddles and patches of snow. The place that I saw from the car is still illuminated though, and so I keep walking toward it.

As I approach I see a large granite rock, almost perfectly square—a perfect lookout on the edge of the riverbank. Touching the stone, it seems to radiate heat. For the first time I allow myself to touch the spot just below my left eye. Three deep breaths and now sobs.

"Tough night?"

The words come from my right. A woman approaches me. I see her long, grey hair clearly in the dark. She looks vaguely familiar.

I nod and say nothing.

"I hope I didn't scare you," the woman says, sitting down next to me. "Here, use my hankie."

"Well," I say, blowing my nose, "I did come looking for you, so I shouldn't be surprised."

"You flatter me, but I know that's not true," the woman says simply. "And you do look surprised. Frankly, I'm surprised, I don't get many people around here unless they're looking for a bush party."

"I am surprised to see you." I say, folding my hankie neatly. "I discovered a book of your poetry in my dad's office. I think that if I had not read those words I might have stayed here."

"I heard you had left rather abruptly," she says, pulling out a pack of cigarettes and offering me one.

I light a cigarette and inhale deeply; I haven't had a smoke in a while and it helps me lose the shakes in my hands.

"Your dad actually drove down here demanding to know where you were," she says, laughing.

"What? How on earth did he connect you with me?"

"Well, he's particular, your father. He could tell that you had been through his things and he figured out you had taken my little book of poetry."

"You know, it makes me think—all the whisperings I heard about you when I was a kid—the witch near the river, the woman who had done things that were so horribly wrong that it couldn't be uttered. I can only imagine what's said about me. Maybe I shouldn't have left."

"Thank God you did." Her gaze sets on the area below my left eye. "What is this?" she says, taking my chin to put the bruise in a better light for her to see.

"Dad was drunk. It was an honest-to-God accident."

"When's the last time you talked to them?"

"The day before I left. Five years ago."

"Wow," she exhales. "David did this to you?"

My legs are starting to fall asleep and the rock is making my bum numb, so I get up and start pacing in front of the woman. "Why didn't you just leave?"

"I have a child. There's no way I could have left him."

"I have a brother."

"Yes."

"Did you love my father?"

"He wanted to marry me, when I told him I was pregnant. But by then I had met..." she stops for a moment, maybe in reverence, maybe out of hurt, "I had met her, and I was in love." She lights another cigarette. "Yes, to answer your question, I did love him, to the best of my ability, until I realized that I couldn't." She shrugs her shoulders.

"I don't know what I expected but I didn't expect him to be drunk."

"He's been down here a few times, drunk, like he wanted a safe place to be drunk. The last time I greeted him with my .22. I haven't seen him since. Not that I mind drunks, but I am not the right person for your father to come to. Unfortunately, your story is being influenced by the narration of a voice that is not your own. Most of your dad's shit has nothing, and yet everything, to do with you because he is your father. Just try to take it one issue at a time and don't try to correct a history that isn't yours; it's not your job." She butts her cigarette on the rock, caches it in her front jacket pocket, and gets up. "Why don't you come and have a sleep before you head back."

I follow her, crumple onto her couch, and watch as she builds the fire up. My eyes flutter shut when I feel the heat of the fire reach me.

I wake up, my eye throbbing. A cracking sound is coming from outside; it's Martha chopping wood. Something's baking in the oven; it looks like Martha's second batch of buns for the day.

I'm putting on my coat when she comes back into the house, arms full of wood.

I want to tell her that I'm writing my thesis about her. I want to interview her and get the answers I've been looking for, but I don't.

Nodding, she puts the wood beside the fireplace and hugs me. She says nothing. Finally, it's time to go.

178

NEGOTIATING WITH THE DEAD

I let the car idle in the driveway for a second before turning it off. At the threshold of the house mom stands, hands on hips. An apron covers her. A light dusting of flour covers it. She looks at me, puzzled. Do I hug her?

"It took me all day to get it out of your father—where his car was and what was going on." She shakes her head, "Look at you, you're thinner than ever." She walks forward and brings me into her arms. She's sniffing me, "And now you're smoking. Some Lied äahre Kjinja," she says, but without the usual exasperation, more like remorse. "Some people's children," she says again. Maybe she thinks I've forgotten Low German. I haven't.

Stepping away, she stares, still shaking her head. I let her stare and then take the reins.

"I think that we have a lot to talk about."

"I think that it's good that you're home." She's absent-mindedly wipes her clean hands on her apron. "We've been praying so long that you would come home. We love you so much."

This would be easier if I was drunk; maybe my mom and I could sit down and have a beer. I almost suggest it, but then remember that it's my mom. "Mom, I don't really know why I came back here. I guess I wanted to know if things could be different. I just don't understand, if you love me so much, why you pretended not to know who I was when I called or why you never searched for me. That's fucked up, mom, I was just a kid."

She seems startled by my comments, possibly more startled by my language.

"You were my baby, Jess. You were my baby and I couldn't protect you. I couldn't think about where you were and what you were doing because I would have wanted to find you." She's starting to cry. "You think that the whole world revolves around you, but it doesn't. Other people have problems, too."

I stand frozen. "What do you mean you would have wanted to find me? You mean you didn't want to?"

Mom gently moves me aside to close the curtain behind me. "Of course I wanted to find you. I wanted to bring you home and put you under a safe roof and clothe and feed you and hug you every day, but I couldn't. I knew you wouldn't stay here no matter what I did. You had to go and I don't know why. I don't regret a thing," she says, her tone changing to something that sounds rehearsed.

My shoes are still on and I still have the keys to dad's car. I can leave.

"I'll call your brother John. Your grandfather is coming for dinner. What am I supposed to do, I can't tell him not to come. I'll call John," she says again. "I have to start supper if it's going to be on time. I suspect Francis will be here shortly, too."

"What's wrong with dad?"

Mom looks at me with horror, her mouth constricting. She's unable to speak. She grips a chair and looks like she might fall. Half a second later, she regains her composure. "Nothing. Nothing's wrong with your father, other than his sciatic nerve."

I can't push her. I want to but I can't. I know from that half-second pause that there's so much going on in her heart. It makes me want to wrap my arms around her and tell her to let it out. She's my mom, and she shouldn't have to live like this—whatever "this" is. Mom quickly turns away and exits.

Outside, the sun is setting. The past five years of urban life leaves me awestruck by view of the sunset from the front steps. "So, the boys are coming," I say to the sunset. "This should be interesting."

John arrives first, already on his way when mom called unless he drove 200 kilometres an hour to get here. He runs toward me, yelling "Jessie, Jessie, Jessie!" He grabs me tight and swings me around in circles. "I can't believe you're home," he says shaking his head, "Do you wanna sit?" he's motioning to the front steps as if they didn't exist where I've been living.

I'm shaking, but it's just because I'm cold. John reaches for my cigarettes, lights one up, and starts puffing.

"Aren't you afraid that mom or dad will catch you?" I say in my best mocking tone.

"I think my smoking is the least of this family's concerns right now." He inhales, "And thanks, by the way, for not stealing my truck and taking it to Winnipeg with you."

"How did you know?"

"Lucky guess. I found the truck at the station—or rather the cops did. I told them that someone played a prank on me. I assumed from the time of night it was left there that you had headed west. When I heard that you had left a note I was just relieved that you hadn't tried to kill yourself. It sounded like you had a plan. I guess mom thought you'd come back. Then weeks turned into months and, well, we just didn't talk about it."

I'm staring at John in disbelief, "You guys never talked about me being gone? I've been gone for five years."

John doesn't respond immediately; I'm getting angry.

"Well, what were we supposed to do? You can't have it both ways— you can't leave and tell us not to contact you and then hope we spend our lives obsessing about where you are and what you're doing."

John is smiling as he says this.

I inhale deeply. "I was a kid."

"I know, but it's what you wanted to do. What would have happened if we had dragged you home? "It would have been a disaster and maybe you would have killed yourself." He's looking at his hands, scratching his left palm. "I'm glad that you've come home."

"Was it a bad idea that I came here? Is this going to work?"

"Nope," John says simply while rubbing my back.

I can't tell what he's saying no to. I assume both.

"No to which part John?"

John laughs, rolling his eyes as though the answer is obvious. "I think mom could use some help with supper. I think grandpa's coming, too."

Inside, mom is busy preparing supper. She's rolled the dough out and is filling small circles of pastry with a cottage cheese filling. She pinches with machine-like precision.

"John, how are you?" Mom says warmly.

"I'm absolutely thrilled to see Jess," John says.

Mom reaches out and squeezes my hand. "Jess, do you remember how to pinch the verenikje shut?"

"I think I can handle it, mom." I feel like a child again, hearing mom use the tone of a cooking instructor she had always been fond of.

"John, you set the table, and make sure there's a place for your grandpa."

I set about filling the small pockets of dough with cottage cheese. Eventually we move on to filling them with saskatoon berries with some sugar mixed in.

We're focused, as though our lives depend on getting everything perfectly pinched shut in time for the magical supper hour.

The door opens, "Hey everyone, it's Frank!" Francis says as he rushes into the kitchen.

When the hell did Francis become Frank?

"Mom said you were here, but I wouldn't believe it until I saw you in the flesh and there you are." Francis extends his hand. I put my hand in his, attempting the strongest grip possible. Instinctively our thumbs emerge from the grip, pass each other three times before entering into a thumb war. We thumb wrestle for what seems like ten minutes before Francis finally pins me.

"Ha, haven't lost my form," Francis says.

"No you haven't," I agree.

"You put up a good fight, though. Come here! Give me a hug."

It's the first time Francis has ever hugged me, apart from head-locks in our childhood. He has never been one for hugs. Francis lets me go and immediately opens the fridge, thrusting his head in like an anteater who's found a healthy colony. He emerges victorious with a Tupperware container filled with some meaty pasta dish.

"Francis, aren't we making supper right now? Why are you eating that?"

"A working man has got to eat, Jess," he says, swallowing a fork full of pasta without chewing.

"Still selling tractors?"

"Yeah. I'm moving up in the ranks every year. Grandpa, he's finally starting to trust me. I've earned it, though," Francis adds. "It's not like he handed me the business or anything, I've worked for it and pretty soon it's going to be all mine. I definitely learned about working from the best." He sits down at the table and puts his feet up on the chair beside him. He stretches, lacing his fingers behind his head, and I can't help but notice that he's grown a little paunch.

I smile, thinking how dad's work ethic is not even a consideration for Francis. Grandpa has effectively indoctrinated him into believing that what dad does is not real work and therefore requires no real work ethic. One thing that our dad could never be accused of is a lack of a work ethic—at least, not the David Klassen I knew. I don't remember dad taking time off; if anything, his sabbaticals always meant seeing less of him as he sequestered himself in his office. Without the daily grounding of interaction with students, dad would work himself into a frenzied state most days and was completely unbearable by suppertime. I remember it being especially bad just before I left, which probably meant that he was all the more clueless when mom was screaming at me for leaving church that fateful Sunday afternoon.

"So, Jess, what was the problem, they don't have telephones where you were? Somebody kidnap you or something, you couldn't get on a bus?" Francis changed his tone sharply and suddenly.

John and mom stop their work and stare at me. It's obviously something they all wanted to say, and Francis has never had any qualms about stating the obvious.

I want to say yes, I was kidnapped, to tell him about Freya and how my ability to trust was shattered. I want to tell him that I'm still recovering and that arriving on the doorstep is a miracle I can't explain. I want to tell him about the conversation I had with mom and dad in the basement after church. I want to remind him that I was about to be sent away before I left on my own. But all I can say is, "Kind of, yeah."

"Well, you scared the shit out of all of us. How long has it been now? Five years? You couldn't call?" Francis is insistent, and I can't blame him.

"Jess did call, Francis," mom says from the kitchen, not looking up from her dough, "we just never discussed it with you."

Tears sting my eyes; she knew it was me on the phone that Sunday afternoon.

Francis casually grabs the newspaper from the chair on the other side of him, then drops it quickly. "What the heck happened to your face?"

"So you're Frank now?" I say, changing the topic. I'll need to come back to the phone call later but for now I don't have the strength to broach the topic.

"Well, people think that they're dealing with a woman if it's Francis, so I just changed it a bit. Do I have to remind you that you weren't always Jess?"

I don't know how to respond; again, it's a fair comment. I've been Jess for so long, it didn't dawn on me that it might be an issue. From his tone, it seems Francis has been thinking about it.

The doorbell rings.

"Oh, that's got to be grandpa," Francis says excitedly, like a child. "I'll get it."

I panic, afraid of what questions he might have. I look to John.

"It's OK," John whispers, "I don't think he even knows that you've been gone. That's why Francis is taking over more of the business, grandpa is kind of," John hesitates, wagging his head from side to side, "he's kind of losing it."

"Oh," I say, unable to imagine our mighty grandfather not being in complete control. I can't imagine what it means for grandpa to be losing it because the man has always been a weird mixture—wrapped up in himself yet keeping his hand in everyone's business. It seems like he lost it a long time ago.

"Jessie, how's my Jessie?" He extends his arms, bringing me in for a hug. "Been keeping well?" he says, slipping a twenty into my hand and winking.

I'm still ten years old in his eyes, ready to accept his money and be thankful. At least the denominations have increased.

"I'm OK, gramps, not too bad, nice to see you too. I hear that Francis is working hard." I settled on the topic because of its relative safety.

"This boy has ambition," he says enthusiastically, his voice filling the room, "he's got a good head for business, too, and he didn't have to go to university for that."

I smile, "I'm almost finished my degree, grandpa. Worked myself all the way through university without a student loan."

"Without a loan? Well, good for you, no sense in borrowing money when you don't need to," he says.

I have no idea why I'm feeding him these false notions of who I am or what I care about, but it seems like the path of least resistance.

It's time for supper and dad hasn't returned. My family has a lot of practice ignoring the elephant in the room. Never before would we have started supper without dad sitting at the table. Grandpa leads us in prayer and for I my mouth along, *Come Lord Jesus, be our guest, may this food to us be blessed, amen.*

All eyes open and I realize that I had not closed mine, or bowed my head; I had given thanks, but just barely. After five years, my previous sixteen years of training are wearing off. I'm confused by the feeling permeating my core, which I finally identify as guilt. I feel very much at home again.

Mom is already up and out of her seat going to the kitchen to find the mustard that we forgot to put on the table. Then she's busy pouring water into everyone's glass.

"Mom," I say, as I'm about to lift another piece of sausage to my mouth, "just sit down and relax." She seems hurt by that comment which makes me realize that fluttering about probably keeps her calm. "I've missed this particular meal and all its components more than I realized. Thanks."

"You just let your mother feed you Jess, you look like you haven't eaten in weeks! You're taking after your grandma Klassen, that's for sure. She always could keep the weight off." Grandpa doesn't acknowledge mom as she fills his coffee mug—he's always believed with religious fervour that coffee is the only beverage that can be consumed with a meal.

"Mom," Francis says, pointing his chin in the general direction of something at the end of the table. Mom responds by passing him the bowl of saskatoon berry verenikje.

"Francis," I say, "have you lost your ability to form full sentences?"

"Yeah, Francis," John gives Francis a hearty shove, "speak in full sentences."

Mom shakes her head, "Some Lied äahre Kjinja. You boys are grown, stop it already."

Some people's children. It's the ultimate Mennonite parental conceit: it could be perceived that the children are behaving badly and just to make sure that others are aware that I am aware of this I must denounce them but really they are doing no harm and I'm glad they get along so well so I won't tell them directly to stop.

"Jessie," Francis says, "are you married yet?"

I've been gone for five years. I realize now that I have no idea whether my brother is married or not.

"No," I say shaking my head, "not married. Are you?"

Grandpa looks confused. "No, he's not married."

The table is silent until John jumps in. "I'm so glad that we're all sitting around the table together and eating this wonderful meal. It's been way too long."

But we're not intact. I look at grandpa and wonder if he even notices that his son isn't there. I wonder if he notices anything at all, maybe that's what happens after awhile; reality simply suits your needs.

I sat myself in the place I had always sat in for every meal. Francis and John are in their spots, too. Even after John moved out to live in Saskatoon, Francis and I held our spots at the table, leaving a chair between me and dad.

"Na, waut de Kuckuck? Where's Doft?" Grandpa says, finally noticing that his son isn't at the table.

"He's working, dad," mom answers.

"It sure takes him a lot of time to do it," he says.

The rest of us are quiet, leaving mom to respond to anymore questions grandpa might have. I'm about to feel guilty for leaving mom hanging but it's not my problem.

"Worscht," grandpa says just above a grunt.

I shake my head.

Worscht—I haven't heard the Low German word for sausage in a very long time. In fact, I haven't eaten any meat in five years.

My most vivid memory of grandpa losing his cool is from when the subject of vegetarianism came up one family gathering. I can't recall exactly how it came up but I do remember grandpa pounding his fist on the table, spitting out a large chunk of the worscht in protest to the suggestion that one shouldn't eat meat. "I should have been so lucky to eat like this when I was your age!" he said, enraged. It wasn't that anyone was suggesting that he should become a vegetarian, but he took the mere suggestion that anyone would choose that "lifestyle" was an affront to his being. Though he had not wanted for meat growing up; with his parents had already established a successful farm by the time he was my age.

We eat quickly and finish supper minutes after first sitting down. That's a sure sign of a Mennonite family—people ingesting food as quickly as possible. I theorize that it's because more than half an hour spent away from work is something God disapproves of. I'm convinced that this eat-and-run mentality is now a genetic trait.

"Frank, let's go," Grandpa barks.

"We're in the middle of going through the accounts, it's gotta get done." Francis looks at me and shrugs. "Are you going to be here tomorrow?"

I can't say anything because I honestly don't know. My silence drags on for a little too long.

"Well, then, maybe I'll come back later on tonight then."

My stomach turns, but I can't figure out if it's from the infusion of meat or the usual ailment. I guess it's a blessing, eating quickly—not having to sit at the table with grandpa for too long.

Food is a necessity—it makes the body able to work. The world that I grew up in was neatly divided into things that were necessary and not necessary, or "nich needig." I remember as a kid asking mom many times if I could go to a friend's house for a sleepover. The response would be a muttered "nich needig" from dad and a tired "Yes" from mom. For all the days I lived under their roof, my dad insisted on waking me up no later than nine in the morning on Saturdays. When I asked him why he replied, "It's necessary." I always countered with "Why? Why is it necessary?" He never felt obliged to respond.

Mom is loading the dishwasher and putting leftovers into Tupperware; I'm just standing there watching her. Mom looks more haggard than I remember. I can't help but wonder what part I play in that.

"You were always so private and sneaky." Mom says continuing to load the dishwasher. "Do you remember when you would hide things like chocolate bars and your collection of toques? Always so afraid that we would steal what was most precious to you."

"Maybe I wished that someone would have cared enough to try."

Mom dries her hands on the tea towel closest to her. "I think it's how you feel now."

Her insight belies the cover of ignorance that she tends to hide under, and I'm too caught off guard to respond.

"I'm going to take a bath," mom says thoughtfully, "because I don't know what else to do with myself."

"Jess," John says from behind me, "do you remember when you decided to call yourself Jess?"

I pull my cigarettes out of my pocket. "If you're going to ask questions you'll have to take them outside for a cigarette with me."

John laughs, "Oh Jess, I'm glad to see that none of your hostility has died."

"It's increased tenfold. Now, are you coming out for a smoke or what?" I reach for the door and let myself out. The garden gnome perched by the door is smiling manically and it reminds me of John, of the many times I tried to nickname him "Smiley," though it never caught on.

We crouch on the front steps, smoking. "John, where's dad?"

"I don't know; you were the last one to see him," John responds as stubbornly innocent as possible. I wonder if he gets it from mom.

"I didn't really see him, John, I saw a shadow of him."

"That's not true at all." John inhales and changes the subject. "So, what brings you home?"

"Him and her," I say pointing into the house, "I think that we have some shit to work out."

John laughs again. "Ya think?"

"John, since you are the only supportive person in this family, I allow you to be sarcastic, but I want you to answer a question, and I'm serious now." I look into his eyes.

"Ask away."

"How long has dad been drinking?"

"I'm going to answer, but first I want you to promise you're going to listen to everything that I say."

"Promise," I say, looking at him and then toward the ground.

"Dad started drinking the day you left," John exhales. "But, before you start blaming yourself and feeling guilty like the good Mennonite that you're not, you need to know that it's not your fault."

"I know."

John touches my shoulder. "You're crying."

"I know."

John hugs me, likely regretting telling me the truth.

"Jess, it's way more complicated than you think it is. You're biggest problem is thinking that you created every event, choice, consequence, success, and failure in dad's life. It broke his heart when you left, but it just wasn't everything that was going on."

"So what you're saying is that I pushed him over the edge." I laugh, but I'm still crying.

"No, that's not what I'm saying at all. The whole notion that someone can drive someone else to drink is bullshit, and you're smart enough to know that. What I'm saying is that he loves you and that it's much more complex than his sixteen-year-old daughter walking out the door."

"I phoned, John," I say, crying a little harder, "but she acted like she didn't know who I was and hung up."

John puts his hands on his knees and leaves the cigarette in his mouth for a minute. He's shaking his head, which makes me think that it's news to him.

It's been so long, but conversations are still easy with him; those things don't just go away.

I jump in, not sure if he's going to speak. "I think mom and dad were going to send me away because they knew I was queer and they didn't want anything fucking with dad's career. It's that simple."

"No, it's not, Jess," John says.

"Yes it is and you know it. And I know that his drinking is not my problem. He feels guilty for the choice he made and that's not my fault."

"Jess," John takes a deep breath, "mom's on an anti-depressant and she takes sleeping pills."

"That would explain why dad drinks at night—she sleeps like the dead." I light another cigarette and squeeze my eyes shut tight.

A silence falls between us. Truthfully, I feel like laughing.

"Where did that bruise come from?" John says.

"I tried to grab dad last night, he was drunk, he flailed, he hit me. It was an accident."

John's jaw shakes, but he forces back his tears. "The problem is that I don't think that this is a choice for him anymore, Jess. I'm not surprised and I really wish I was."

"Have people here not noticed? He's one of the top three faces of Mennonite academia, and his colleagues in other parts of the country are certainly starting to notice. How do people in church not see it?"

"Because, that's the way it always is—a bunch of Mennos walking around with their clothes on inside out. What is private is public and what is public is private." John picks at his teeth nervously.

"I'm not even angry about the bruise. I'm angry that he embraced his fear instead of embracing love. It's that simple."

"Do you really think he knew about you being gay before you left? He didn't. And since when have you become so fond of simple answers to complex questions?"

I say nothing. How do I explain the fear I felt, so primal that I needed no direct words or actions from my parents to make it real.

"Do you remember when your name became Jess?"

"Honestly, I've told so many different stories that I can't remember which one is true."

"You were maybe only seven. We were at grandma and grandpa Klassen's for Sunday afternoon faspa. You were running around the house like a little bantchi and whining about something. Grandma was starting to experience dementia. She was in the middle of cooking but couldn't remember what was going on, so it was taking a long time. You were half starved and half crazed, so dad yelled at you, 'Ruth Klassen, you calm yourself down right now.' Grandma freaked out because she thought she was being yelled at and maybe didn't know where she was or which day. Do you remember?"

I feel like crying, I don't want to remember because it's the only painful memory of grandma Klassen that I have. "Yeah, of course, I was named after her and she was so confused and embarrassed because she thought that dad was mad at her for faspa being late. She turned around and had this venomous look I had never seen before and she said, 'How dare you speak to me like that.' Dad didn't want to point out the obvious—that she was losing it—so he just said, 'I'm terribly sorry, mom, I didn't mean it.' He walked away. I felt so terrible."

"You threw up, didn't you?"

"I did. And then I went to find dad and I told him that from now on my name was going to be Jess. Don't ask me where I got Jess from; I needed something in a pinch, and that's what I came up with. I didn't ever want him to feel that way again because of me. I didn't entirely understand what was going on—how sad he was that his mom was losing her mind. How unfair it was that the parent who loved and respected him was disappearing before his eyes. I just knew that if I had behaved myself he wouldn't have had to yell my name and then she wouldn't have yelled at him."

PANCAKES

Around two in the morning I finally allow myself to attempt sleep. John offered to stay and is snoring on the couch in the living room. He says he wants to be around when dad gets home. To calm my mind and body, I put on my headphones and listen to music. I'm sitting in the rocking chair, staring at him. I couldn't bring myself to go downstairs into the bedroom that used to be mine.

I realize that I've never been in Shea's childhood bedroom due to the fact that I've never been on the second floor of her house. They've successfully divided it into dad space and daughter space, meeting on the main floor to mutually agree not to enter each other's worlds.

I see headlights in the driveway. The driver pops out of the truck and goes around to the side door to help the slumping passenger out.

"John." I walk over and tap his shoulder. "John, I think it's Francis and dad."

"Yip, yup, I'm awake."

John walks to the door and opens it as Francis makes the "shhh" sign. Dad is neither awake nor sober.

"Jesus," I whisper, "where did you find him?

John and Francis walk dad to the couch and lay him down. The couch hits the wall behind it with his weight.

"I found him at a bar in Dundurn."

"What? That's on the other side of the city; that's forty-five minutes from here."

"You think I don't know that."

"Don't be a fucking idiot, I'm just asking how you found him?"

Francis unzips his jacket and waves us into the kitchen where he opens the fridge and pulls out the leftover sausage. He puts it into the centre of the table and then finds the ketchup and mustard. Pulling a piece of sausage from the casserole dish, he dresses it with the condiments and swallows it down in two bites. He starts the process all over again. John and I join him.

"A buddy I played hockey with lives down there and bartends. He had this old guy on his hands at close and didn't know who the hell he was. He grabs his wallet, looks at the driver's licence, and thinks 'Holy shit, this is Francis' dad.' So he called me up and I drove down there." He eats another piece of sausage and goes to get a glass of water. "He's drunker than a fucking skunk. He threw up in the truck before he passed out."

I look at John and giggle. I don't know where it's coming from but I can't stop. John can't resist and bursts out laughing.

"At least it wasn't my truck," John says.

I laugh harder. Finally, Francis joins in.

After the dust settles I look at Francis. "Do you want to know where I've been?"

"Do I get to know?"

"What's that supposed to mean?"

"You and John and your little club, I never got to know what was going on. You guys just kept your secrets."

"That stops tonight, Francis. OK?" I'm starting to tear up again.

He looks a little choked himself. He takes a deep breath. "We gotta stick together."

John nods.

"I left because I came to the realization—I am a homosexual," I say slowly, wanting to make sure that there's no room for interpretation. "I tried to talk to mom and dad about it and it didn't go well. They wanted to ship me off to boarding school. I felt like dad would always be choosing between his church, his God, his career and me and so I left before I was forced to leave. I lived in Winnipeg for a while and now I live just outside of Toronto where I'm going to university."

"Holy shit," Francis gives a whistle. "This family is so fucked up."

His words feel like a knife square in my back.

Francis reads the look on my face. "That's not what I mean. That's not what I mean at all. I don't care about that, Jess, it doesn't make a difference to me. I just mean," he stops, looking around the dark house, "look around. Dad's passed out—wasted. Mom doesn't notice a damn thing, apparently. You run away from home and don't speak to your family for five years because you're scared shitless, and we all convince ourselves that you've gone to boarding school—well, at least I did. We're supposed to be this perfect family and we're fucked."

Francis passes the sausage around. John and I each take another slice.

"What do we do now, John?" Francis asks, sincerely looking for an answer.

"Watch a movie?"

Francis nods.

"There's not much we can do until they wake up."

"I can't sleep anyway," I offer.

So we watch a movie. Then another. Finally, around 7:00, I suggest we make pancakes. The three of us start cooking.

Mom greets us in her housecoat. She smiles warmly, but her expression changes. "What's going on here? Why is everyone here so early? Your father already went to work."

Francis turns around, spatula in hand. "No, mom. Dad has not gone to work, he's sobering up on the couch."

John and I are impressed. Mom looks stunned, like her son just peed on her foot. But she says nothing.

I hear a rumbling behind us. Dad is awake and coming into the kitchen.

"What's going on?" His hair wild and the smell of booze is wafting off him.

"We're having a family meeting. Why don't you sit down and we'll get you some pancakes."

"What?" He's none-too-pleased, probably because he didn't plan the meeting, but he sits down and accepts his plate of pancakes from John.

The four of us sit down at the table.

Francis crosses his arms and sits up straight. Dad grudgingly slices into a pancake. His eyes are bloodshot and he's a pale shade of green.

"Dad," John says, "do you know how Jess got that bruise on her cheek?"

Mom takes a deep breath; she's clued into where this is going.

John continues. "Francis had to pick you up last night after a buddy of his found you passed out at Dundurn Bar. But more

193

importantly, the bruise on Jess' cheek is there because you smacked her in the face the night before last. You were drunk."

Mom starts to cry. She stands and pushes her chair away from the table but then sits back down again.

Dad puts his head in his hands, then runs his hands through his hair.

"I know that I've been gone for a long time, but this family is going to start talking. If you want me to stick around here and not say goodbye to you two," I point at mom and dad, "we're all going to start talking."

"What's there to talk about?" Mom says between sobs. "Can't we just leave the past in the past? Can't we just be happy that we're all together again?"

"Mom," John says, reaching for her hand, offering her comfort, "I know that it might seem easier to just leave things in the past, but Jess needs to speak and we need to listen." He looks at me and nods.

"Mom and dad, what I tried to say to you, all those years ago in my bedroom after church, is that I'm gay."

Everyone remains silent, like they didn't hear what I said, so I say it again, "I'm gay."

"I know," mom says. She's quiet for a while, as though trying to remember something. "I didn't know what to do. I felt I needed to find a way for us all to be OK and so I thought that if you just didn't mention it…if you would just not talk about it…."

"I felt like you knew and that's why you wanted me to go to boarding school. I didn't feel I had a choice, I never thought for a minute you would accept me for who I was. I was scared."

"We didn't know what else to do," dad says out of his stupor. "You were always so outspoken and you were getting so wild."

"You were afraid that you were going to lose your job, weren't you? You couldn't have a queer kid, could you?" I feel my voice sharpen.

Dad stands up from the table and rubs his forehead. "I," he starts, "I don't know," he stumbles backward but regains his balance. "It wasn't like that."

Mom looks at him. "Did you hit our daughter?"

"You knew?" he says, looking back at her. "You knew and you didn't tell me."

"You knew, you figured it out, too." She wipes her cheeks with the back of her hand. "Would that have stopped this," she's waving her hands at him. "Would that have stopped you from this?"

"Just sit down everyone," I say sharply. It works, they obey my command. John looks angry; he's never been one for shouting. "Just sit down and eat your pancakes. This is not going to be the last time that we talk about this."

Dad shakes his head. "Jess, the Bible is very clear about the issue of homosexuality." He looks pained; maybe it's just the hangover. "In terms of our Confession of Faith...the Mennonite church has been clear about our position. People have made very strong theological arguments."

"Dad, I'm not a theological argument, I'm not a church policy, and I am not an issue of biblical interpretation. I'm your daughter."

He reaches for his coffee cup but his hands are shaking too wildly to bring it to his mouth to sip. He lifts his sleeve and looks at his watch. "I have to lead chapel in an hour. I have to go."

The doorbell rings. Everyone jumps out of their seats. No one moves, though, so I push my chair back and head to the front door. As I open the door it occurs to me that the person standing there—a neighbour, a friend, the minister from the church, an aunt or uncle— might recognize me and ask me why they haven't seen me in five years. I'm not prepared to answer that question.

I open the door and my stomach drops. My breath quickens and I'm shaking my head. And then, everything relaxes. She is here, and I feel calm.

POWERFUL SENSATION OF LIFE UNDER THE TONGUE—
NICOLE BROSSARD, *MUSEUM OF BONE AND WATER*

I want you and me. I want my mother's hug and my father's bad breath urging me, lovingly, to try harder. I want my brothers' pick-up trucks parked outside. I want my words, saying the right things. I want my body aligned in perfect action. I want to go home.

And here I am, with one arm wrapped around the garden gnome, a cigarette glowing between my fingers, and the other arm wrapped around Shea. My heart sits beside me waiting for my body to invite it back inside. My eyes aren't distracted by trees, soaring mountains, or a mighty ocean—it's just my town, a bunch of houses on a bald prairie, the smell of cow shit from a nearby dairy farm. There's plenty of room for my body to take up a little space of its own.

I want to call myself the prodigal son, but the story doesn't fit— I haven't come grovelling and I won't say I'm sorry. But I feel at the mercy of my family tonight because somewhere on the way home I made a promise to myself to stay, and it's time to trust myself and stop running. It's also time to trust them.

I'm proud of myself tonight. If there's a moment when I'm tempted to trivialize—to tell myself that it wasn't so bad, that these years of separation and hurt weren't so hard—I will remind myself that getting to the steps of my parent's house was no easy task. I've always loved my family, even in the midst of my numb heart because embedded in the stitches that bind my skin, climbing the hundred-foot banks of my soul, sitting in the wooden church benches of my heart is the community of me.

The light in the front porch is not lit. On the edge of this small, prairie town the stars still have a chance of shining to earth. I'm holding my lover's hand, and mom and dad have gone to bed. She and I are taking in the stars—trying to orient ourselves according to the bright map above. John and Francis are watching bad late night television, and soon, Shea and I will join them.

Acknowledgements

Mom, Dad, Shelley, Gene, Jolene, Matthew, Julie.

The editorial committee: Roewan Crowe—you took a leap, and I'm still not sure why but I'm forever thankful. John K. Samson and Richard Wood—two steady hands at the tiller.

Julia Gingrich, you've edited almost everything I've written. You've been unselfish in celebrating with me, and you never hesitate to remind me of the glass half full. Thank you.

More editorial thanks to Rachel Loewen Walker, Jennifer Code, Joni Church.

My thanks/apologies to some housemates: Alison, Thom, Ryan J. Weston, Jen and Dylan, Shauna and Daniel, Kelsey, Rachel, Clint, Sarah and Charlie.

My Organic Planet Worker Co-op family for every impromptu kitchen dance party, for every battle waged (I learned to speak it), for the forgiveness of mistakes, for white-board messages, for ideals and actions, for difference.

The odds and sods (an extension of the biological family): Marieke Meyer and Thane Ladner. Erika MacPherson and Jacki Hagel. Allison, Heather, Joel, Marlis, Nichole, Diane. Meagan and Dan, Joc, Rob, Dave, Greg. Laura, Kath, Tina and Paul, Nat, Natasha.

I am indebted to Vergil Kanne, web designer. Please go to <www.vergilkanne.com> to see more of his work.

Thanks to Chris Cox for his help in making the Low German consistent and somewhat correct, whatever that may be.

Dedicated to the saints that have gone before me. To the countless queer Mennonites who have stayed silent. This story does not pretend to speak for all of us; it is only an attempt to add a voice to the choir. One day we will dance through the doors of our churches unafraid and with joy. For those whose pain is too deep to ever dawn the church door again even if one day the dogma crumbles to the ground, thank you for having the courage to begin.

About the author

Jan Guenther Braun, originally from a farm near Osler, Saskatchewan, now lives in Winnipeg, where she is one-sixth of a worker co-op selling organic groceries. She graduated with a Bachelor of Theology in 2000 from Canadian Mennonite Bible College where she participated in the summer pastoral internship program. In 2004, Jan graduated from the University of Waterloo with a BA in English Literature. She was the Manitoba winner of the 2005 CBC Poetry Face-Off competition and selected for the Manitoba Writers' Guild Sheldom Oberman mentorship program. In 2006, Jan was an invited lecturer for the Margaret Laurence Women's Studies Speakers Series, University of Winnipeg, presenting a paper called "Queer and Mennonite: Putting My Protestant Work Ethic to Good Use."